Nine

and

One Rogue

Nine Man-Eaters
and
One Rogue

Kenneth Anderson

RUPA

Published by
Rupa Publications India Pvt. Ltd 2014
7/16, Ansari Road, Daryaganj
New Delhi 110002

Sales centres:
Allahabad Bengaluru Chennai
Hyderabad Jaipur Kathmandu
Kolkata Mumbai

ISBN: 978-81-291-1642-0

Third impression 2015

10 9 8 7 6 5 4 3

The moral right of the author has been asserted.

Printed at Nutech Photolithographers, New Delhi

*To the memory of the jungles of southern India, their birds and animals,
particularly elephant, and panther, and their forest-people Chensoos,
Sholagas, Karumbas and Poojarees, 1 proudly and gratefully dedicate this
book, in return for twenty-five years of unadulterated joy they have given
me in making and keeping their acquaintance.*

Contents

Introduction

The Man-Eating Tiger is an abnormality, for under normal circumstances, the King of the Indian Jungles is a ~~gentleman~~ GENTLEMAN and of noble nature. He kills only for food, never wantonly, and his prey are the wild beasts of the forest, or, where temptation offers, the village cattle that are sent to graze in the government reserves.

Occasionally a tigress will teach her half-grown cub, or cubs, the art of killing their prey in the way a tiger should kill—by breaking the vertebrae of the neck. Under such special circumstances three or four cattle may be killed at a time, to provide practice for the youngsters, but such slaughter is never performed wantonly by a single tiger for the sheer joy of slaying. A tigress normally brings up two cubs at a time—although I have personally seen four—and it is said that the male limits the species by eating half the litter shortly after their birth.

The tiger's skill in breaking the neck of its prey, in contrast to the method of leopards and panthers, which strangle their prey by seizing its throat and holding on, has often been debated by hunters. In fact, when attacking, the tiger rises up besides its victim, generally places a paw over its shoulder and seizes the beast by the back of the neck or throat, according to its size, pressing the head to the ground. The paw is then used as a lever to cause the victim to topple over itself, while the tiger continues to hold the head down. Thus, the weight of the animal's own body is the factor that breaks the neck rather than any twisting action by the tiger, although I am personally of the opinion that the latter does exist to a considerable extent. Because of the tiger's ability to open its jaws very widely, it is sometimes difficult to judge whether the prey was seized by the back of its neck or by the throat, the fang marks being so positioned that either could have happened.

The panther and leopard are for all practical purposes the same animal although even here much argument has arisen from the great contrast in size between the 'Thendu', or forest variety of panther, which kills its prey by breaing the neck after the manner of a tiger, for which it is sometimes mistaken, and the smaller variety of leopard haunting the outskirts of villages, which kills goats and dogs by strangling, and even descends to feeding on rats and domestic fowls. The panther is a much less powerful animal than the tiger, generally of a cowardly disposition, but nevertheless one of the most picturesque inhabitants of the forests of the Indian Peninsula, and of Asia and Africa.

Man-eaters of both varieties have generally been created by the interference of the human race. A tiger or panther is sometimes so incapacitated by a rifle or gunshot wound as to be rendered incapable, thereafter, of stalking and killing the wild animals of the forest—or even cattle—that are its usual prey. By force of circumstance, therefore, it descends to killing man, the weakest and puniest of creatures, quite incapable of defending himself when unarmed. The same incapacity may sometimes occur through accidental injury, such as a porcupine quill in the foot; and sometimes the habit of man-eating is passed on by a tigress to her cubs. Occasionally the taste for human flesh is acquired by a panther that has devoured corpses that have been thrown into the forest, as happens when epidemic diseases attack villages in those areas, though this is very uncommon. Equally rare are instances where none of these circumstances appear to account for the propensity.

A man-eating tiger, or panther, when it exists, is a scourge and terror to the neighbourhood. The villagers are defenceless and appear to resign themselves to their fate. Victims are killed regularly, both by day and night if the killer is a tiger, and by night only if a panther, the former often repeatedly following a particular circuit over the same area. While the death roll increases, superstition and demoralisation play a very considerable part in preventing the villagers from taking any conceited, planned action against their adversary. Roads are deserted, village traffic comes to a stop, forest operations, wood-cutting and cattle-grazing cease completely, fields are left uncultivated, and sometimes whole villages are abandoned for safer areas. The greatest difficulty experienced in attempting to shoot such animals is the extraordinary lack of cooperation evinced by the surrounding villagers, actuated as they are by a superstitious fear of retribution by the man-eater, whom they believe will mysteriously come to learn of the part they have attempted to play against it.

A 'rogue' elephant is generally the result of the periodic disease of 'musth', from which all male elephants suffer for a period of about 90 days. An oily discharge from an orifice behind the eye is the outward evidence. They are then extremely aggressive and dangerous, but afterwards they generally regain their normal harmless composure. Sometimes it is the result of a particularly ambitious young elephant coming into battle with the big tuskers of a herd for the favour of a female, when he gets badly beaten up and expelled by the larger beasts. He then becomes very morose and surly, and takes his revenge on whatever he comes across—again the easiest being man.

It must not be imagined, however, that the forests of India are always stocked with man-eating tigers and leopards, or rogue elephants. Generally they do not exist, and the jungles are then safer to wander in than any busy street of a capital city, where the possibility of being run over by motor traffic at any moment is considerable. Further, the beauties of nature, of the flowers, insects, birds and animals—the glories of an Indian jungle dawn, and of the glowing red sunset, and of the silvery moonlit night that bathes the swaying tops of feathery bamboos the mystery of the dark nights, the sky set with a myriad stars—above all the peaceful solitude and sense of nearness to Nature and to God, fill the wanderer with an assurance that he has at last found a home, from which he will not willingly be torn.

I hope I may be forgiven if, in some of these stories, I have devoted considerable space to geographical and natural descriptions and conditions, and have tried to mimic, in writing, the calls of birds and beasts of the forest. I have done so deliberately, in an attempt to recapture, for the benefit of some of my readers who have been in India and have visited her glorious forests, memories of those days and of those jungles from which I am sure they are sorry to have been separated. I dread the day when that separation must come to me.

In closing, I have to record my grateful thanks to my late father, who taught me how to use a gun when I was seven; although he was not a jungle-lover himself, he delighted in shooting duck, partridge and small game. My thanks are due also to Byra, a wild Poojaree whom I discovered living in a burrow on the banks of the Chinar River in the district of Salem; more than twenty-five years ago, he taught me most of what I now know about the jungle and its fauna, and bred in me a deep love of his home in the wilds. I am grateful, too, to Ranga, my faithful old 'Shikaree', also of the Salem District, who has accompanied me on many trips, has patiently looked after me, guided me, helped me and been staunchly faithful and fearless in the face of danger; Sowree, his assistant and almost his equal in shikaring; and my old hunting friends, Dick Bird and Pat Watson, who between them have killed more tiger than any men I know, for their many tips and instructions in my early days.

KENNETH ANDERSON

1

The Man-Eater of Jowlagiri

Those who have been to the tropics and to jungle places will not need to be told of the beauties of the moonlight over hill and valley, that picks out in vivid relief the forest grasses and each leaf of the giant trees, and throws into still greater mystery the dark shadows below, where the rays of the moon cannot reach, concealing perhaps a beast of prey, a watchful deer or a lurking reptile, all individually and severally in search of food.

All appeared peaceful in the Jowlagiri Forest Range, yet there was danger everywhere, and murder was afoot. For a trio of poachers, who possessed between them two matchlocks of ancient vintage, had decided to get themselves some meat. They had cleverly constructed a hide on the sloping banks of a waterhole, and had been sitting in it since sunset, intently watchful for the deer which, sooner or later, must come to slake their thirst.

The hours wore on. The moon, at the full, had reached mid-heaven and the scene was as bright as day. Suddenly, from the thicket of evergreen saplings to their left, could be heard the sound of violently rustling leaves and deepthroated grunts. What could be there? Wild-pig undoubtedly! A succulent meal, and flesh in addition that could be sold! The poachers waited, but the beasts, whatever they were, did not break cover. Becoming impatient, Muniappa, the marksman of the trio, decided to risk a shot. Raising his matchlock, he waited till a dark shadow, deeper than its surroundings, became more evident, and fired. There was a snarling roar and a lashing of bushes, followed by a series of coughing 'whoofs' and then silence.

Not pigs, but a tiger! Fearfully and silently the three poachers beat a hasty retreat to their village, there to spend the rest of the night in anxiety as to the result of their act.

But morning revealed that all was apparently well, for a male tiger just in his prime lay dead, the chance shot from the ancient musket having sped straight to his heart. So Muniappa and his friends were, for that day, the unsung and whispered heroes of the village.

But the next night produced a different story. With sun set came the urgent, angry call of a tigress seeking her dead mate. For it was the mating season, and this tigress, which had only just succeeded in finding her companion the night before, was decidedly annoyed at his unaccountable absence, which she quite rightly connected with the interference of human beings.

Night after night for a week she continued her uneasy movements, calling by day from the depths of the forest and in darkness roaring almost at the outskirts of the village itself.

Young Jack Leonard, who was keen to secure a trophy, and who had been summoned to the village by an urgent letter, arrived on the morning of the eighth day, and acquainted himself with the situation. Being told that the tiger wandered everywhere, and seeing her many pugmarks on the lonely path to the forest-bungalow, he decided to try his luck that evening, concealing himself by five o'clock behind an anthill that stood conveniently beside the path.

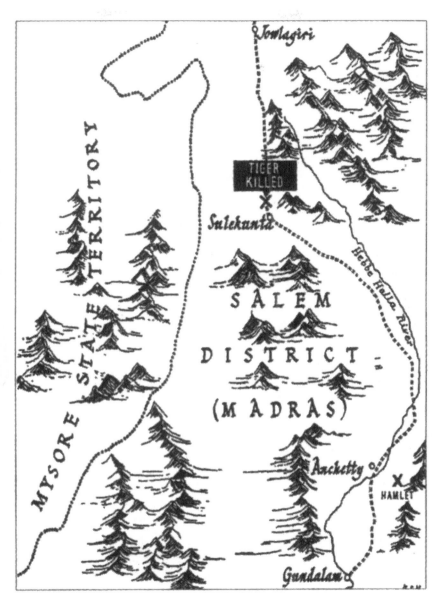

Sketch map of localities referred to in the
story of the man-eater of jowlagiri.

The minutes passed, and at 6.15 p.m. dusk was falling. Suddenly there was a faint rustle of leaves and a loose stone rolled down the bank a little to his right. Leonard strained his eyes for the first sight of the tigress, but nothing happened. The minutes passed again. And then, rapidly moving along the edge of the road towards him, and on the same side as himself, he could just discern the form of the tigress. Hastily transferring the stock of his rifle to his left shoulder, and leaning as far out from his sheltering bush as possible, so that he might see more of the animal, Leonard fired at her chest what would have been a fatal shot had it carried a little more to the right.

As it was, Leonard's bullet ploughed deeply into the right shoulder, causing the beast to roar loudly before crashing away into the jungle. Bitterly disappointed, Leonard waited till morning to follow the trail. There was abundance of blood everywhere, but due to the rocky and difficult country, interspersed with densely wooded ravines and close, impenetrable shrubbery, he failed to catch up with his quarry.

Months passed, and the scene changes to Sulekunta, a village deeper in the forest and about seven miles from Jowlagiri, where there was a little temple occasionally visited by pilgrims from the surrounding region. Three of these had finished their devotions and were returning to their home: a man, his wife and son aged sixteen. Passing under a wild tamarind tree, hardly a quarter mile from the temple, the boy lingered to pick some of the half-ripe acid fruit. The parents heard a low growl, followed by a piercing, agonised scream, and looked back to see their son carried bodily in the jaws of a tiger, as it leapt into a nullah bordering the lonely path. The aged couple bravely turned back and shouted abuse at the marauder as best they could, only to be answered by two more shrieks from their only son, then all was silent again.

Thereafter, death followed death over a wide area, extending from Jowlagiri in the extreme north to the cattlepen of Gundalam, thirty miles to the south; and from the borders of Mysore State, twenty miles to the west, to the main road to Denkaflikota, for about forty-five miles of its length. Some fifteen victims, including three girls, one just married, had fallen a prey to this monster, when I received an urgent summons from my friend, the sub-collector of Hosur, to rid the area of the scourge.

Journeying to Jowlagiri, where the sub-collector had told me the trouble had begun, I pieced together the facts of the story, deducing that this was no tiger but a tigress, and the one that had been robbed of her mate by the poachers and later wounded by Leonard's plucky but unfortunate shot. From Jowlagiri I tramped to Sulekunta in the hope of coming across the fresh pug marks of the marauder, but I was unlucky, as no kills had occurred at that place in recent days, and what tracks there were had been obliterated by passing herds of cattle. Moving on to Gundalam, twenty-three miles away at the southern limit of the affected area, I decided to pitch camp, since it was at this cattle-pen that the majority of kills had been reported, seven herdsmen being accounted for in the last four months.

Three fat buffalo calves had been very thoughtfully provided as bait by my friend the sub-collector; I proceeded to tie them out at likely spots in the hope of securing a kill. The first I tethered a mile down the river bordering Gundalam—at that time of the year a mere trickle of water—at a point where the river was joined by a tributary named Sige Halla, down which the tigress was reported to keep her beat; the second I tied along the path to the neighbouring village of Anchetty, four miles away; the remaining calf I secured close to the watershed, whence both herdsmen and cattle obtained their daily supply of drinking water.

Having myself attended to the securing and comfort of these three baits, I spent the next two days in tramping the forest in every direction, armed with my .405 Winchester, in the hope of picking up fresh pug marks, or perhaps of seeing the man-eater herself.

Early in the morning of the second day I located the footprints of the tigress in the soft sand of the Gundalam river. She had descended in the night, walked along the river past the watershed—and my buffalo bait, which, as was evident by her foot-prints, she had stopped to look at but had not even touched—and up and across a neighbouring hill on her way to Anchetty Here the ground became too hard for further tracking.

The third morning found me searching again, and I had just returned to camp, preparatory to a hot bath and early lunch, when a group of men, accompanied by the headman of Anchetty, arrived to inform me that the tigress had killed a man early that morning at a hamlet scarcely a mile south of Anchetty. Apparently a villager, hearing restless sounds from his penned cattle, had gone out at dawn to investigate and had not returned. Thereafter his brother and son had followed to find out the cause of his absence, and at the outskirts of the cattle-pen had found the man's blanket and staff, and, indistinct in the hard earth, the claw marks of the tigress's hindfeet as she reared to attack her victim. Being too alarmed to follow, they had fled to the hamlet and thence to Anchetty, where, gathering strength in numbers and accompanied by the headman, they had hastened to find me.

Foregoing the bath and swallowing a quick lunch, we hastened to Anchetty and the hamlet. From the spot where the tigress had attacked and—as was evident by the fact that no sound had been made by the unfortunate man—had killed her victim, tracking became arduous and slow, owing to the hard and stony nature of the ground. In this case, the profusion of thorny bushes among the shrubbery assisted us; for, on casting around, we found shreds of the man's loincloth impaled on the thorns as the tigress carried him away. Had the circumstances not been so tragic, it was instructive to learn how the sagacious animal had detoured to avoid such thorns and the obstruction they would have offered.

Some 300 yards away she had dropped her burden beneath a thicket at the foot of a small fig-tree, probably intending to start her meal. Then she had changed her mind, or perhaps been disturbed, for she had picked her victim up again and continued her retreat towards a deep nullah that ran southwards towards the main Cauvery River, some thirty miles away.

Thereafter, tracking became easier, for the tigress had changed her hold from the man's neck and throat; this had accounted for the lack of blood-spoor. Now she held him by the small of his back. Drops of blood, and smears across the leaves of bushes and thickets, now made it comparatively easy for us to follow the trail, and in another hundred yards we had found the man's loincloth, which had completely unwound itself and was hanging from a protruding sprig of 'wait-a-bit' thorn.

Continuing, we reached the nullah where, in the soft dry sand, the pugs of the tigress were clearly imprinted, with a slight drag-mark to one side, evidently caused by one of the man's feet trailing downwards as he was carried.

As there was no need of a tracker, and numbers would create disturbance, apart from needless risk, I crept cautiously forward alone, after motioning to the rest to remain where they were. Progress was of necessity very slow, for I had carefully to scan the heavy undergrowth on both banks of the nullah, where the tigress might have been lurking, waiting to put an end to her pursuer. Thus I had traversed two bends in the nullah when I sighted a low outcrop of rock jutting into the nullah-bed itself. Keeping as far as possible to the opposite side of the rock, I increased the stealth of my approach. Closer scrutiny revealed a dark object on the far side of the rock, and this duly proved to be the body of the unfortunate victim.

The tigress had already made a fair meal, having consumed about half her prey in the process, severing one leg from the thigh and one arm. Having assured myself that she was nowhere in the vicinity, I returned to the men, whom I summoned to the spot to help construct some sort of place where I might sit up and await the return of the assassin to its gruesome meal, which I was confident would be before sunset that day.

A more unsuitable spot for sitting-up could hardly be imagined. There was a complete absence of trees on which a hide or machan could be constructed, and it soon became evident that there were only two possibilities. One was to sit close to the opposite bank of the nullah, from where the human victim was clearly visible. The other was to ascend the sloping outcrop of rock to a point some ten feet above the bed of the nullah, where a natural ledge was formed about four feet from its upper edge. The first plan I rejected, as being too dangerous in the case of a man-eater, and this left me with the prospect of sitting upon the rockledge, from where I could not only view the cadaver but the whole length of the nullah up to its bend in the direction from which we had come, and for about twenty yards in the other direction, where it swung abruptly to the right.

Working silently and quickly, at a spot some distance up the nullah, whence the sound of lopping would not be heard, the men cut a few thorny branches of the same variety as grew in the immediate vicinity of the rock, so as not to cause a contrasting background. These they deftly and cunningly arranged below the ledge, so that I would not be visible in any direction from the nullah itself. Fortunately I had had the forethought to bring my blanket, water-bottle and torch, although there would not be much use for the last of these during the major portion of the night, as the moon was nearing full and would rise comparatively early. By 3 p.m. I was in my place and the men left me, having been instructed to return next morning with a flask of hot tea, and sandwiches for a quick snack.

The afternoon wore slowly on, the heat from the blazing sun beating directly on the exposed rock and bathing me in sweat. Looking down the nullah in both directions, all was still and nothing disturbed the rays of shimmering heat that arose from the baked earth. Absence of vultures could be accounted for by the fact that, in the position the tigress had left it beneath the sharply-sloping rock, the body was hidden from the sky. About

5 p.m. a crow spotted it, and by its persistent cawing soon attracted its mate. But the two birds were too nervous of the human scent actually to begin picking the kill. Time wore on, and the sun set as a fiery ball beneath the distant rim of forest-clad hills. The crows flapped away, one after the other, to roost in readiness on some distant tree in expectation of the morrow when, overcome by hunger, they would be more equal to braving the feared smell of human beings. The cheering call of the jungle-cock broke forth in all directions as a farewell to the dying day, and the strident '*ma-ow*' of a peacock sounded from down the dry bed of the stream. I welcomed the sound, for I knew that in the whole forest no more alert watchman than a peacock could be found and that he would warn me immediately of the tigress's approach, should he see her. Now was the expected time, and with every sense intently alert I awaited the return of the man-killer. But nothing happened, the peacock flapped heavily away and dusk rapidly followed the vanquished day.

Fortunately the early moon had already risen and her silvery sheen soon restored a little of my former range of vision. The birds of the day had gone to roost by now, and their places had been taken by the birds of the night. The persistent '*chuck-chuck-chuckoo*' of nightjars resounded along the nullah, as these early harbingers of the night sought their insect prey along the cooling banks. Time passed again, and then a deathly silence fell upon the scene. Not even the chirrup of a cricket disturbed the stillness, and my friends, the nightjars, had apparently gone elsewhere in their search for food. Glancing downwards at the human remains, it seemed that one arm reached upwards to me in supplication or called perhaps for vengeance. Fortunately the head was turned away, so that I could not see the frightful contortion of the features, which I had noticed earlier that afternoon.

All at once the strident belling of an alarmed sambar broke the silence and was persistently followed by a successsion of similar calls from a spot I judged to be about half a mile away.

These were followed by the sharp cry of spotted-deer, and echoed up the nullah by a restless brainfever bird in his weird call of '*brain-fever, brain-fever*', repeated in rising crescenao. I breathed a sigh of relief and braced my nerves and muscles for final action. My friends, the night-watchmen of the jungle, had faithfully accomplished their task and I knew the tigress was approaching and had been seen.

The calls then gradually died away. This meant that the tigress had passed out of the range of the callers and was now close by. I strained my eyes on the bend to the right, twenty yards down the nullah, around which, at any moment, I expected the man-eater to appear. But nodiing happened. Thirty minutes passed, then forty-five, by the hands of my wristwatch, clearly visible in the moonlight. Strange, I thought; the tigress should have appeared long ago. She would not take forty-five minutes to cover half a mile.

And then a horrible feeling of imminent danger came over me. Many times before had that obscure sixth sense, which we all possess but few develop, stood me in good stead in my many wanderings in the forests of India and Burma, and on the African belt. I had not the slightest doubt that somehow, in spite of all my precautions, complete screening and absolute stillness, the tigress had discovered my presence and was at that moment probably stalking me preparatory to a final spring.

In moments of danger, we who know the jungle think quickly. It is not braveness that goads the mind to such quick thinking, for I confess that at this moment I was very afraid and could feel beads of cold sweat trickling down my face. I knew the tigress could not be on the nullah itself, or below me, or I would have seen her long before. She might have been on the opposite bank, hidden in the dense undergrowth and watching my position, but somehow I felt that her presence there would not account for the acutely-growing sense of danger that increasingly beset me. She could only be above and behind me. Suddenly it was borne home to me that the four-foot wall of rock behind me prevented me from looking backwards unless I raised myself to a half-crouching, half-kneeling position, which would make a steady shot almost impossible, apart from completely giving away my position to any watcher on the opposite bank, or on the nullah-bed itself. Momentarily, I cursed myself for this lack of forethought, which now threatened to become my undoing. As I hesitated for another second, a thin trickle of sand slid down from above, probably dislodged by the killer, now undoubtedly very close above me, and gathering herself for a final spring.

I hesitated no longer; I forced my numbed legs to raise me to a half-crouching position, simultaneously sling the cocked .405 around, till the end of the muzzle was in line with my face. Then I raised myself a fraction higher, till both my eyes and the muzzle, came above the ledge.

A fearful sight revealed itself. There was the tigress, hardly eight feet away and extended on her belly, in the act of creeping down the sloping rock towards me. As our eyes met in surprise, we acted simultaneously, the tigress to spring with a nerve-shattering roar, while I ducked down again, at the same moment contracting my trigger finger.

The heavy blast of the rifle, level with and only a few inches from my ears, mingled with that demoniacal roar to create a sound which often till this day haunts me in my dreams and causes me to awaken, shivering with fear.

The brute had not anticipated the presence of the ledge behind which I sheltered, while the blast and blinding flash of the rifle full in her face evidently disconcerted her, deflecting her aim and deviating her purpose from slaughter to escape. She leapt right over my head, and in passing her hind foot caught the muzzle of the rifle a raking blow, so that it was torn from my grasp and went slithering, butt first, down the sloping rock, to fall dully on the soft sand below, where it lay beside the half-eaten corpse. Quicker than the rifle, the tigress herself reached the nullah-bed, and in two bounds and another coughing roar was lost to view in the thickets of the opposite bank.

Shocked and hardly aware of what had happened, I realised I was unarmed and helpless, and that should the tigress return on her tracks, there was just nothing I could do. At the same time, to descend after the rifle would undoubtedly single me out for attack, if the animal were lying wounded in the bushes of the opposite bank. But anything seemed preferable to indecision and helplessness, and I dived down the slope to retrieve the rifle and scramble back, expecting at each second to hear the awful roar of the attacking killer. But nothing happened, and in less time than it takes to tell I was back at the ledge.

A quick examination revealed that no harm had come to the weapon in its fall, the stock having absorbed the shock. Replacing the spent cartridge, I fell to wondering whether I had hit the tigress at all, or if I had missed her at ridiculously close range. Then I noticed something black and white on the ledge behind me and barely two feet away. Picking it up, I found it was the major portion of the tigress' ear, which had been torn off by my bullet at that close range. It was still warm to my touch, and being mostly of skin and hair, hardly bled along its torn edge.

To say that I was disappointed and chagrined could not describe one-tenth of my emotions. I had failed to kill the man-eater at a point-blank range, failed even to wound her in the true sense. The tearing-off of her ear would hardly inconvenience her, beyond causing slight local pain for a few days. On the other hand, my foolish miss would teach her never to return to a kill the second time. This would make her all the more cunning, all the more dangerous and all the more destructive, because now she would have to eat when she killed, and then kill again when she felt hungry, increasing her killings beyond what would have been normally necessary. She might even alter her sphere of activities and remove herself to some other part of the country, where the people would not be aware of the arrival of a man-eater and so fall still easier prey. I cursed myself throughout that night, hoping against hope that the tigress might show up again, but all to no purpose. Morning, and the return of my men, found me chilled to the marrow, disconsolate and disappointed beyond expression. The hot tea and sandwiches they brought, after my long fast since the previous forenoon, followed by a pipeful of strong tobacco, somewhat restored my spirits and caused me to take a slightly less critical view of the situation which, after all, might have been far worse. Had it not been for my sixth sense, I would undoubtedly have been lying a partially devoured corpse beside that of the previous day's unfortunate victim. I had something to be really thankful for.

Approaching the spot into which the tigress had leapt, we cast about for blood-spoor, but, as I had expected, found none, beyond a very occasional smear from the damaged ear against the leaves of bushes, as the tigress had retreated from what had turned out for her a very surprising situation. Even these we eventually lost some distance away, so that it was an unhappy party of persons that returned to the hamlet and Anchetty, and eventually Gundalam, to report complete failure.

I remained at Gundalam for a further ten days, persistently tying out my buffalo baits each day, although I had little hope of success. Whole mornings and afternoons I devoted to scouring the forest in search of tracks, and nights were spent in sitting over waterholes, game-trails and along the bed of the Gundalam River in the hope of the tigress showing up, but all to no avail. Parties of men went out in the daytime in all directions to secure news of further kills, but nothing had happened. Apparently the tigress had deserted her haunts and gone off to healthier localities.

On the eleventh day I left Gundalam, tramping to Anchetty and Denkanikota. From there I travelled to Hosur, where I told my friend the sub-collector of all that had happened and extracted from him a promise that he would tell me immediately of further kills, should they occur, as I now felt myself responsible for the welfare of the people of the locality. Then, leaving Hosur, I returned to my home at Bangalore.

Five months passed, during which time I received three letters from the sub-collector, telling of vague rumours of human tiger-kills from distant places, two being from across the Cauvery River in the Coimbatore District, one from Mysore State territory, and the fourth from a place still further away.

Then suddenly came the bad news I feared, but had hoped would not eventuate. A tiger had struck again at Gundalam, killing her eighth victim there, and the next evening had snatched, from the very door of the little temple at Sulekunta, the old priest who had attended to the place for the last forty years. The letter concluded with the request to come at once.

Such urgent invitation was unnecessary, for I had been holding myself in readiness for the worst; within two hours I was motoring to Jowlagiri.

Arriving there I was fortunate in being able to talk to one of the party of pilgrims who had almost been eyewitnesses to the death of the old priest of the temple at Sulekunta. Apparently a party of men had been on pilgrimage and, as they approached the temple itself, were horrified to hear the low growl of a tiger, which then leapt into the forest from the roots of a giant peepul tree that grew some thirty yards away. Bolting for shelter into the temple itself, they were surprised to find it tenandess, and looking out were aghast to see the body of the old priest lying within the folds of the gnarled roots of the old peepul tree that directly faced them. After some time, and very timidly, they approached in a group, to find that the old man had apparently been attacked in, or very near, the temple, and then been carried to this spot to be devoured. The tiger had already begun its meal, consuming part of the skinny chest, when it had been disturbed by the pilgrim party.

I particularly inquired as to whether my informant, or his companions, had noticed anything wrong with the tiger's ears, but obviously they had all been too frightened to observe any defects.

I hurried to Sulekunta with my party of three and arrived near dusk; I must confess that the last two miles of the journey had been very uncomfortable, traversing a valley between two steeply sloping hills that were densely clothed with bamboo. But we heard and saw nothing, beyond the sudden trumpeting of a solitary elephant, which had been inhabiting these parts for some time and had been a considerable annoyance to pilgrims, whom he apparently delighted to chase if they were in small parties. But that is another story.

There was no time to make a proper camp, so we decided to sleep in the deserted front portion of the temple itself, a proceeding which I, and very decidedly my followers, would have declined to do under normal circumstances. But nightfall and the proximity of a man-eater are apt to overcome all scruples and principles. I stood guard with the loaded rifle, while my three men frenziedly gathered brushwood and rotting logs that lay in plenty nearby, to build a fire for our warmth and protection, for on this occasion there was no friendly moon and it would soon be dark. Under such circumstances, attempting to situp for the man-eater, in the hope of its passing near the temple, would have been both highly dangerous and futile.

Soon we had a bright fire blazing, on the inner side of which we sat, away from the pitch-black jungle night, which could easily have sheltered the murderer, all unknown to us, within a distance of two feet. Listening intently, we occasionally heard the deep belling boom of sambar, and I could discern the harsher note of a stag, but these did not follow in persistent repetition, showing that the animals had not been unduly alarmed by any such major foe as the king of the Indian jungle. After midnight we arranged to keep watch in twos, three hours at a time, and I elected, with one of my companions, to take first turn. The other two were soon asleep. Nothing untoward happened, however, beyond the fact that the solitary tusker, who had approached near enough to catch a sudden sight of the fire, trumpeted once again and crashed away. A kakur, or barking-deer, uttered its sharp cry around 2 a.m., but as this was not continued, I decided it had been disturbed by a wandering leopard. Three o'clock came, I awoke the two sleeping men, and in turn fell into a dreamless sleep, to awaken to the early and spirited cry of a grey jungle cock, saluting the rising sun.

Hot tea, made with water from the well nearby, and some food gave us new life and heart, after which I walked across to the giant peepul-tree and inspected the remains of the old priest. The vultures by day, and hyenas and jackals by night, had made a good job of him, for nothing remained but a few cleanly-picked bones, at the sight of which I fell to reminiscing about the old man who had tended this temple for the past forty years, looking daily upon the same view as the one I now saw, hearing the same night-sounds of sambar, kakur and elephant as I had heard that night, and was now but a few bones, folded in the crevices of the hoary peepul-tree.

For the next hour we cast around in the hope of finding pug marks and perhaps identifying the slayer, but although we saw a few old trails, I could not with any certainty classify them as having been made by my tigress.

By 9 a.m. we left on the long 23-mile trek to Gundalam, where we arrived just after 5 p.m. Here, upon making inquiries about the recent killing, I gleaned the first definite information about the slayer from a herdsman who had been attending to his cattle at the same watershed where I had tied my buffalo bait on my last visit. This man stated that he had had a companion with whom he had been talking, and who had then walked across to a nearby bush to answer a call of nature. He had just squatted down when, beyond the bush, the devilish head of a tiger arose, with only one ear, soon to be followed by an evil, striped body. The man had shrieked once when the fangs sank into the face and throat, and the next instant tiger and victim had disappeared into the jungle.

Here at last was the information I had been dreading, but somehow wanting, to hear. So, after all, it was now confirmed that the killer was none other than my old enemy, the tigress, who had returned at last to the scene of her former depredations, and for whose return and now vastly increased cunning I was myself responsible.

Everywhere I had heard reports that no cattle or buffaloes had been killed by this beast, so I did not waste time, as on the previous occasion, in setting live baits, realizing that I had an adversary to deal with whom I could only hope to vanquish in a chance encounter, face-to-face.

For the next two days I again searched the surrounding jungle, hoping by luck to meet the killer, but with fear and dread of being attacked from behind at any moment. Pugmarks I came across in plenty, especially on the soft sands of the Gundalam River, where the familiar tracks of the Jowlagiri tigress were plainly in view, adding confirmation to the thought that by my poor shot, some five months ago, I had been responsible for several more deaths.

At midday on the third day, a party of men arrived in a lather, having covered the thirty miles from Jowlagiri to tell me of a further kill—this time the watchman of the Jowlagiri Forest Bungalow—who had been killed and half-eaten within a hundred yards of the bungalow itself, the previous afternoon.

Hoping that the tigress might retrace her steps towards Sulekunta and Gundalam, as she was rumoured never to stay in the same place for more than a day after making a human kill, I left with my men at once, augmented by the party from Jowlagiri, who, although they had practically run the thirty miles to Gundalam, preferred the return tramp of twenty-five miles to Sulekunta protected by my rifle rather than return by themselves.

Again we reached the temple of Sulekunta as daylight was fading and, as the nights were still dark, repeated our camp-fire procedure within the temple itself. Our party had now been increased to twelve, including myself, a number which, aldiough it made us feel safer, was far too many for my personal comfort.

This time, however, we were not to spend a peaceful night. The sambar and kakur were restless from nightfall, and at 8.30 p.m. we heard a tiger calling from a spot I judged to be half a mile away. This was repeated an hour later from quite close, and I could then easily distinguish the intonations of a tigress calling for a mate. The tigress had also seen the campfire and become aware of the proximity of humans and, obviously hoping for a meal, she twice circled the temple, her repeated mating calls being interspersed by distinctiy audible grunts of anticipation.

All this gave me an idea by which I might possibly succeed in keeping her in the vicinity till daylight, at which time only could I hope to accomplish anything. Twice I gave the answering call of a male tiger, and received at once the urgent summons of this imperious female. Indeed, she came to the edge of the clearing and called solidly as almost to paralyse us all. I was careful, however, not to call while she was in the immediate vicinity, which might have aroused her suspicions. At the same time I instructed the men to talk rather loudly, and not over-stoke the already blazing fire, instructions which were doubtlessly most unwelcome. I hoped by these means, between mating urge and appetite, to keep the tigress in the vicinity till daylight.

She called again, shortly before dawn and, congratulating myself on my ruse, as soon as it became light enough to see I hastened down the path towards Jowlagiri where, but a quarter a mile away, stood the tamarind tree beneath which the boy had been killed over a year ago, and which I had already mentally noted as an ideal sitting-up place, requiring no preparation.

Reaching the tree in safety, I clambered up some twelve feet to a crotch, which was reasonably comfortable and provided a clear view of the path at both ends. Then, expanding my lungs, I called lustily in imitation of a male tiger. Nothing but silence answered me, and I began to wonder if after all the tigress had moved on at dawn. A new anxiety also gripped me. Perhaps she was near the temple, waiting for one of the men she had marked down the night before to come out of the building.

Before departing I had very strictly enjoined my companions not, on any account, to leave the temple, but I felt anxious lest any of them disobey me, perhaps in answer to a call of nature, or to get water from the well that was temptingly near.

I called a second time. Still no answer. After a short interval, and expanding my lungs to bursting-point, I called again. This time I was successful, for my voice penetrated the intervening forest and was picked up by the tigress, who immediately answered from the direction of the temple. I had been right in my surmise; the wily animal had gone there to look for a meal.

After a few minutes I called a fourth time and was again answered by the tigress; I was overjoyed to find that she was coming in my direction in search of the mate she thought was waiting.

I called twice more, my last call being answered from barely a hundred yards. Levelling the rifle, I glanced along the sights to a spot on the path about twenty-five yards away. I judged she would take less than thirty seconds to cover the intervening distance. I began to count, and as I reached twenty-seven the tigress strode into full view, inquiringly looking for her mate. From my commanding height in the tree her missing ear was clearly visible, and I knew that at last, after many tiring efforts, the killer was within my power. This time there would be no slip. To halt her onward movement, I moaned in a low tone. She stopped abruptly and looked upwards in surprise. The next second the .405 bullet crashed squarely between the eyes, and she sank forward in a lurching movement and lay twitching in the dust. I placed a second shot into the crown of her skull, although there was no need to have done so; actually this second shot did considerable damage to the head and gave much unnecessary extra work to the taxidermist.

The dreaded killer of Jowlagiri had come to a tame and ignominious end, unworthy of her career, and although she had been a murderer, silent, savage and cruel, a pang of conscience troubled me as to my unsporting ruse in encompassing her end.

There is not much more to tell. My eleven followers were elated at the sight of the dead marauder. Soon a stout sapling was cut, to which her feet were lashed by strong creeper vines, and we commenced the seven mile walk to Jowlagiri, staggering beneath the burden. Because of the man-eater's presence, no humans were afoot until we practically entered the village itself. Then word went round and throngs surrounded us. I allowed the people a short hour in which to feast their eyes on their onetime foe, while I retired to a tree some distance away, where hot tea soon refreshed me, followed by some food, and two comforting pipes of tobacco. Then I ~~renirned~~ RETURNED to the village, where willing hands helped me to lash the tigress across the rear seat of my two-seater Studebaker, to begin my homeward journey with the comforting thought that I had lived down my error and avenged the deaths of many humans.

2

The Spotted Devil of Gummalapur

The leopard is common to practically all tropical jungles, and, unlike the tiger, indigenous to the forests of India; for whereas it has been established that the tiger is a comparatively recent newcomer from regions in the colder north, records and remains have shown that the leopard—or panther, as it is better known in India—has lived in the peninsula from the earliest times.

Because of its smaller size, and decidedly lesser strength, together with its innate fear of mankind, the panther is often treated with some derision, sometimes coupled with truly astonishing carelessness, two factors that have resulted in the maulings and occasional deaths of otherwise intrepid but cautious tiger-hunters. Even when attacking a human being the panther rarely kills, but confines itself to a series of quick bites and quicker raking scratches with its small but sharp claws; on the other hand, few persons live to tell that they have been attacked by a tiger.

This general rule has one fearful exception, however, and that is the panther that has turned man-eater. Although examples of such animals are comparatively rare, when they do occur they depict the panther as an engine of destruction quite equal to his far larger cousin, the tiger. Because of his smaller size he can conceal himself in places impossible to a tiger, his need for water is far less, and in veritable demoniac cunning and daring, coupled with the uncanny sense of self-preservation and stealthy disappearance when danger threatens, he has no equal.

Such an animal was the man-eating leopard of Gummalapur. This leopard had established a record of some forty-two human killings and a reputation for veritable cunning that almost exceeded human intelligence. Some fearful stories of diabolical craftiness had been attributed to him, but certain it was that the panther was held in awe throughout an area of some 250 square miles over which it held undisputable sway.

Before sundown the door of each hut in every one of the villages within this area was fastened shut, some being reinforced by piles of boxes or large stones, kept for the purpose. Not until the sun was well up in the heavens next morning did the timid inhabitants venture to expose themselves. This state of affairs rapidly told on the sanitary condition of the houses, the majority of which were not equipped with latrines of any sort, the adjacent waste land being used for the purpose.

Finding that its human meals were increasingly difficult to obtain, the panther became correspondingly bolder, and in two instances burrowed its way in through the thatched walls of the smaller huts, dragging its screaming victim out the same way, while the whole village lay awake, trembling behind closed doors, listening to the shrieks of the victim as he was carried away. In one case the panther, frustrated from burrowing its way in through the walls, which had been boarded up with rough planks, resorted to the novel method of entering through the thatched roof. In this instance it found itself unable to carry its prey back through the hole it had made, so in a paroxym of fury had killed all four inhabitants of the hut—a man, his wife and two children—before clawing its way back to the darkness outside and to safety.

Only during the day did the villagers enjoy any respite. Even then they moved about in large, armed groups, but so far no instance had occurred of the leopard attacking in daylight, although it had been very frequently seen at dawn within the precincts of a village.

Such was the position when I arrived at Gummalapur, in response to an invitation from Jepson, the district magistrate, to rid his area of this scourge. Preliminary conversation with some of the inhabitants revealed that they appeared dejected beyond hope, and with true eastern fatalism had decided to resign themselves to the fact that this shaitan, from whom they believed deliverance to be impossible, had come to stay, till each one of them had been devoured or had fled the district as the only alternative.

It was soon apparent that I would get little or no cooperation from the villagers, many of whom openly stated that if they dared to assist me the shaitan would come to hear of it and would hasten their end. Indeed, they spoke in whispers as if afraid that loud talking would be overheard by the panther, who would single them out for revenge.

That night, I sat in a chair in the midst of the village, with my back to the only house that possessed a twelve-foot wall, having taken the precaution to cover the roof with a deep layer of thorns and brambles, in case I should be attacked from behind by the leopard leaping down on me. It was a moonless night, but the clear sky promised to provide sufficient illumination from its myriad stars to enable me to see the panther should it approach.

The evening, at six o'clock, found the inhabitants behind locked doors, while I sat alone on my chair, with my rifle across my lap, loaded and cocked, a flask of hot tea nearby, a blanket, a water-bottle, some biscuits, a torch at hand, and of course my pipe, tobacco and matches as my only consolation during the long vigil till daylight returned.

With the going down of the sun a period of acute anxiety began, for the stars were as yet not brilliant enough to light the scene even dimly. Moreover, immediately to westward of the village lay two abrupt hills which hastened the dusky uncertainty that might otherwise have been lessened by some reflection from the recently set sun.

I gripped my rifle and stared around me, my eyes darting in all directions and from end to end of the deserted village street. At that moment I would have welcomed the jungle, where by their cries of alarm I could rely on the animals and birds to warn me of the approach of the panther. Here all was deathly silent, and the whole village might have been entirely deserted, for not a sound escaped from the many inhabitants whom I knew lay listening behind closed doors, and listening for the scream that would herald my death and another victim for the panther.

Time passed, and one by one the stars became visible, till by 7.15 p.m. they shed a sufficiently diffused glow to enable me to see along the whole village street, although somewhat indistinctly. My confidence returned, and I began to think of some way to draw the leopard towards me, should he be in the vicinity. I forced myself to cough loudly at intervals and then began to talk to myself, hoping that my voice would be heard by the panther and bring him to me quickly.

I do not know if any of my readers have ever tried talking to themselves loudly for any reason, whether to attract a man-eating leopard or not. I suppose they must be few, for I realise what reputation the man who talks to himself acquires. I am sure I acquired that reputation with the villagers, who from behind their closed doors listened to me that night as I talked to myself. But believe me, it is no easy task to talk loudly to yourself for hours on end, while watching intently for the stealthy approach of a killer.

By 9 p.m. I got tired of it, and considered taking a walk around the streets of the village. After some deliberation I did this, still talking to myself as I moved cautiously up one lane and down the next, frequently glancing back over my shoulder.

I soon realised, however, that I was exposing myself to extreme danger, as the panther might pounce on me from any corner, from behind any pile of garbage, or from the rooftops of any of the huts. Ceasing my talking abruptly, I returned to my chair, thankful to get back alive.

Time dragged by very slowly and monotonously, the hours seeming to pass on leaden wheels. Midnight came and I found myself feeling cold, due to a sharp breeze that had set in from the direction of the adjacent forest, which began beyond the two hillocks. I drew the blanket closely around me, while consuming tobacco far in excess of what was good for me. By 2 a.m. I found I was growing sleepy. Hot tea and some biscuits, followed by icy water from the bottle dashed into my face, and a quick raising and lowering of my body from the chair half-a-dozen times, revived me a little, and I fell to talking to myself again, as a means of keeping awake thereafter.

At 3.30 a.m. came an event which caused me untold discomfort for the next two hours. With the sharp wind banks of heavy cloud were carried along, and these soon covered the heavens and obscured the stars, making the darkness intense, and it would have been quite impossible to see the panther a yard away. I had undoubtedly placed myself in an awkward position, and entirely at the mercy of the beast, should it choose to attack me now. I fell to flashing my torch every half-minute from end to end of the street, a proceeding which was very necessary if I hoped to remain alive with the panther anywhere near, although I felt I was ruining my chances of shooting the beast, as the bright torch-beams would probably scare it away. Still, there was the possibility that it might not be frightened by the light, had that I might be able to see it and bring off a lucky shot, a circumstance that did not materialise, as morning found me still shining the torch after a night-long and futile vigil.

I snatched a few hours' sleep and at noon fell to questioning the villagers again. Having found me still alive that morning—quite obviously contrary to their expectations—and possibly crediting me with the power to communicate with spirits because they had heard me walking around their village talking, they were considerably more communicative and gave me a few more particulars about the beast. Apparently the leopard wandered about its domain a great deal, killing erratically and at places widely distant from one another, and as I had already found out, never in succession at the same village. As no human had been killed at Gummalapur within the past three weeks, it seemed that there was much to be said in favour of staying where I was, rather than moving around in a haphazard fashion, hoping to come up with the panther. Another factor against wandering about was that this beast was rarely visible in the daytime, and there was therefore practically no chance of my meeting it, as might have been the case with a man-eating tiger. It was reported that the animal had been wounded in its right forefoot, since it had the habit of placing the pad sidewards, a fact which I was later able to confirm when I actually came across the tracks of the animal.

After lunch, I conceived a fresh plan for that night, which would certainly save me from the great personal discomforts I had experienced the night before. This was to leave a door of one of the huts ajar, and to rig up inside it a very life-like dummy of a human being; meanwhile, I would remain in a corner of the same hut behind a barricade of boxes. This would provide an opportunity to slay the beast as he became visible in the partially-opened doorway, or even as he attacked the dummy, while I myself would be comparatively safe and warm behind my barricade.

I explained the plan to the villagers, who, to my surprise, entered into it with some enthusiasm. A hut was placed at my disposal immediately next to that through the roof of which the leopard had once entered and killed the four inmates. A very life-like dummy was rigged up, made of straw, an old pillow, a jacket, and a saree. This was placed within the doorway of the hut in a sitting position, the door itself being kept half-open. I sat myself behind a low parapet of boxes, placed diagonally across the opposite end of the small hut, the floor of which measured about 12 feet by 10 feet. At this short range, I was confident of accounting for the panther as soon as it made itself visible in the doorway. Furthermore, should it attempt to enter by the roof, or through the thatched walls, I would have ample time to deal with it. To make matters even more realistic, I instructed the inhabitants of both the adjacent huts, especially the women folk, to endeavour to talk in low tones as far into the night as was possible, in order to attract the killer to that vicinity.

An objection was immediately raised, that the leopard might be led to enter one of their huts, instead of attacking the dummy in the doorway of the hut in which I was sitting. This fear was only overcome by promising to come to their aid should they hear the animal attempting an entry. The signal was to be a normal call for help, with which experience had shown the panther to be perfectly familiar, and of which he took no notice. This plan also assured me that the inhabitants would themselves keep awake and continue their low conversation in snatches, in accordance with my instructions.

Everything was in position by 6 p.m., at which time all doors in the village were secured, except that of the hut where I sat. The usual uncertain dusk was followed by bright starlight that threw the open doorway and the crouched figure of the draped dummy into clear relief. Now and again I could hear the low hum of conversation from the two neighbouring huts.

The hours dragged by in dreadful monotony. Suddenly the silence was disturbed by a rustle in the thatched roof which brought me to full alertness. But it was only a rat, which scampered across and then dropped with a thud to the floor nearby, from where it ran along the tops of the boxes before me, becoming clearly visible as it passed across the comparatively light patch of the open doorway. As the early hours of the morning approached, I noticed that the conversation from my neighbours died down and finally ceased, showing that they had fallen asleep, regardless of man-eating panther, or anything else that might threaten them.

I kept awake, occasionally smoking my pipe, or sipping hot tea from the flask, but nothing happened beyond the noises made by the tireless rats, which chased each other about and around the room, and even across me, till daylight finally dawned, and I lay back to fall asleep after another tiring vigil.

The following night, for want of a better plan, and feeling that sooner or later the man-eater would appear, I decided to repeat the performance with the dummy, and I met with an adventure which will remain indelibly impressed on my memory till my dying day.

I was in position again by six o'clock, and the first part of the night was but a repetition of the night before. The usual noise of scurrying rats, broken now and again by the low-voiced speakers in the neighbouring huts, were the only sounds to mar the stillness of the night. Shortly after 1 a.m. a sharp wind sprang up, and I could hear the breeze rustling through the thatched roof. This rapidly increased in strength, till it was blowing quite a gale. The rectangular patch of light from the partly open doorway practically disappeared as the sky became overcast with storm clouds, and soon the steady rhythmic patter of raindrops, which increased to a regular downpour, made me feel that the leopard, who like all his family are not overfond of water, would not venture out on this stormy night, and that I would draw a blank once more.

By now the murmuring voices from the neighbouring huts had ceased or become inaudible, drowned in the swish of the rain. I strained my eyes to see the scarcely perceptible doorway, while the crouched figure of the dummy could not be seen at all, and while I looked I evidently fell asleep, tired out by my vigil of the two previous nights.

How long I slept I cannot tell, but it must have been for some considerable time. I awoke abruptly with a start, and a feeling that all was not well. The ordinary person in awaking takes some time to collect his faculties, but my jungle training and long years spent in dangerous places enabled me to remember where I was and in what circumstances, as soon as I awoke.

The rain had ceased and the sky had cleared a little, for the oblong patch of open doorway was more visible now, with the crouched figure of the dummy seated at its base. Then, as I watched, a strange thing happened. The dummy seemed to move, and as I looked more intently it suddenly disappeared to the accompaniment of a snarling growl. I realised that the panther had come, seen the crouched figure of the dummy in the doorway which it had mistaken for a human being, and then proceeded to stalk it, creeping in at the opening on its belly, and so low to the ground that its form had not been outlined in the faint light as I had hoped. The growl I had heard was at the panther's realisation that the thing it had attacked was not human after all.

Switching on my torch and springing to my feet, I hurdled the barricade of boxes and sprang to the open door way, to dash outside and almost trip over the dummy which lay across my path. I shone the beam of torchlight in both directions, but nothing could be seen. Hoping that the panther might still be lurking nearby and shining my torch-beam into every corner, I walked slowly down the village street, cautiously negotiated the bend at its end and walked back up the next street, in fear and trembling of a sudden attack. But although the light lit up every corner, every rooftop and every likely hiding-place in the street, there was no sign of my enemy anywhere. Then only did I realise the true significance of the reputation this animal had acquired of possessing diabolical cunning. Just as my own sixth sense had wakened me from sleep at a time of danger, a similar sixth sense had warned the leopard that here was no ordinary human being, but one that was bent upon its destruction. Perhaps it was the bright beam of torchlight that had unnerved it at the last moment; but, whatever the cause, the man-eater had silently completely and effectively disappeared, for although I searched for it through all the streets of Gummalapur that night, it had vanished as mysteriously as it had come.

Disappointment, and annoyance with myself at having fallen asleep, were overcome with a grim determination to get even with this beast at any cost.

Next morning the tracks of the leopard were clearly visible at the spot it had entered the village and crossed a muddy drain, where for the first time I saw the pug-marks of the slayer and the peculiar indentation of its right forefoot, the paw of which was not visible as a pug-mark, but remained a blur, due to this animal's habit of placing it on edge. Thus it was clear to me that *the* panther had at some time received an injury to its foot which had turned it into a man-eater. Later I was able to view the injured foot for myself, and I was probably wrong in my deductions as to the cause of its man-eating propensities; for I came to learn that the animal had acquired the habit of eating the corpses which the people of that area, after a cholera epidemic within the last year, had by custom carried into the forest and left to the vultures. These easily procured meals had given the panther a taste for human flesh, and the injury to its foot, which made normal hunting and swift movement difficult, had been the concluding factor in turning it into that worst of all menaces to an Indian village—a man-eating panther.

I also realised that, granting the panther was equipped with an almost-human power of deduction, it would not appear in Gummalapur again for a long time after the fright I had given it the night before in following it with my torchlight.

It was therefore obvious that I would have to change my scene of operations, and so, after considerable thought, I decided to move on to the village of Devarabetta, diagonally across an intervening range of forest hills, and some eighteen miles away, where the panther had already secured five victims, though it had not been visited for a month. ?

Therefore, I set out before XXX a.m. that very day, after an early lunch. The going was difficult, as the path led across two hills. Along the valley that lay between them ran a small jungle stream, and beside it I noted the fresh pugs of a big male tiger that had followed the watercourse for some 200 yards before crossing to the other side. It had evidently passed early that morning, as was apparent from the minute trickles of moisture that had seeped into the pug marks through the river sand, but had not had time to evaporate in the morning sun. Holding steadfastly to the job in hand, however, I did not follow the tiger and arrived at Devarabetta just after 5 p.m.

The inhabitants were preparing to shut themselves into their huts when I appeared, and scarcely had the time or inclination to talk to me. However, I gathered that they agreed that a visit from the man-eater was likely any day, for a full month had elapsed since his last visit and he had never been known to stay away for so long.

Time being short, I hastily looked around for the hut with the highest wall, before which I seated myself as on my first night at Gummalapur, having hastily arranged some dried thorny bushes across its roof as protection against attack from my rear and above. These thorns had been brought from the hedge of a field bordering the village itself, and I had had to escort the men who carried them with my rifle, so afraid they were of the man-eater's early appearance.

Devarabetta was a far smaller village dian Gummalapur, and situated much closer to the forest, a fact which I welcomed for the reason that I would be able to obtain information as to the movements of carnivora by the warning notes that the beasts and birds of the jungle would utter, provided I was within hearing.

The night fell with surprising rapidity, though this time a thin sickle of new-moon was showing in the sky. The occasional call of a roosting jungle-cock, and the plaintive call of pea-fowl, answering one another from the nearby forest, told me that all was still well. And then it was night, the faint starlight rendering hardly visible, and as if in a dream, the tortuously winding and filthy lane that formed the main street of Devarabetta. At 8.30 p.m. a sambar hind belled from the forest, following her original sharp note with a series of warning cries in steady succession. Undoubtedly a beast of prey was afoot and had been seen by the watchful deer, who was telling the other jungle-folk to look out for their lives. Was it the panther or one of the larger carnivora? Time alone would tell, but at least I had been warned.

The hind ceased her belling, and some fifteen minutes later, from the direction in which she had first sounded her alarm, I heard the low moan of a tiger, to be repeated twice in succession, before all became silent again. It was not a mating call that I had heard, but the call of the King of the Jungle in his normal search for food, reminding the inhabitants of the forest that their master was on the move in search of prey, and that one of them must die that night to appease his voracious appetite.

Time passed, and then down the lane I caught sight of some movement. Raising my cocked rifle, I covered the object, which slowly approached me, walking in the middle of the street. Was this the panther after all, and would it walk thus openly, and in the middle of the lane, without any attempt at concealment? It was now about thirty yards away and still it came on boldly, without any attempt to take cover or to creep along the edges of objects in the usual manner of a leopard when stalking its prey. Moreover, it seemed a frail and slender animal, as I could see it fairly clearly now. Twenty yards and I pressed the button of my torch, which this night I had clamped to my rifle.

As the powerful beam threw across the intervening space it lighted a village cur, commonly known to us in India as a 'pariah dog'. Starving and lonely, it had sought out human company; it stared blankly into the bright beam of light, feebly wagging a skinny tail in unmistakable signs of friendliness.

Welcoming a companion, if only a lonely cur, I switched off the light and called it to my side by a series of flicks of thumb and finger. It approached cringingly, still wagging its ridiculous tail. I fed it with some biscuits and a sandwich, and in the dull light of the star-lit sky its eyes looked back at me in dumb gratitude for the little food I had given it, perhaps the first to enter its stomach for the past two days. Then it curled up at my feet and fell asleep.

Time passed and midnight came. A great horned owl hooted dismally from the edge of the forest, its prolonged mysterious cry of 'Whooo-whooo' seeming to sound a death-knell, or a precursor to that haunting part of the night when the souls of those not at rest return to the scenes of their earthly activities, to live over and over again the deeds that bind them to the earth.

One o'clock, two and then three o'clock passed in dragging monotony, while I strained my tired and aching eyes and ears for movement or sound. Fortunately it had remained a cloudless night and visibility was comparatively good by the radiance of the myriad stars that spangled the heavens in glorious array, a sight that cannot be seen in any of our dusty towns or cities.

And then, abruptly, the alarmed cry of a plover, or 'Did you-do-it' bird, as it is known in India, sounded from the nearby muddy tank on the immediate outskirts of the village. '*Did-you-do-it, Did-you-do-it, Did-you-do-it, Did you- do-it*', it called in rapid regularity. No doubt the bird was excited and had been disturbed, or it had seen something. The cur at my feet stirred, raised its head, then sank down again, as if without a care in the world. The minutes passed, and then suddenly the dog became fully awake. Its ears, that had been drooping in dejection, were standing on end, it trembled violently against my legs, while a low prolonged growl came from its throat. I noticed that it was looking down the lane that led into the village from the vicinity of the tank.

I stared intently in that direction. For a long time I could see nothing, and then it seemed that a shadow moved at a corner of a building some distance away and on the same side of the lane. I focussed my eyes on this spot, and after a few seconds again noticed a furtive movement, but this time a little closer.

Placing my left thumb on the switch which would actuate the torch, I waited in breathless silence. A few minutes passed, five or ten at the most, and then I saw an elongated body spring swiftly and noiselessly on to the roof of a hut some twenty yards away. As it happened, all the huts adjoined each other at this spot, and I guessed the panther had decided to walk along the roofs of these adjoining huts and spring upon me from the rear, rather than continue stalking me in full view.

I got to my feet quickly and placed my back against the wall. In this position the eave of the roof above my head passed over me and on to the road where I had been sitting, for about eighteen inches. The rifle I kept ready, finger on trigger, with my left thumb on the torch switch, pressed to my side and pointing upwards.

A few seconds later I heard a faint rustling as the leopard endeavoured to negotiate the thorns which I had taken the precaution of placing on the roof. He evidently failed in this, for there was silence again. Now I had no means of knowing where he was.

The next fifteen minutes passed in terrible anxiety, with me glancing in all directions in the attempt to locate the leopard before he sprang, while thanking Providence that the night remained clear. And then the cur, that had been restless and whining at my feet, shot out into the middle of the street, faced the corner of the hut against which I was sheltering and began to bark lustily.

This warning saved my life, for within five seconds the panther charged around the corner and sprang at me. I had just time to press the torch switch and fire from my hip, full into the blazing that

eyes that showed above the wide-opened, snarling mouth. The .405 bullet struck squarely, but the impetus of the charge carried the animal on to me. I jumped nimbly to one side, and as the panther crashed against the wall of the hut, emptied two more rounds from the magazine into the evil, spotted body.

It collapsed and was still, except for the spasmodic jerking of the still-opened jaws and long, extended tail. And then my friend the cur, staunch in faithfulness to his new-found master, rushed in and fixed his feeble teeth in the throat of the dead monster.

And so passed the 'Spotted Devil of Gummalapur', a panther of whose malignant craftiness I had never heard the like before and hope never to have to meet again. When skinning the animal next morning, I found that the injury to the right paw had not been caused, as I had surmised, by a previous bullet wound, but by two porcupine quills that had penetrated between the toes within an inch of each other and then broken off short. This must have happened quite a while before, as a gristly formation between the bones inside the foot had covered the quills. No doubt it had hurt the animal to place his paw on the ground in the normal way, and he had acquired the habit of walking on its edge.

I took the cur home, washed and fed it, and named it 'Nipper'. Nipper has been with me many years since then, and never have I had reason to regret giving him the few biscuits and sandwich that won his staunch little heart, and caused him to repay that small debt within a couple of hours, by saving my life.

3

The Striped Terror of Chamala Valley

The Chamala Valley is part of the north-eastern tip of the District of Chittoor in the Presidency of Madras, where it adjoins the District of Cuddapah immediately to the north. It is a comparatively small valley, its main portion extending northwards for some seven miles by five wide, with two branches at its extremity, like the letter 'Y', running respectively north-west and north-east, somewhat narrower than the main valley and each about four miles long. The branches terminate below the bluff crags of a towering escarpment that forms the southern boundary of Cuddapah.

A beautiful stream, called the Kalayani River, flows down the north-eastern valley, having its twin sources just below the escarpment, in magnificently wooded forest glens named Gundalpenta and Umbalmeru, where pools of translucent, ice-cold water are always to be found even in the hottest part of summer. The Kalyani then flows south ward through the main valley and eventually enters a cultivated area at the hamlet of Nagapatla, with an ancient lake at which the kings of Chandragiri, and afterwards the all-conquering Mohammedan hero, Tippoo Sultan, attempted to construct a dam to feed water to the parched countryside in the terribly hot months of summer. A heavily thatched, but snug forest bungalow has been constructed by the Forest Department on the southern side of the lake, bordering the ancient aquaduct. The sleepy village of Arepalli Rangampet lies about a mile and a half distant, and is of almost recent origin.

The Chamala Valley is entirely forested and in the days of British rule was a game preserve. Westward lies the Bakhrapet Forest Block, and eastward the Tirupati Forest Range, which culminates in the great pilgrim shrines of Tirupati, famous throughout India. Southward is the ancient town of Chandragiri, with its age-old fort, a mute tribute to the glory of its former kings.

A metre-gauge railway line passes close to Chandragiri, on its way to Tirupati and Renigunta, where it joins the arterial broad-gauge line from Madras to Bombay. A narrow cart-road leads from Chandragiri railway station for about three and a half miles to Rangampet; then it turns north wards for a mile and a half to Nagapatla, whence it continues still further north and becomes a Forest Departmental path for all the seven miles of the Chamala Valley till it reaches a spot named Pulibonu, which means Tiger's Cage, where it abruptly ends. Two flat, square, cemented campsites, and a well to provide a continuous supply of drinking water, have been constructed at this spot by the Forest Department.

The valley and its branches are beautiful, and when I first visited them, eighteen years ago, were a paradise for game. Large herds of chital, or spotted deer, roamed the main valley, some of the stags carrying heads the like of which I have nowhere seen in Southern India. The slopes of the foothills running into the Bakhrapet range on the west, and the Tirupati range on the east, as well as along the foot of the whole northern escarpment, were the home of magnificently proportioned and antlered sambar. The black or sloth bear could be found everywhere, but was especially numerous and dangerous in the dense forest below the escarpment. Kakar, or the 'muntjac' or barkingdeer, as it is known, also abounded. The main valley and its north-eastern appendage were the regular beat of tiger, which came from the Bakhrapet range, passed up the valleys, crossed the escarpment and into the Cuddapah Forests, thence to the Mamandur range and onwards to Settigunta. Panther were everywhere, and the area abounded in pea-fowl, spurfowl and grey jungle fowl, the latter especially being very numerous. This was the only forest in Southern India where I have found jungle fowl crowing even at midday, and regularly at 2 a.m., and at about 4.30 a.m., apart, of course, from their usual chorus at sunrise and sunset.

Into this peaceful area one day, early in 1937, came the striped terror of which I shall tell you. He was a tiger of normal size, and his tracks indicated no deformity that might have accounted for his partiality for human flesh. He suddenly appeared, no one knew from where, nor had any rumour been heard of the activities of a man-eating tiger in any of the adjoining forest areas, far or near. Strange as was his sudden and unheralded coming, it was soon well-known that a man-eater had entered the valley, for he killed, and wholly ate, a bamboo-cutter near the pools of Gundalpenta. Within three days thereafter, he practically entirely devoured a traveller on the Nagapatla-Pulibonu forest track, close to the fourth milestone.

Thereafter his killings became sporadic and irregular, extending throughout the length and breadth of the three valleys, where in all he killed and devoured, or partly devoured, seven people in the space of about six months.

One day the Forest Range Officer from Bakhrapet, in whose area the Chamala Valley is included, was on his way to take up residence in the Forest Bungalow at Nagapatla, during his rounds of inspection. He travelled by bullockcart, in which he was also bringing provisions, personal effects and other necessities for the period of a fortnight he would stay at Nagapatla.

It was 5 p.m., and the cart was hardly two miles from its destination, when a tiger walked on to the road in front of the vehicle. I should have told you that this road, leading from Bakhrapet to Nagapatla, ran through the reserved forest for practically its whole length, the last two miles being across the beginning of the Chamala Valley itself.

Seeing the tiger on the road before him, the cart-driver brought his vehicle to a stop and called out to the range officer and the forest guard who were with him. As the cart was a covered one and they were inside, neither had seen that there was a tiger on the road.

The three men commenced to shout, when the tiger, walking along the clearing that bordered the road, passed the cart and so came into view of the two men inside. At this juncture the forest guard, for no understandable reason, jumped out of the cart and commenced waving his hands and shouting, to frighten the beast away. However, he sealed his own fate, for with a succession of short roars the animal charged, seized him in its jaws, and bounded back into the concealing forest. The action had been so unexpected and abrupt that the range officer had no opportunity to do a thing, although what he could have done in any event was problematical, as he himself was unarmed.

The cart was then driven to Nagapada in great haste, but it was not until the following morning that a large group could be assembled, armed with matchlocks, hatchets and staves, to attempt to find the unfortunate forest guard, or rather what was left of him.

The remains were eventually located in a ravine, less than a furlong from the road; only the head, hands and feet, and his bloodstained and mangled khaki uniform and green turban, were left to tell the tale, the latter lying where it had fallen when the tiger jumped with its victim across the clearing that bordered the road.

This tragedy received a great deal of official attention, and was published by the Press throughout the country. A reward

Sketch map of localities referred to in the story of the Striped Terror of Chamala Valley.

was offered by the government for the destruction of the man-eater, and several venturesome hunters, both local and from, the city of Madras, arrived at the valley to destroy the creature. But after its last killing, and as if it had become aware that it had attracted too much attention, the terror completely disappeared for a while, nor could any trace of it be found anywhere in the valley. The assumption was that it had escaped, either by traversing the escarpment northwards into the Cuddapah District, or had wandered into the Bakhrapet or Tirupati blocks. The whole locality was on the alert, but nothing was heard of the animal for the next two months.

Then one day a railway ganger, patrolling the broadgauge railway track near the station of Mamandur, which stands on the Madras-Bombay arterial line, and is situated in a wide, densely-forested plateau, encircled with hills, some eighteen miles north-east of the Chamala Valley, failed to report at the terminal point of his patrol. No particular notice of his absence was taken for a day or two, as sudden absenteeism on trivial grounds is a common occurrence in the East; but when after that the man still failed to put in an appearance, the matter was regarded more seriously, and a squad was sent out to try to find him.

Walking along the railway, the first clue to the missing man's fate was the large hammer he had been using, which was found lying beside the track. Gangers are issued with such hammers to keep in place the wooden blocks used to wedge the rails against their supports, known as chairs. On the hard, sun-baked earth, no signs of any struggle was evident, but not far away were a few drops of blood that led down an embankment and into the neighbouring forest. Following this trail, the party came across an odd chapli (or country-made slipper) as worn by the missing ganger, together with traces of blood that had been smeared against the leaves of bushes. A little further on they crossed a strip of dry, soft sand, traversing which they clearly found the pug marks of a tiger.

This established that the missing man had been taken by a tiger. The fame of the man-eater of the Chamala Valley had spread far and wide during the past months, and naturally it was concluded that this animal was responsible for the latest tragedy. Incidentally, the remains of the ganger were never found.

Thereafter, two kills occurred during the succeeding months. The first at Settigunta, n miles north-west of Mamandur, and the second at Umbalmeru, which, as you will remember, was one of the twin sources of the Kalyani River before it entered the Chamala Valley

At this time, I was on a business visit to Madras and had had occasion to visit the chief conservator of forests with regard to a complaint I had earlier lodged against the activities of local poachers in the Salem District. While talking to the chief conservator, he mentioned the activities of the tiger—of which I had read a great deal in the Press—and suggested I make an attempt to bag the animal.

Fortunately, I had not availed myself of privilege leave during the past year, and as I had some months to my credit, I decided to spend one of them in making such an effort. Returning to Bangalore, I spent the next few days in getting together all the many necessities for such an undertaking and ten days later I was at the Nagapatla Forest Bungalow, which I had decided to make my headquarters in conducting the campaign against the man-eater of Chamala.

The first thing to do was to make exhaustive local inquiries, visit the spots in the Chamala Valley where the kills had occurred, and try to establish some sequence in the localities where the various incidents had taken place, so as to arrive, if possible, at a knowledge of the beat the tiger followed. This I entirely failed to do; it became obvious that this particular animal was a wanderer, who visited the valley there for some time, snatched a human victim wherever opportunity offered, and climbed over the escarpment in the direction of Mamandur or into the Cuddapah District.

Not without considerable difficulty, I purchased four young buffaloes. These I tied up at widely separated points; one at Gundalpenta, another at Umbalmeru, a third at a waterhole called Narasimha Cheruvu, close to the fourth milestone of the Nagapada-Pulibonu forest road, and the last at a rocky stream named Ragimankonar, a tributary of the Kalyani River, as it issued from the rocky hills of the Timpati block about two miles east of the road.

On the second day the bait at Narasimha Cheruvu was killed, but examination showed this to be the work of a large Tendu', or forest panther, and not of a tiger, as I had hoped. As baits are costly and I could not afford to lose them to interfering panthers, I sat up for this animal by the waterhole, and was lucky enough to bag him by 6.45 p.m., while it was still daylight, when he returned to the kill.

I then bought another bait, to replace the one the panther had killed, and secured it to the same spot at Narasimha Cheruvu.

The next week was spent in idleness at the forest bungalow, except for long walks throughout the forest every morning and evening in all directions in the hope of accidentally meeting the tiger. On the morning of the ninth day, when driving early in my Studebaker in the direction of Pulibonu, from where I intended starting out on another stroll through the jungles, I came across the pug-marks of a tiger which had joined the road at the sixth milestone and had walked down the middle of it to beyond Pulibonu. No distinguishing peculiarities about the man-eater's tracks had been so far observed, so that it was impossible to tell whether the animal that had made these fresh tracks was the slayer I was seeking, or just a casual wandering tiger. These pugs were, in places, very clear in the soft roadside sand, and I was able to examine them minutely; but beyond enabling me to say that they had been made by a male tiger of average size, no other peculiarity or distinguishing mark of any sort presented itself.

Leaving the car at Pulibonu, I walked up the north-eastern valley, the forest track crossing and re-crossing the Kalyani River, where I saw that the tiger had preceded me for some distance. I visited both Gundalpenta and Umbalmeru that day, in high hope that one or other of my baits had been taken, but found both of them alive, placidly chewing at the large piles of hay I had left them so that they might be as comfortable and as contented as possible.

After lunch that afternoon I returned and attempted to follow the tiger's tracks from the place I had last observed them. But I only partly succeeded, losing the tracks in some heavy bamboo that clothed both banks of the river along its higher reaches. It was fairly late that evening when I turned back towards Pulibonu. Proceeding a half-mile, and still within the heavy bamboo belt, I came upon a sloth bear which had made an unusually early appearance, as these creatures do not begin their wanderings till after sun down. He was standing up against a large white anthill, with his nose and a part of his head inside the hole he had made, drawing the white ants into his ready mouth with powerful inhalations. He looked for all the world like a very black, hairy man, standing against the anthill, while the noises he was making in his efforts were extraordinary, resembling the buzzing of a million bees, interspersed with loud, impatient snufflings and shufflings, as of a giant bloodhound on the trail.

I drew quite close to the bear, yet he did not see me, so engrossed he was in his congenial task. I could have come still closer, but this would have meant that, when eventually he did become aware of my presence, he would probably attack, and I would have to shoot him. This I did not want to do, as personally I have no quarrel with bears, and secondly, the sound of my shot would disturb the jungle and might result in driving the tiger away. So I stopped at the distance of about forty yards and coughed loudly. The bear heard me, ceased his buzzing and snuffling, and whirled around on his hind feet, to face me with an expression that was amusing, to say the least of it. Annoyance, fear, chagrin and resentment were writ large across his mud-covered features. For a moment he watched me, rising still higher on his hind-legs, and I thought at first he would make a blind charge, which is the habit of the sloth-bear when disturbed at close quarters. But better judgement prevailed; he sank to all fours and bolted for all he was worth, bounding away like a black hairy ball, muttering, '*Aufl Aufl Aufl!*'

Early next morning found me back at Pulibonu. There were no pug-marks on the road to indicate the tiger's return, leaving the inference that he was somewhere in the north-eastern valley, or that he had departed across the escarpment.

Leaving the car, I trudged to Gundalpenta, but found my bait alive, still chewing hay as if nothing else in the world mattered. Then I went on to Umbalmeru, and upon approaching the spot where my other bait had been tethered, found that it was missing. Examination revealed that it had been killed by a tiger, which had then succeeded in dragging it away after first snapping the strong tethering rope with which I had secured it.

To follow the drag mark was easy, and after proceeding about 100 yards, my attention was attracted by a solitary crow, perched on the low branch of a tree, looking downwards in expectation.

This could only mean one thing—that the tiger was there and in possession of his kill. If he were not there, the crow would have descended to feed on the carcase, instead of sitting on a branch looking so dejectedly downwards, as he was doing at that moment.

The tree on which the crow was sitting overlooked a downwardly sloping bank of spear-grass, at the foot of which was a small depression densely covered by a thicket. It was somewhere in this thicket that the tiger, and his kill, were sheltering.

To approach this thicket directly was inadvisable. To begin with, the tiger would probably hear me and decamp. On the other hand, and especially if he were the man-eater, he would undoubtedly charge, and the proximity of the surrounding bushes and the length of the spear grass gave me a very poor chance of being able to stop him before he reached me.

I therefore backed away some fifty yards and began casting about for a detour by which I could approach the spot from some other angle, or perhaps from the opposite side, where I could glimpse the tiger from more favourable ground.

To my good fortune, a shallow nala ran diagonally across, roughly from north-west to north-east, on its way to join the early reaches of the Kalyani River. Tiptoeing up this nala, I soon judged I was abreast of the thicket in which the tiger lay. Continuing for another twenty-five yards, I cautiously climbed the right-hand bank and found, as I expected, that I was now some little distance beyond the thicket. A half-grown tamarind tree lay a few yards ahead of me, and creeping up to this, I swung myself into its sheltering branches, and then climbed higher in the hope of being able to look down into the thicket.

But I was disappointed, in that I could see nothing. Not even the crow was visible from this position, as the low branch on which he was perched was obscured from my view by the intervening thicket. I had therefore no means of knowing whether the tiger was still there, or had moved on.

I remained in this position for about half an hour, hoping that the jungle—or rather its inmates—would indicate the movements of the tiger if he came out of the bushes. The sun was well up by now, and I knew the tiger would soon move off to one of the water-pools of Umbalmeru, to quench his thirst after the heavy meal he had undoubtedly had.

Then I heard the peculiar alarm cry of a grey langur monkey, '*Ha-aah! Har! Har!*' he called, from a hundred yards to my left. This he repeated steadily, to the accompanying, '*Cheek I Cheek!*' of a female of the tribe.

The tiger had moved at last, and the langur watchman had seen him.

There is no need for me to tell those of my readers who are familiar with the Indian forests about the wise ways of langur monkeys. Those who are not will be interested to know that these great grey arboreans, with black faces and enormously long tails, live in tribes in the forests, where they exist entirely on wild fruits, certain leaves, and of course the multifarious caterpillars and insects which form a particular delicacy. The flesh of the langur is an outstanding attraction on the menu of tigers and panthers, and of some jungle tribes, so that generations of hard experience have taught them to post a watchman, who invariably takes up his position on the highest tree and keeps an intent lookout for prowling felines. It might do some humans good to take a leaf out of the langur watchman's book, for while he is on duty this langur will not feed or allow his attention to be in any way distracted from his job. He realises that the safety and lives of the babies, females and other members of his tribe depend entirely on his vigilance. You will see him on top of the highest tree, sitting alert and looking around. Not a movement within visible range escapes his beady, black eyes. Eventually, and only after he is relieved by another watchman, will he think of feeding himself.

The normal calls of langurs at play are a series of resounding 'Whoomp—Whoomps', that echo down the hillsides and the deep forest glens. When he spots danger, however, the watchman barks, 'Ha-aah! Har! Har!' in a successive series of calls, and the tribe seeks safety in the highest trees.

Alas, for all the wisdom of the astute langurs, tiger and panther have also developed an instinctive technique to overcome the cleverness of these monkeys, for they too must eat. When they hear the watchman's call, tigers and panthers who have been stalking the tribe know they have been discovered, and that the monkeys will take to the highest trees. So they now change their tactics, and after having located a tree on which a number of the apes are seated, rush with a series of blood-curdling roars towards it and possibly leap to the lowest fork, as if to climb the tree themselves. Seated on the highest branches, the langurs would be quite safe if they would only stay put. But the horrid snarls and roars, together with the terrible striped or spotted form charging towards them with wide-open jaws, unnerves the poor beasts, and they jump wildly from their perches of safety, either in attempts to reach neighbouring trees, or from the great height on to the ground itself, where one of them invariably falls an easy prey to the tiger or panther anticipating the foolish act.

But I have digressed, and must return to what happened after I heard the langur watchman's '*Ha-aah! Har! Har!*'

Clambering down the tree, I crept forward with my rifle at the ready diagonally towards the spot from which the langur watchman was giving his warning. Knowing the tiger to have fed well, I did not anticipate it would attempt to molest the monkeys on this occasion, but that when seen by the watchman he was making his way towards one of the pools. Spear grass and 'wait-a-bit' thorn grew prolifically in this area and progress was both slow and difficult.

Proceeding very cautiously about half a furlong, I caught sight of the langur watchman on the top-most branch of a wild-cotton tree, at the same instant as he saw me. He. now had two possible enemies to observe, and I knew if I watched carefully enough I would be able to get a rough idea of the tiger's whereabouts by noting in which direction the langur was looking. I accordingly squatted down on my haunches in the long grass and 'froze'.

The watchman looked in my direction for a few seconds, then looked away to his left, then back again at me, then back again left, still voicing his alarm.

I knew by these glances that he was watching both me and the tiger and judged the latter to be ahead of me by at least a hundred yards. Getting to my feet, and bent double, I shuffled forward as rapidly as possible in the direction I judged the tiger to be, much to the consternation: of the already excited langur watchman, who could not make out whether I contemplated an attack against the tribe or against the tiger. His alarm call redoubled both in tempo and volume, a fact which began to worry me as I knew the tiger was listening to him too, and would sense, by this increased excitement, some fresh source of danger to the monkeys and so also, perhaps, to himself.

And I was right. I covered the hundred yards rapidly, and after another twenty-five yards I judged that I must now be pretty near the tiger and that it was time to redouble my caution. Momentarily I glanced back at the langur watchman. He was looking intently in my direction, confirming the fact that both the tiger and myself were now in the same area of his vision.

'Freezing' again, I listened and watched minutely the space before me, and on either side. It consisted of the usual clumps of thorn-bush, interspersed by short glades of speargrass, about four foot high. As I watched I saw a slight movement of the grass to my left, about thirty yards away. I raised myself in order to get a better view, and the tiger saw me. A low growl followed by two bounds, and he had disappeared.

I knew it was now both futile and dangerous to follow him, having made him aware of my presence and the fact that he was being followed. Cautiously guarding my rear against a surprise attack, I crept back towards the thicket in which I knew the kill was lying, and I soon found it. The calf had been half-eaten; it was resting on its left side, sheltered by the grass and thicket from vultures, and very fortunately overlooked by a wild mango tree.

I had now to make a quick decision. There was a chance of the tiger returning to his kill, in spite of having seen me, which I would miss if I were to lose this opportunity of sitting up for him. At the same time, I had not come equipped for a night vigil, and was carrying no torch, blanket or food. If I decided to sit up, I would have to remain in the tree till morning, as the nights were dark at that time and there was no moon. It would hardly be possible to negotiate the pitch-black forest and return to my car at Pulibonu, apart from the fact that I would be entirely at the man-eater's mercy. If I remained, I was in for a night of extreme discomfort in the bitterly cold breeze that would blow down from the escarpment, against which I could not shield myself. I thought of going back to the car to get the necessary things. The distance was roughly four miles each way, and I feared the tiger might come back in my absence and entirely remove the kill.

Finally I decided to abandon all thought of personal discomfort and sit it out. Ascending the mango tree, I settled myself in its second fork, where I was able to be fairly comfortable with my back against a branch. I folded my feet crosswise, in Indian fashion, after removing my shoes, and stood the cocked rifle against the branch before me. From this position I had a clear view of the kill to my left, then an interruption by the branch before me, then another view, then a branch, then a view over my right shoulder at an angle from which it was impossible to shoot, and finally the branch against which my back rested. This precluded any view of the rear. At the same time I was about fifteen feet from the ground and safe from the tiger's spring. To reach me he would have to pass the first crotch in the tree, where he would be almost at point-blank range.

The time was 12.50 p.m., and I settled down to what I felt would become one of the coldest and most unendurable vigils of my whole career as a hunter.

I will not weary my readers by recounting how the hours dragged by until 6.30 p.m., when the fowl and daybirds of the forest had gone to roost, and the langurs had long since moved away from the hated presence of their two enemies, tiger and man. I was alone, except for an occasional nightjar that flitted, chirping, around my tree. At 6.45 p.m. it was almost dark. The nightjar had now settled below me, and commenced its squatting call of 'Chuckoo-chuckoo-chuckoo', when I met one of the strange experiences that sometimes, but very rarely, fall to the lot of a wanderer in the Indian forests.

I had been told stories by jungle men, and had also read, that tigers, in particular localities only, imitate sambar and emit the belling call of a stag, presumably to decoy other animals of the same species to them, particularly the does. I had never placed much credence in this story, and never experienced it myself. That evening, shortly after 6.45, the sudden solitary *'Dhank'* of a sambar stag rang out from a thicket in the waning light, in the space still visible between the branch against which my rifle rested before me, and that immediately to the right, and from out of this thicket almost simultaneously stepped the tiger.

Now there could not have been any sambar stag in that thicket, along with or just in front of the tiger, for I could not have missed its hoof beats as it ran from the spot. No sambar would have stood there and allowed the tiger practically to touch it in passing. Beyond that one *'Dhank'* there was no other sound, when, as I have said, the tiger stepped into the open, and there was no possible doubt that the tiger had made the sound. Why it did so is a mystery, as it was not hunting. It had fed well earlier that morning and was now returning to another repast, so that there could have been no thought in its mind of decoying a sambar by imitating its call. I can only recount what actually happened, and what I experienced, and the fact that, beyond doubt, there was no sambar in that thicket when the tiger stepped out. I leave the rest to your own conjecture and conclusion. For my part, having heard it with my own ears, I have no alternative but to believe the old tales I had read and heard of a tiger's ability to mimic this sound.

The animal walked towards the kill and was lost to view behind the branch before me, which opportunity I seized to get my rifle into position. It then reappeared to my left, and very shortly seized the kill in its jaws and lifted it. My shot struck it squarely behind the left shoulder. It spun around to receive my next shot in the neck, then collapsed, kicked and twitched for another minute, and was still.

The tiger being dead, I now felt that it was safe for me to walk to the car, provided I could find my way in the darkness. With all the difficulties involved, I felt this to be preferable to sitting all night in the tree, cramped and shivering, with the cold and on an empty stomach. Abruptly making up my mind, I shinned down the tree without approaching the tiger, and hurried off to find the bed of the Kalyani River before total darkness set in, for I realised it would be possible, even in darkness, to stumble along the bed of the dry river which would ultimately bring me to Pulibonu and the car, although the distance would be about six miles through all the bends of the river. I would almost surely lose the narrow footpath, the only alternative, in the darkness, and have to spend the night in the jungle.

Trying to negotiate the stony bed of the Kalyani in darkness proved a real nightmare. On many occasions I slipped on the rounded boulders that strewed the bed of the stream in profusion, or barked my shins against hidden tree-stumps and rocks. More than once I was in danger of twisting an ankle, or perhaps breaking a leg in jumping from one boulder to another, and twice I fell while holding my precious rifle aloft to prevent dashing it against the rocks. The journey required absolute concentration, and it took me four hours to reach Pulibonu, stepping into the car at ten minutes past 11 p.m.

You may suppose that in driving back to Nagapada I was congratulating myself on having slain the man-eater. But in actual fact I was not, for many circumstances forced themselves on my mind and made me uneasy as to the degree of success I had achieved. First, the tiger had killed a buffalo bait; second, it had remained at that bait when discovered by me and then casually retreated, with me following; third, after becoming aware of my presence it had turned tail and fled; fourth, it had returned to its buffalo-kill; last, it had emitted a close imitation of a sambar's call. All these facts individually and collectively far from indicated the actions or behaviour of a man-eater, but pointed instead to an ordinary tiger, more particularly a game-killer. The more I thought about it, the more doubtful I became that I had shot the man-eater. It was good for my peace of mind that, when concentrating on my struggle along the Kalyani River in the darkness, I had not had time to think of these things, or of how I had placed myself entirely in the power of the real man-eater, had he met me in those circumstances.

Next morning I returned with a party of men, carried the tiger to the car and brought it to Nagapatla, where general joy prevailed at the death of the man-eater. Before skinning the beast I examined it very carefully and found it to be a flawless specimen of adult male tiger, with a beautiful coat and in perfect physical condition. This made me doubt even more that I had bagged the real man-eater.

That evening I left for Bangalore, spending the night with the Collector at Chittoor, to whom I recounted my misgivings, and extracted a promise that he would let me know by telegram should any human kills recur.

On the afternoon of the eleventh day from that date, I received his wire, stating that a woman cutting grass, just within the boundary of the reserve forest forming the Chamala Valley, and within a mile of Nagapatla, had been carried away by the man-eater. I had failed. I had shot the wrong tiger, exactly as I feared had been the case.

Next morning found me journeying back to Nagapatla, arriving at the little forest bungalow late that afternoon.

Early the following morning, I was shown the spot where the tiger had attacked his most recent victim. The woman had been cutting grass, which she had gathered into a bundle preparatory to carting it away on her head. This bundle she had placed beneath the shade of a tree, and was evidently in the act of tying it up when the tiger, which had stalked her from the adjacent jungle, launched his attack. Another woman, who had also been cutting grass and was about a hundred yards away at the time, had heard a piercing scream, and, looking up, had been in time to see a tiger disappearing into the forest with her companion in its jaws. She had fled to Nagapatla and told the tale, whence news had been conveyed to Rangampet and onwards to Chandragiri, where the tahsildar had taken immediate steps to inform the Collector at Chittoor, who in turn had telegraphed me.

No attempt had been made to follow the tiger, or to rescue the woman. Three days had now elapsed since the occurrence, and the ground was too dry to reveal any tracks. Casting around in a broad semi-circle, we succeeded in finding the woman's saree, which had unravelled itself from her naked body and lay on the ground some quarter mile away. Blood tracks we could not find, showing that the tiger had not released its original grasp of her throat, for there had been no other cries from the unfortunate victim after her first desperate scream for help.

We never succeeded in locating the remains of that woman.

Returning to the village, I procured the three remaining buffalo calves, which had been my baits on the last visit and had been left behind; I tied one close to the roadside by the fourth milestone, one at Pulibonu, and this time I tied the third only two miles from Nagapatla, in the bed of the Kalyani River before it entered cultivated areas.

The following morning all three baits were alive, but there were also tiger pugs along the Pulibonu forest road. The tiger had joined the track just before the third mile, passed my bait on the fourth mile without touching it, and had left the road again at the sixth mile, shortly before reaching Pulibonu, making eastwards towards a large, stony hill, known as 'Monkey-hill', that jutted out from the Tirupati block.

The pug-marks were distinct and revealed no deformity in the animal. Nevertheless, it had passed within a few feet of my live-bait, which I had tied by the roadside on the fourth mile, without even stopping to look at it, as the tracks very clearly indicated. This was certainly much more like the behaviour of a man-eater, and I felt a sense of elation that at last I seemed to be up against the real thing.

As I have said, the tiger had gone towards 'Monkey Hill'. It was either sheltering on its jungle-clad slopes, or had perhaps skirted the base of the hill and rejoined the track towards Gundalpenta and Umbalmeru, and thence onward to the escarpment, further away. In any case, there was a faint chance that it might return along the road that night, and as now there was a good moon, nearing full, I determined to make an attempt to shoot the animal on this path.

A large teak tree stood by the roadside some 150 yards from my bait at the fourth milestone. Like most of its kind, this tree had an upright stem practically impossible to climb, but by seating myself at its base with my back to the bole, I commanded a view of my bait, the road in both directions, and over a hundred yards on all sides, since that section of the forest had suffered from fire about a year before and was therefore free of undergrowth.

I took up my position by 5 p.m. As darkness set in the moon, which had just topped the trees to the east, restored visibility by casting its pale, silvery light over the silent forest. Although in daylight I considered that the position I had selected was quite safe, nightfall had its accustomed effects, and I began thinking of the possibilities of the tiger stalking me from the rear. Common sense came to my rescue however, and told me this was impossible, unless the tiger first saw me, or heard me for tigers have practically no sense of smell. But to be seen or heard I would have to move first, so you may be certain I sat absolutely still and without a sound, with my back resting against that big tree. I could not smoke nor eat, but had taken the precaution of dressing warmly against the chill that would set in with the early hours of the next day. I remember that the jungle was exceptionally silent that night, leading me to conclude the tiger was not in the vicinity. As I had anticipated, the early hours brought with them a sharp drop in temperature, and as a consequence an equally sharp dewfall, till my clothes were soaking wet and the ice-cold barrel of the rifle streamed with moisture.

Several times I glanced towards my buffalo-calf, to see how it was reacting. The first part of the night it spent in placidly chewing the cut grass I had provided, but in the early hours it settled down on the ground apparently to rest and get what warmth it could against the chill that had set in.

Dawn eventually came to the relief of a very dispirited hunter, and I made my way back the four miles to Nagapatla. Here a wash, followed by steaming tea, bacon and eggs, and two hours' snatched sleep, made me feel a new man again and fit for any eventuality.

I motored up the road to Pulibonu, two trackers seated on each mudguard while I drove at a snail's pace, the men scanning the road as we went. But the tiger had not passed anywhere along it that night. Arriving at Pulibonu, we skirted the vicinity of the Kalyani River in both directions, as well as a mile up each of the tracks leading north-west and north-east, but again we found no evidence of the tiger's recent passing.

About noon we returned to Pulibonu, where I sat down by the forest well to smoke and consider my plan of action for that night.

Just across the Kalyani, and two furlongs from where I was sitting, grew a tamarind tree which overlooked the bifurcations in the forest paths, leading respectively to Pulibonu, and branching off north-eastwards to Umbalmeru and the escarpment. I had heard that several tigers had been shot from this tree in recent years; indeed, I had myself bagged a small leopard as it passed below me while I sat in that tree some eighteen months earlier, so that I eventually decided to commit myself to the safety of its sheltering branches for the next few nights, at least while the moon was on, in preference to the danger always present while sitting on the ground.

Having come to a decision, I instructed my two men to make a machan on the same branches I had occupied previously, and while they did so I fell fast asleep at the foot of the tree. The men knew what they were doing, and some thirty minutes later awoke me to examine their handiwork and put the few necessary final touches.

I always carry the frame of a charpoy, or Indian rope cot, constructed in two half-sections, in the rear seat of the Studebaker. Experience has taught me that this makes the best machan. It is light but strong, makes no noise even if you move about on it, is very comfortable, and most important of all, lends itself to easy erection on any tree as a machan, easy concealment by a screen of leaves, and easy removal when the time comes to go home. Moreover, it is both cheap and portable.

This charpoy had been strung across two branches, to which it had been securely bound with cotton rope, which I also carry for such purposes. The whole had been well concealed by twigs, which had also been built up along the sides to provide further concealment for myself. An opening had been provided through which I could see the crack where it branched immediately below me, and also some 100 yards in each direction, towards both Pulibonu and Umbalmeru. A similar opening in the screen of leaves behind me allowed me to see the road back to Nagapatla for quite 200 yards.

All being to my satisfaction, I drove the men back to Nagapatla, had a hearty lunch and a further short nap till 4 p.m., when I got together the necessary blanket, water-bottle, gun-torch, sandwiches and tea, and returned alone to Pulibonu, where I concealed the Studebaker in a forest glade adjoining the well. Walking back to the tree, I was settled for the night before 6 p.m.

The hours dragged by practically undisturbed by jungle sounds till 11 o'clock, when a panther made its sawing call from the direction of the Umbalmeru track. *'Ah-hah! Ah-hah!'* it sawed, the sound being an almost exact imitation of somebody sawing wood, the expiration and inspiration of breath at each double sound faithfully resembling the forward and backward motions of a saw in action.

Then around the bend he strode, a beautiful specimen of 'Thendu', or large forest panther, the rosettes on his hide showing up clearly in the brilliant moonlight. He walked towards the tree in which I was sitting, crossed the road below it and disappeared into the forest on the other side.

Filled with admiration, I watched the pretty sight, but let the animal go, for fear of disturbing the tiger which might hear my shot if he was anywhere in the vicinity.

Nothing further turned up that night, and the following night was exceptionally uninteresting, in that I did not hear or see a thing.

Returning to Nagapatla next morning, I fell asleep, but was wakened about 10 a.m. with the news that a herdsman had been killed by the tiger scarcely half-an-hour before.

Hastily dressing and grabbing my rifle, I followed the bereaved brother of the missing man and a few others for about three-quarters of a mile down the Pulibonu road, where we branched to the right and were soon on the banks of the Kalyani River The man had been grazing his buffaloes in this vicinity, when the tiger had sprung upon him from the thicket of rushes which here bordered the river. The man had screamed, and his brother, who was attending the same herd and driving on the stragglers, had seen the whole incident. In this case the tiger had grasped his victim by the shoulder, so that it was possible for him to continue to scream as he was dragged away into the same bank of rushes from which the tiger had sprung. His brother had then run back to the village to spread the news, and on to the forest Bungalow where I was sleeping.

Reaching the actual spot from which the man had been taken, we followed into the rushes, where the slightly bent reeds indicated the direction from which the tiger had approached, while a much more evident path showed how he had left, carrying his victim in his mouth. The victim's turban lay among the reeds, after traversing which we reached the dry bed of the river. The man had possibly been struggling, or his screams may have annoyed the tiger, for he had here released his hold of the man's shoulder and probably grasped his throat. From this place a fresh blood-trail became evident, as well as a drag-mark, where the man's legs had trailed along the ground as the tiger hastened with its victim across the exposed sands that formed the bed of the river, into the jungle that clothed the further bank.

Cautiously advancing, we traversed the dense shrubbery that immediately bordered the river on its further bank and came out on to a grassy glade. The tiger with its burden, in crossing the glade, had bent the heads of spear-grass and they had not yet had time to recover. Following along land that sloped slightly upwards, I crested a long hillock, beyond which the ground dropped sharply into a small stream as it wended its way to join the Kalyani further down. I felt that the tiger would decide to begin his gruesome meal in the hidden recesses of that stream, and at the moment was in all probability engaged on this task.

To follow the trail directly into the stream would be useless, as, no matter how cautiously I might move, I was bound to make some slight sound among the thorns that would put the tiger on the alert and acquaint him with the fact that he was being pursued. A man-eater in such circumstances is an extremely dangerous animal to deal with, and I knew that he had all the advantages of cover and concealment in his favour. He might decide to abandon his human victim and bolt, or even carry it with him; he might decide to remain by his kill and fight it out; most dangerous of all, he might decide to ambush me in the thick undergrowth, by launching a rear or flank attack. Very quickly reviewing the situation, I therefore decided to cut across to my right in a diagonal fashion, enter the stream about a quarter of a mile down its course, and then work upwards along the soft sand which at least would emit no sound if I covered it on tiptoe. By this means I hoped to surprise the tiger on its kill.

Retreating accordingly across the small hillock I had just crested, I bent double on its further side, where I knew I would be lost to view from the nala-bed, and in this position I shuffled forward as rapidly as possible for a furlong or so. Then again cresting the ridge, I noted the direction of the stream by the undergrowth along its banks, and descended in a half-right declination to meet it a furlong further down. Eventually reaching the sandy bed, I halted for a minute to regain my breath, after moving in the doubled position I had been doing, and then, with rifle cocked and held to my shoulder, I began to tiptoe up the soft sand, keeping as much as possible to the centre of the stream-bed and avoiding the thickets and bushes that clothed its banks.

I will always remember that nightmare walk. The stream narrowed in places to ten yards; at its widest point it was never more than thirty. I tiptoed forward slowly, every sense alert, scanning every bush and shrub on both banks, looking below them and around them, and as far as I could see. Periodically, I stopped to listen intently, but no sound disturbed the abysmal silence, like that of the land of the dead. How I longed for the slightest living sound, the chirp of an insect, or the call of a bird! Nothing but total silence enveloped me, broken only by the very faint, grating sounds of my own footsteps as I cautiously tiptoed forward along the sand.

I might have progressed about half a furlong in this way when the stream took a slight turn to the left. Before reaching this point I halted in my tracks to listen, and it is well that I did so, for next instant, soundlessly and unheralded, appeared the tiger, carrying its human victim by the back, just 25 yards away.

The surprise was mutual. Evidently the tiger had heard or sensed he was being followed, and without getting down properly to his meal had decided to convey it to some remoter spot downstream.

On my part, although I had moved so cautiously at every step, I had not actually anticipated meeting the tiger just yet.

Inaction for both of us was only momentary, however. Dropping its prey, the tiger sank its head between its forelegs, its hindlegs gathering beneath it, with tail erect, tensed for the spring. At the same time the rifle spoke, the bullet striking the animal, as I later discovered, just a half inch below the centre of a straight line between the eyes. But this slight inaccuracy was sufficient to have missed the vital brain-shot that would have dropped it instantly in its tracks, and with a gurgling roar it rushed forward, lurching over its victim and stumbling onward in its stunned efforts to reach me. Leaping to one side I fired round after round into the striped form, till I stood with empty magazine before the twitching monster at my feet, from whose smashed and mangled skull the blood literally spurted in a heavy red stream.

Next instant I felt faint and sick from reaction, I reached the bank, where for a moment I almost passed out. But a strong constitution came to my rescue and I was able to return to the men whom I had left on the main stream of the Kalyani; they had heard my five shots, which told them that now indeed the man-eater was dead.

You may be interested to know that, although we examined that tiger closely, both before and after skinning, and actually held a post-mortem on the carcase, absolutely no trace could we find of any physical or functional disorder or derangement that might have caused it to become a man-eater. Here indeed was a finely proportioned adult animal, able, from all the evidence that could be gathered by external examination, to hunt its natural food, the game of the forest, or even an adopted diet in the form of cattle from the village. But it had deliberately repudiated both these forms of food to follow a perverse taste for human flesh, which had eventually resulted in encompassing its end, and incidentally, very nearly mine. Where it had originally come from nobody knew, but all were glad that it had now gone to the jungles from which there was no return.

4

The Hosdurga-Holalkere Man-Eater

Holalkere is the second-largest town in the District of Chitaldroog, which itself is the northernmost district of the native State of Mysore and borders on the neighbouring division of Bellary in the Province of Madras towards the north-east, and on the Province of Bombay to the north-west. It has long been the centre of sporadic instances of man-eating by tigers, and there is good evidence to believe that the locality is the habitat of tigers which have inherited a taste for human flesh.

About ten years ago several instances of human kills were reported in this area, which was thrown open, by advertisement in the Mysore Gazette, to the free shooting of tigers without the requirement of a big-game licence.

At that time there was a very sporting couple in Bangalore, Angus Mactavish and his wife, who were keen on killing a tiger, particularly a man-eater, and suggested to me that we make a party of three and spend some four weeks in the attempt.

Accordingly we motored in Mactavish's car from Bangalore to Chitaldroog, the capital town of the district of the same

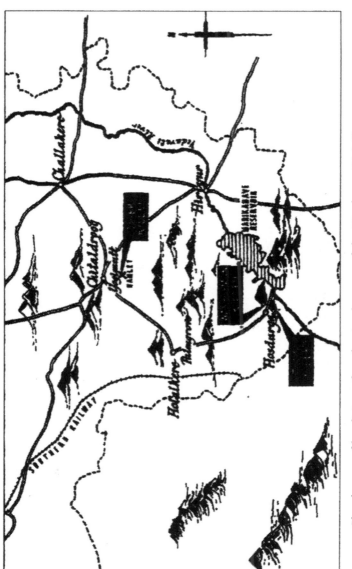

Sketch map of localities referred to in the story of the Hosdurga-Halalkere man-eater.

name, where we called on the district forest officer to obtain all possible information about the most recent kills and where they had taken place.

This officer was most cooperative and informed us that the existing man-eater's beat extended from the very outskirts of Chitaldroog town itself to the town of Holalkere, which lay some ten miles away in a south-westerly direction, and thence southward nine miles to the small village of Hosdurga, where the two recent human victims had been taken.

From Hosdurga the line of the tiger's activities was reported to proceed eastwards to the borders of the huge reservoir of Marikanave or Vani Vilas, as it is sometimes known, five miles away, an enormous lake inhabited by huge fish and crocodile; all along the shores of this lake, and back northwards in a rough line to Chitaldroog town itself. Indeed, he assured us, the man-eater had been reported among the ruins of an old fort which crested a small hill named Yogi Mutt, rising abruptly to the south of the town.

I knew that the environs of this old fort had long been frequented by stray bears and panthers, with an occasional tiger, but after further consultation it was decided to move on to Holalkere and Hosdurga, where we would establish our centre of operations, as circumstances warranted, after hearing local reports.

Leaving early next morning, we reached Holalkere within an hour, where the usual condition of nervous excitement and fear that accompanies the proximity of a maneater always prevail. We were told all sorts of stories, some of them completely contradictory, and from this mass of statements were able to gather only that the man-eater was a very astute animal, wandered everywhere and had the knack of appearing unexpectedly at most unlikely places. A prevailing rumour was that it very often frequented a vast plantation of date palms, interspersed with a dense undergrowth of lantana that bordered both sides of the road leading from Holalkere to Hosdurga. This plantation commenced just beyond the outskirts of Holalkere itself. We were told that its pug-marks could be seen almost daily on the road, and were advised to motor up and down the nine miles that connected the two places all night, when we would surely meet the man-eater, sooner or later, particularly when passing the palm-grove.

Accordingly we set out at 7 p.m. that night, and had left Holalkere a mile behind when the tall, spreading leaves of the palm-trees came into view, the close array of their spiky trunks being entirely hidden from view at the base by a dense and continuous stretch of lantana undergrowth. From this point we motored onwards at a snail's pace, flashing the spotlight in all directions, while the gleaming headlights pierced the road before us. Proceeding in this fashion for a half-mile, we came upon what looked Uke a very black, hairy man who had climbed a palm-tree some 15 feet high to the right of us, and was busy gulping down bunches of the small, yellow half-ripe palm dates that hung in clusters from among the spiky fronds.

We approached closer and stopped the car, when this strange man began to climb down. Descending half-way, however, he stopped and looked around at us, and my companions were surprised to discover that their 'strange man' was a sloth-bear, disturbed at a feast of dates. I had known from the onset that it was a bear, but had wanted my companions to learn for themselves. With her .3005 Spring field rifle, Mrs Mactavish brought off a good shot from the car, dropping the creature to the ground with a resounding thud.

We then motored on to Hosdurga without seeing a thing, returned to Holalkere, and twice more backwards and forwards in each direction, seeing nothing beyond a hyaena near the carcase of the bear on our final return journey. Fearing, therefore, that if we left the carcase there any longer it would be destroyed, by herculean effort the three of us managed to hoist the heavy body on to the space between the engine and the front mud-guard of Mac's car. Although long, the hair of a bear is slippery, and it was most difficult to keep a firm hold of any part of the animal, which began to slip out of one's fingers as soon as its weight was lifted.

Next morning we had tea at the Travellers' Bungalow at Holalkere, together with steaming porridge and bacon and eggs, which Mrs Mactavish prepared in excellent fashion. Then after skinning the bear we decided to move on to Hosdurga to obtain first-hand information about the two latest human kills.

Traversing the date-palm plantation in daylight enabled us to realise fully the denseness of the surrounding, all-enveloping lantana, which it was impossible to fathom the night before, and of what little hope there was to see or shoot a tiger in such a place.

At Hosdurga, we were told the story of the two earlier tragedies. The first had happened some three weeks before. A girl aged eleven years, and incidentally a distant relation of the amildar of the taluq, was living with her parents in a house on the outskirts of the village. At 8 p.m. she had gone outside, probably to answer a call of nature, and had never been seen again, nor had any cry or sound, explaining her fate, been heard. Anxious about her failure to return, her parents followed with a lantern, but nothing was seen of her, nor were any marks evident on the hard ground. Becoming increasingly alarmed, they aroused the village, and in about two hours a party of some fifty persons, armed with lanterns, staves, hatchets and two muzzle-loading guns, went forth to search for the girl. Nothing could they find, however, in the darkness that night. Next day further efforts were made, and a few fragments of tattered underwear were found entangled among thorns a half-mile away. Nothing was ever found of the remains of that little girl.

The second kill had occurred twelve days ago, in the following fashion. The reservoir of Marikanave lay some five miles away to the east. About halfway to its shore, and The Hosdurga Holalkere Man-eater 85 crossing the track that led there, was a tiny brook that formed, close to the track-side, a small but fairly deep pool. This pool was used by two brothers of the village, who were professional 'dhobies' or washermen, as a convenient place in which to wash clothes. They possessed three donkeys, which were used for conveying the washing to and from the pool. That evening they had finished their task at about 5 p.m., loaded the donkeys and were returning homewards. These animals, being their only stock-in trade, so to say, were taken particular care of, one brother walking in advance followed by the three donkeys in line, and the other brother bringing up the rear. They were a mile from Hosdurga when a tiger leapt from concealment, seized the leading man and disappeared with him before he could utter a sound. His brother in the rear, seeing what had happened, lost his head and bolted back towards the pool which they had just left.

When 8 p.m. came and neither the donkeys nor the brothers had turned up at Hosdurga, the two wives became alarmed and spread agitation throughout the village. By 10 p.m. a second search-party of some three-score men, armed with lanterns, staves and, of course, the two muzzle-loading guns, set forth in search.

In due course they came upon one of the three missing donkeys, complacently sitting in the middle of the track, the bundle of washing still tied to its back. Farther on, a furlong short of the pool, they came upon the man who had turned tail and fled. He had fainted with terror at finding himself alone in the jungle after seeing what had happened to his brother, and was in a state of collapse. He frothed at the mouth and his eyes were turned upwards. It was nearly an hour before he was in a condition to whisper hoarsely the terrifying news. Together with him the party then returned to the spot where the attack had taken place, when a half-hearted attempt was made to search for the missing man. Naturally it proved unsuccessful and it was decided to return next day

Accordingly daylight found the party back again, when extensive search revealed bits of tattered clothing, a blood-trail, and finally the remains of the unfortunate man, which had been three-quarters eaten during the night. All that was left was his head, two arms, one whole leg and just the remaining foot, which were duly gathered together and brought back to Hosdurga for cremation. Contentedly grazing a furlong from the track were the two remaining pack-donkeys.

An additional piece of news was now offered, in that four days ago a bullock-cart, with a double-yoke of oxen, proceeding to Holalkere, had been attacked by a tiger three miles from Hosdurga at about 3 p.m. In this instance the driver had jumped out of the cart and escaped, returning by a circuitous route through the forest to the village. A party had gone out next morning to find the cart, with one bull still yoked to it, standing by the roadside. Hardly 50 yards away lay what was left of the other bull, which the tiger had killed, wrenched free of the yoke, carried this distance and then eaten in full view of its unfortunate companion.

Along with all this news we were also told that a rival party of two huntsmen were in occupation of the small one-room Travellers Bungalow of which the village of Hosdurga boasted, having arrived by car some five days earlier.

This indeed cramped our style, as it would not be cricket to commence attempts at shooting the man-eater when the other sportsmen had preceded us. Further, in keeping with the good old adage of 'too many cooks spoil the broth', too many huntsmen generally achieve nothing beyond frightening off their quarry, that is, if they do not in the meantime accidentally shoot each other.

It was nearing ten o'clock by the time we had gathered all this information, and we were just debating the advisability of returning to Holalkere, when the two sportsmen in question turned up. They were both youngsters, and although inexperienced, were exceedingly keen on the game. Introducing themselves, they repeated all the news we had already heard, and added that they had tied out a buffalo bait for the last two nights in the vicinity of where the washerman had been eaten. Nothing had happened during the first night and their party of coolies had gone out that morning to ascertain how the bait had fared the previous night.

We wished these gentlemen the best of luck, and told them we would return to Holalkere so as not to be in their way. They would not hear of the idea, however, considered our action to be a personal affront and begged us to join them in the bungalow till the next morning, when, they stated, they were due to return to Bellary, where they had come from.

In the midst of all this friendly talk, their party of coolies arrived to announce that the bait had been killed and half-eaten the night before. Those two boys were the acme of hospitality and offered us the chance of sitting over their bait. Needless to say, of course, we would not consent to this.

After a combined lunch, we set out with them to see the kill and render any possible assistance. We found the boys had chosen rather unwisely in tying their bait in a region scattered with boulders. Moreover, they had not secured the animal properly, with the result that the tiger had broken the tethering rope and dragged its victim partly behind a rock, and completely out of view of the tree in which they had intended to construct their machan.

To the spot where the kill had been dragged were two possible lines of approach by the man-eater, if in fact it was a man-eater that had killed the bait; the first being from the direction of the track where the 'dhoby' had been killed, and the other from a hillock lying a quarter-mile away, approximately south-east of the kill. Two separate boulders, among the many that lay around, were so positioned as to command each a view of these possible lines of approach, as well as of the kill and of each other.

The two sportsmen therefore elected to sit, one behind each of these boulders. I ventured to suggest that, as the adversary they were dealing with might also turn out to be the man-eater, it would be safer if they sat on top of the boulders behind a concealing wall of thorns. They did not agree to this, however, and decided to sit on the ground with their backs to the boulders.

Roughly sheltering them behind a few cut thorny bushes, we left these doughty lads by 4 p.m. to return to the bungalow. I was anxious about their welfare and would have liked to linger within calling-distance, to render help if necessary, but finally decided that my presence might frighten the tiger off, and my motive be misunderstood. Little did we know that afternoon, that our hearty good wishes for a lucky night were the last words that any of our party would utter to one of those fine boys.

We spent the evening in the bungalow, drinking tea, smoking and chatting, while interviewing as many villagers as possible to gain additional information. A strong wind was blowing from the south-west, so that it would be impossible to hear any rifle shot fired by the two lads, who were over a mile away. We had an early dinner, and Mactavish and his wife then turned in. I decided, however, to sit on the verandah and listen to any jungle sounds I might possibly hear.

It was nearing 11 o'clock, the village had been silent for the past hour and I was thinking of going to bed, when I heard a peculiar noise, which I soon recognised as running, stumbling footsteps in the distance. Realising that my intuitive fear of impending trouble, experienced so strongly earlier that evening, had not misled me, I hastily grabbed my rifle and torch and ran out to meet the runner.

It turned out to be Ince, the elder of the two sportsmen. His clothes were tattered, he was lathered in sweat and staggered like a drunken man, looking behind him continually as he stumbled forward. Supporting him by the shoulder, I asked what had become of his companion. The poor boy was so exhausted that he could hardly speak, but he finally gasped out the awful words,

Tiger—got him—carried him off, ooh! ooh! and began to weep on my shoulder like a child.

I hurried him to the bungalow, where I awoke Mactavish and his wife. We gave Ince a stiff dose of brandy, laid him down and covered him with two blankets, for he was now shaking like an aspen with the reaction that had set in. Then, with Mrs Mactavish chafing his hands, we impatiently waited for his story, and it was indeed an extraordinary tale.

He had sat below the rock commanding the approach from the track, while his companion, Todd, behind the other rock, commanded the approach from the hillock. Shortly before dark, Ince thought he had seen a long, red dish object move in the bushes quite some distance away and beyond Todd, where the land sloped gently down from the hillock. Of course he had no means of apprising Todd of what he had seen, and knew that the latter did not know about it, as that area was hidden from his view by the very boulder below which he—Todd—was sitting. Ince had continued to watch the bushes, but had seen nothing thereafter.

Then darkness fell, and the hours passed wearily by until about 10 p.m. The kill was not visible in the shadows, although the stars shed a faint light that enabled Ince to see in his immediate vicinity. Suddenly Ince heard a faint thud, a slight dragging noise, and then the unmistakable sound of crunching bones. Guessing that the tiger had returned and was eating its kill, Ince waited awhile to give his companion a chance to take the shot, knowing, as he did, that the kill was equidistant, if not a little nearer to Todd, who must also be hearing the sound of the tiger feeding.

Nothing happened, however, and nobody will know why Todd remained inactive.

Then the thought came to Ince that perhaps his companion had fallen asleep, and with that he decided to take the shot himself. Aligning his rifle in the direction of the kill he pressed the button of his rifle-torch, the bright beam immediately revealing a huge tiger devouring the remains of the buffalo.

At the same time there was a piercing scream from Todd, a horrible growl from that direction, a slight scuffling noise, another half-muffled cry, and then silence. In the meantime Ince had shifted the beam of his rifle-torch from the tiger and his kill to the rock, at the base of which Todd had been sitting earlier that evening. The last glimpse he had of the former was as it bounded away from the remains of the buffalo into the concealing shrubs.

Of Todd he could see no sign. Calling to his friend repeatedly, Ince rushed blindly to the spot where he had been sitting. Todd's rifle, water-bottle and half-empty packet of sandwiches lay on the ground, but he was nowhere to be seen. Becoming hysterical with the realisation that his friend had been taken by the man-eater, ~~Ince~~ floundered about and attempted to search the jungle for INCES him, only to lose his own way. Demented with grief and growing more desperate each minute, he rushed aimlessly about when, by sheer good luck, he succeeded in stumbling on the track leading to Hosdurga, up which he had run top speed.

It was now clear from Ince's story that we had two tigers to deal with: one an avowed cattle-lifter and the other an even more determined man-eater. They were probably a pair, male and female, although this was not necessarily so. Never in my life had I met such an unusual combination. The possibility that they were two grown cubs from the same litter, one of which had acquired man-eating tendencies, appeared to be ruled out by Ince's description of the cattle-lifter as a. 'huge tiger' and by no means half-grown. The man-eater nobody had seen.

Within fifteen minutes we aroused the village, and assembled some twenty rather reluctant helpers, although the owners of the two muzzle-loaders were again to the fore, with lanterns, sticks, staves and matchets. Mrs Mactavish insisted on coming too, and so did Ince, although he was almost spent. The search-party, together with Mactavish and myself, were soon at the rock from which Todd had been taken.

Casting around, it was not long before we found an odd rubber-soled shoe that had fallen from his left foot. From *the* place where we found it we judged the tiger was making with its burden towards the little hillock from which it had apparently come. Pressing forward with all possible speed, we eventually reached a spot where the animal had first laid its victim down. From then, probably alarmed by the noise created by Ince in his shouting and floundering, it had moved on. As usual, a blood trail now commenced, which led us to the base of the hillock, which it followed towards the right-hand side.

Led by Mactavish and myself, and keeping close together for fear of unexpected attack, we persevered in our search, but it was 3.30 that morning before we came upon what remained of poor Fred Todd. The tiger had eaten quite half of him, and it was a ghastly sight. A severe reaction now overtook Ince, who began to retch, wept and finally collapsed. It was past 6 a.m. that terrible day before we managed to get the remains to Hosdurga, together with a now totally incapable Ince.

We put what was left of Fred Todd into Mactavish's car, while I drove Ince in what had been his poor friend's motor, and we reached Chitaldroog by 9 o'clock. Here Ince was taken into the Local Fund Hospital, and we spent the major part of the day on the tedious official inquiries that follow an incident of this kind, so that it was almost sunset before we returned to Hosdurga, and a very empty, silent Travellers' Bungalow. We fell asleep that night, sad and disheartened, but grimly determined on revenge. Mrs Mactavish, in particular, had endured the nervous strain of the past twenty hours in heroic fashion, and was of untold assistance throughout the whole time.

Early next morning found us back at the scene of the tragedy, where we spent the next three or four hours in piecing together the evidence. The ground was hard, as no rain had fallen for several weeks, and it was impossible to find an imprint of the man-eater to enable us to determine its size and sex. Ince's description of the cattle-killer led us to think it was a male. The man-eater was therefore, in all probability, a female, although, as I have said earlier, this was not necessarily so.

Finding nothing in the vicinity, we followed the trail once more to the spot where we had found Todd's body, but nowhere could we see a solitary pug-mark of the killer. We even attempted to look further, but the hard ground hid its secret well, and in spite of all our efforts, the maneater's size and sex remained a secret.

During our absence at Chitaldroog, the vultures had completely demolished what had remained of the buffalo kill. We now had to make a fresh start in our operations.

After due consultation it was decided to secure a fresh buffalo bait close to the original track where the washerman had been killed. Mactavish could sit over it, while I determined to lie prone on top of one of the boulders close to where Todd had been taken. Our plan was roughly this. Should the two tigers move in company, the cattle-lifter would kill the bait, when, in all probability, although a man-eater, the other tiger would not be able to resist the temptation of a feast, and would also join in. That would provide Mac with a shot. On the other hand, even if it did not join in, the man-eater would probably be in the vicinity; and as the rock on which I was going to lie was in a direct line with the hillock, and along the direction of his approach the previous day, I hoped to be able to hear and see him if he should pass near me.

As there were no trees along the track where Mac was to sit up, we solved the problem of protection by scooping a shallow hole in the earth, over which we decided to place an inverted 'Sugar-cane pan'. These pans resemble huge saucers, and are some six to eight feet in diameter, eighteen inches deep, and beaten from sheet iron about one-eighth of an inch thick. They are used throughout India as containers in which to melt the juice from the sticks of cane-sugar, previously gathered by means of crushing through a press. This juice is boiled in the pan and becomes a goldenbrown liquid, which is then allowed to cool and solidify, before being cut into four-inch squares to form what is known as 'jaggery' or brown sugar. Jaggery is the only form of sugar used in Southern Indian villages, white sugar being unknown, and practically every village in any fertile area possesses its own cane-sugar plantations, with accompanying 'Sugar-cane pans'. We had already seen a few of them in Hosdurga.

It was not long before we were back from the village with one of these pans, carried by half-a-dozen men, a length of camouflaged tarpaulin which Mac had brought in his car, and the other necessities for a night sit-up. This pan we inverted over the shallow hole we had dug and was raised from the ground at four points by rocks, so as to provide a six-inch gap for vision and ventilation, and a space through which to shoot. Over the pan we spread the camouflaged tarpaulin, covering this again with a sprinkling of sand dug from the shallow hole, and with a few thorns, cut-bushes, leaves, etc., to give it a realistic appearance. We made a good job of the whole effort, so that the pan looked no more, from a fair distance, than a small hump in the ground.

A further complication now arose as Mac was about to get in, when his wife insisted on sitting with him. We both did our best to dissuade her, but she was adamant, with the result that finally the men and I raised the pan at one end, allowed the Mactavishes to creep in, and then rearranged the whole affair. Actually, I felt it was quite safe inside, the inverted pan providing a sort of armoured turret. The bait was then tied, and before going off to the rock on which I was to lie, it was agreed that, in case of need, we were to signal each other by three sharp whistles.

I ascended my rock by 5 p.m., settled myself comfortably, and lay prone to await events. I recollect that the stone was uncomfortably hot after having been exposed to direct sunlight throughout the day.

There was no sound as the hours dragged by and the forest seemed empty of any form of life. Even the familiar nightjar, welcome at the moment, was absent. The silence was deep and complete, and the stars twinkled down on me in eerie stillness. I fell to thinking of poor Fred Todd, and of what had happened to him.

Midnight passed, when suddenly I heard a clear whistle twice repeated. It was the agreed signal from Mac, and wondering what had happened to ail him, I slid down from the rock, switched on the torch, and cautiously approached the place where he and his wife were stationed. I came upon them standing beside the buffalo bait, which was alive and untouched. To one side lay the pan that they had overturned in getting out, and this is what they told me.

They had seen and heard nothing till about midnight, when Mrs Mac, sitting directly behind her husband who was facing the buffalo, thought she heard a faint sigh or moan behind her. Glancing around slowly, and endeavouring to look through the space between the pan and the ground, she had at first noticed nothing. Then she observed what appeared to be a boulder, as big as a bathtub, just six feet away. Remembering that there had been no boulder there earlier in the evening, she had brought her head closer to the opening, and was horrified to see a tiger, lying on the ground on its belly, its forelegs stretched out in front, intently meeting her gaze. Stifling the gasp of surprised horror that almost escaped her, she endeavoured, by vigorous nudging, to attract her husband's attention. From his position Mac had seen nothing, and it was almost impossible for him to turn around, for the hole, that had originally been dug for one person, was too small to allow for the movement of two.

Sensing by her continued nudges that something unusual was afoot, Mac had then made a determined effort to turn himself, with the result that the muzzle of his extended rifle contacted the edge of the pan with a slight metallic clang. There was a loud 'Woof' and a thud, as the tiger jumped lightly over the contraption. Knowing that they had been discovered and that no purpose was likely to be served by remaining any longer, they then summoned me by the agreed signal.

To remain longer was useless, so we decided to return to the bungalow at Hosdurga, leaving the bait where it was for the night, pending a decision on some other plan.

Early next morning I despatched a party of men to bring in the bait. They returned with the astounding news that the animal had been killed and entirely devoured. Hastening to the spot, we found their story true. Practically nothing remained of our bait but its head and hooves. Close examination of the ground revealed that two tigers had partaken of the meal, in close proximity, moreover, to the overturned sugar-cane pan and tarpaulin sheet, lying in a heap nearby, both of which had failed to frighten the beasts away.

The deduction to be drawn from this latest development was, therefore, that our man-eater was also a cattle-eater when opportunity offered. Alternatively, there was the possibility that three tigers were operating in the vicinity; a man-eater, and two cattle-killers.

For the following night we decided to work to the same plan, tying a fresh bait a quarter-mile further along the same track, and to plant the sugar-cane pan beside it as before, this time making the shallow hole large enough to accommodate both Mac and myself. Mrs Mac very reluctantly consented to remain in the bungalow. The camouflaged tarpaulin was spread over the pan, under a layer of loose sand and rubble, with grass, thorns and small cut bushes, to give the whole a very realistic appearance of a small rise in the ground. Mac and I sat back to back, rifles ready, with Mac facing the bait. On this occasion we also provided for a slightly greater apperture to allow more shooting space, by using larger stones at the four opposite ends of the pan.

Mac and I sat thus throughout three nights in succession, but we saw and heard nothing. But about 10 o'clock on the fourth morning, while we were having a nap in the bungalow, news arrived that a man had been killed a mile from Holalkere, in the same date-palm grove where we had shot the bear some days earlier, and almost at the same spot.

Hastening there by car, we were both disgusted and annoyed to find that the relations of the latest victim had in the meantime removed his body for cremation, so that we lost the chance of sitting-up over this human kill, to which the tiger might possibly have returned.

We then procured another buiffalo bait at Holalkere, and tied it within fifty yards of the place where the man had been killed. A convenient tree overlooked the road at this spot, and on this tree I erected a machan. As Mac was feeling a bit seedy, and was tired after his vigil of four consecutive nights, he decided to rest on that occasion and I sat up alone.

Again nothing happened, and 6 a.m. found me trudging the mile towards Holalkere with mixed feelings of tiredness, disappointment and disgust. Arriving there, I sent men out to bring back the bait. They came running back in half-an-hour with the news that, as they were about to untie the animal, a tiger had growled in the jungle within a few yards of them. They had then rushed pell-mell back to Holalkere, leaving the buffalo where it was.

Jumping into the car, we hastened to the spot and were truly surprised to find our bait still alive. This was very unexpected, as we were certain that the tiger, or tigers, would have killed the buffalo as soon as the fleeing men were out of sight. Taking a chance, I went up into the machan at once, instructing Mac to return to Holalkere. There was just a possibility, I felt, that the tiger might turn up.

Nothing happened, and as at 1 p.m. I was feeling both hungry and sleepy, I then got down, untied the bait, and walked along with it to Holalkere.

That night, we retied the bait at the same spot, and I sat up once again. Mac and his wife went to Hosdurga in the car, and sat up together under the sugar-cane pan, beside the bait we had left there, in the spot where he and I had sat for three consecutive nights.

Again nothing happened, and by 6.30 a.m. they came along in the car from Hosdurga, picked me up, and proceeded to the bungalow at Holalkere, where we all went to sleep after lunch.

At 4 p.m. we were awakened by a great hubbub. Restoring some order in the throng that had collected in the verandah, we came to learn that a company of a dozen men had left Holalkere before noon to drive a herd of cattle to Chitaldroog for market, intending to cover the intervening distance long before sunset. About three miles from Holalkere one of the cattle had strayed from the main road for a short distance of perhaps twenty-five yards. A man who had gone to drive it back was attacked by a tiger that had evidently been flanking the party, and was in hiding in the very bushes that bordered the roadside. Being cut off from retreat to his friends on the road, he had rushed up a rock that happened to be nearby. The whole scene had occurred in full view of the party, all of whom stood huddled together in a bunch and failed to render help of any sort, so stricken were they with fear.

The tiger had then sprung up the rock and fastened the claws of a forepaw in the man's thigh, attempting to pull him down. The man, continuing to scream for help, had clung with both hands to the branch of a tree that overhung the rock, to save himself from being dragged down.

The first attack failed, and the tiger slipped backwards to earth, its claws practically peeling the skin from the man's thigh, till it hung like the skin of a partially stripped banana.

Becoming infuriated, and no doubt urged on by the sight of human blood, the tiger then made a second attempt, this time fastening both its forepaws squarely in the body of the man and dragging him from his feeble hold. Once it got him down from the rock it had seized him by the neck and bounded off into the forest.

It was a matter of minutes to reach the spot by car. Evidence of the fresh tragedy was available in abundance, the bits of human skin and finger nails embedded in the broken branch testifying to the intensity of that last desperate hold. Spattered blood could be seen everywhere, and there was a distinct trail where the victim had been carried away.

We followed this up in all haste, the trail leading downwards to a valley of dense jungle. It was past 5 p.m. and we had exactly an hour to find the body before dark. Soon we discovered the usual pieces of tattered clothing, then a dark pool of blood where the tiger had deposited his victim, only to go on downwards into the dark valley.

Perhaps six furlongs had been covered in this way when we came upon a low outcrop of rock, interspersed with bushes. I was surprised to find that the tiger had not yet stopped to begin its meal, as this was a quiet and secluded spot; but hardly had the thought entered my mind, when a distinct growl came from behind a large rock, followed by the sound of a small stone being dislodged, as the tiger bounded away before we could even see it. Rounding the bend, we encountered the corpse, weltering in its own blood, and about one-third devoured.

Time was passing, there was no suitable tree nearby, and the only possible place to sit was on top of the largest of the neighbouring rocks, which was about twelve feet high. This rock rose steeply on three sides and was fairly safe against a tiger's spring, but unfortunately it sloped on the fourth side, and still more unfortunate was the fact that this sloping side did not face the dead man but was a little more than a right angle from the body's position. This meant that if I lay on top of the rock I would have to keep a careful watch in two directions, namely, on the corpse below me to the left, and on the sloping side of rock to my right, for fear that the tiger might make a sudden rush up this side and be on to me before I was aware of it. As I have said, I considered my rear, which faced one of the sides where the rock dropped steeply, fairly safe against a sudden spring, to do which the tiger would have to leap a clean twelve feet to the top of the rock. If he did not clear that height in one jump, he would have no hold at all and would slip backwards, which would give me ample time to shoot. No tiger, in my opinion, would risk such an uncertain jump.

Screening the top of the rock on the sloping side with a few small stones and bushes, I scrambled up, after telling the Macs to spend part of the night in driving up and down between Holalkere and Hosdurga in the hope of meeting the tiger on the road, in case it had abandoned the kill.

With the departure of my friends and the villagers, I was now alone with the mangled remains that were strewn on the ground below me. The hours passed, while I kept an intent watch on the sloping rock to my right. The jungle beyond was hidden in darkness, and appeared just a blur in the hazy background, against which it was impossible to distinguish any animal smaller than an elephant. In the gloom the corpse to my left could no longer be seen.

At about ten o'clock a sambar belled in the distant forest a mile away. This was followed by a tiger calling, which was answered shortly by another tiger in the direction of the road from which we had come.

The complexity of the situation was now fully apparent, as I thought the matter over during those silent hours. We had at least two tigers operating in the area, possibly three. Of these, one was a man-killer, daring, cruel and ruthless. The other was a cattle lifter, equally daring and cunning by nature. But this did not necessarily mean that either of the tigers refrained from indulging in both habits, when occasion presented. Again there was the possibility of a third tiger operating in the district, which might itself be a man-eater, or a cattle-lifter, or both. So far, due to the dry weather and hard ground, we had been prevented from picking up any distinguishing pug-marks to be able to identify these various animals.

The tigers had ceased calling by now, and all was silent again in the surrounding forest except for the chirping of the tree crickets, the occasional hoot of an owl, and the periodic sound of a gust of wind bending the tops of the giant trees, a sound like the roar of a distant sea.

Then suddenly, and without warning or premonition, it happened! There was a thud against the rock behind me, a violent scratching and scraping against the stone, mingled with a snarling growl, and then another thud as the tiger fell backwards to the ground. Before I could turn and peer over the edge of the rock, he was gone. That man-eater had done the unexpected thing! Having somehow become aware of my presence, he had stalked me from behind and attempted a sheer leap of twelve feet to the top of the rock where I was lying. By good fortune he had failed to make it by a few inches.

I spent the rest of the night sitting up and fully alert, but nothing occurred. I waited till the sun had risen high next morning before venturing to scramble down and return to the road, as I feared the tiger, having discovered my presence, might be lying in ambush for me, but again my luck held out and I reached the road in safety, where Mac came for me in the car in a few minutes, having himself spent a fruitless night in driving up and down between Holalkere and Hosdurga.

Immediately upon arrival at the bungalow I instructed a party of men to return to the human remains and cover them with branches to protect them against vultures, as I intended to sit up again on the rock that night. These men were just setting out, however, when the relatives of the dead man arrived from his village and demanded the remains for cremation. I attempted to persuade them to allow the body to stay where it was for another day, they were adamant, and so any opportunity that might have presented itself of avenging the death of that poor man that night was lost to us through the obstinacy of his relations.

Two hours later, a party of men arrived from Hosdurga to inform us that our bait, which had been left tied near the sugar-cane pan for the past week, had at last been killed.

Evening found Mac and myself sitting under the pan, and about midnight we heard a tiger moving around in the vicinity, by the intermittent low grunt it was making every now and then. We waited anxiously for it to come on to the kill but this it would not do, and kept circling the area for the best part of three-quarters of an hour. Quite obviously it had discovered our presence near the kill. A brave—but foolhardy—idea now entered Mac's mind, which was that he should get up and walk away to give the tiger the impression we had left and that his kill was alone. He hoped it would then approach and I could deal with it.

The plan was likely to meet with success, as you will remember that this is exactly what happened on the last occasion we had left the pan and our bait. At the same time it was a very dangerous thing for Mac to do, in view of the fact that the tiger hovering near might be the maneater itself, or might be accompanied by the man-eater, as on an earlier occasion. It took me quite thirty minutes to drive the idea from the head of that stubborn but magnificently brave Scotsman, that to venture out in the dark jungle with a man-eater about would be to sign his own death warrant.

In the meantime the tiger continued to prowl around, but went off in the early hours of the morning, and we returned to the little bungalow at Hosdurga, after yet another night of disappointment.

Nothing happened the two following days, the nights of which we spent driving up and down between Hosdurga, Holalkere and Chitaldroog, flashing the spotlight in the hope of meeting one of the tigers on the road.

Early on the morning of the third day a party of Lumbani woodcutters reported that they had been camped in the forest four miles away the previous night, in the protection of a huge campfire, around which they had drawn their five carts in a rough circle, and within which they and their five bullocks were sheltering. At dead of night the fire having burnt low, a tiger had crept past the carts and attacked one of the bulls. The rest had stampeded around, awakening the men, who had shouted and thrown fire brands at the tiger. It had then decamped. The bull had been bitten through the neck and severely scratched as well, but it was alive. At dawn they had come on to Hosdurga with four carts and the injured bullock, abandoning the fifth cart which the bullock was too badly hurt to haul.

One of these Lumbanis, who had been in the area from childhood and knew the forest like the palm of his hand, mentioned that six miles away, in the heart of the forest, was a small stream leading to a clear pool surrounded by sloping rocks, under giant trees. It was in this locality, he asserted, that the tigers had their permanent abode. Now that it was summer, they spent the hours of noonday heat in this cool retreat, and invariably one or other of them would drink at this pool in the evening before setting out on its hunt for prey, or in the early hours of the morning, after returning from the hunt.

This man evidently knew what he was talking about, for intimate speech with him revealed that he was a poacher and a bootlegger to wit, who made quite a lot of money by illicitly distilling in the fastnesses of the forest a very potent liquor called 'arrack' from the bark of the babool tree. Evidently few knew of this place, and those who did dared not venture there, for fear of the tigers. The upshot of the conversation was that it was agreed Mac and I would leave with him after lunch that day to spend the evening, night and following morning at this pool.

3 p.m. found us at the spot, and a more likely tiger-haunt I have seldom seen. The pool was a small one, entirely surrounded

by sloping rock, but the banks of the tiny stream that fed it amply revealed the presence of tiger, by repeated tracks that led down to and crossed it. A rough survey of these tracks indicated the pug-marks of two separate animals, a large male and an adult female. From the repeated reports of its large size, the former was in all probability the cattle-lifter, leaving now definite cause for suspicion that his companion, the female, might be the man-eater unless, of course, there was a third tiger in the party.

A wild mango tree overhung the pool at almost the spot where the stream ran in, and on the lower branches of this tree, at about the height of fifteen feet, we put up my portable 'charpoy' machan, which we had brought along with us for just such an occasion, carried by the Lumbani. 4.30 p.m. found all three of us sitting on this machan, it being dangerous to send the Lumbani away by himself, for fear of the man-eater.

On account of the overhanging big trees, it was pitch dark by 7 o'clock, nor did any animals visit the vicinity; no doubt they avoided it because of the habitual proximity of the Kings of the Jungle. The hours dragged by in solemn silence, disturbed once or twice by the distant calls of Sambar and Kakur, or barking-deer.

It must have been past 4 a.m. when we heard a slight sighing, moaning sound, and then the unmistakably heavy but softly muffled tread of a tiger on the carpet of fallen bamboo leaves that covered the sloping bank that faced us. Minutes passed, but we could see nothing in that Stygian darkness. Then we heard the distant sound of the lapping of water from the edge of the pool down below in the darkness, and to our right.

The time had come, and as previously agreed, I gently nudged Mac to take the shot. Pointing his rifle in the direction of the sound, while I kept ready for a covering shot if necessary, Mac depressed the torch-switch and the bright beam streamed down upon the form of an immense tiger crouched over the water's edge.

The beast looked up, his eyes reflecting the light in two large, gleaming red-white orbs, and then Mac fired. There was a roar as the tiger sprang into the air to turn a complete somersault and fall over backwards, biting the ground and lashing out in a furious medley of bubbling, snarling growls. Mac followed up with two more shots before the tiger rolled over, half into the water, to twitch in the ~~dirocs~~ THROES of approaching death, then to lie still.

With the dawn we descended, to find that Mac had shot the male of the party. He was a truly magnificently proportioned tiger and a wonderful trophy, but we were all disappointed to know that the man-eater was still at large. Mac's first shot had struck the animal at the top of its nose, smashing the upper jaw and palate, and passing into the throat, which accounted for the bubbling sound we had heard with its snarls. His second shot had passed through the right shoulder and into the abdomen. The third had missed.

I will pass over the events of the next four days, during which no reports were received, and the local population began congratulating us on having slain the man-eater, the opinion of some being that it was this same tiger that had killed both man and cattle. But we knew better and lingered on, certain that sooner or later we would receive news of another human kill, unless of course the man-eater had left the area after the death of its companion. The nights of those four days we spent in driving along the road up to Chitaldroog, and along all passable forest tracks, in the hope of meeting the man-eater, but without success.

Shortly before noon on the fifth day came the news we had feared but anticipated, in the form of three runners despatched by the amildar at Chitaldroog to acquaint us with the fact that, late the previous evening, a lad aged fourteen years had been carried away by a tiger from a hamlet at the base of the southern slopes of the hillock of Togi-mutt, which I have already told you lay to the south of the town of Chitaldroog itself, and boasted an ancient, abandoned fort on its summit.

Driving there by car, we visited the hamlet and were shown the small hut on its outskirts, from the very door of which the lad had been snatched at sun-down the previous evening. As the country to the ~~south~~ south of the hamlet was practically bare, there was good reason for believing, along with the inhabitants of the village, that the tiger had carried its victim up the hill, and was probably at that moment sheltering in the ruins of the fort.

No organised attempt at searching for the body had been made and only four hours of daylight remained to us when we assembled a party of half-a-dozen men and began to climb the hill.

It was soon apparent that the tiger had not carried its victim up the main footpath leading to the top of the hill, which we more than half ascended without finding a vestige or trace of the victim. Climbing neighbouring boulders as we advanced, I instructed men to look in all directions for anything that became visible, and when about three-quarters of the way up one of these men reported vultures sitting in a tree about a quarter-mile to our left. Scrambling across the intervening rocks and thorny bushes, we eventually came upon the remains of the boy, completely devoured, by this time, by the vultures.

There appeared little use or hope in sitting up over the bones, especially as we knew from experience that the killer seldom returned to such a meal. Nevertheless, Mac and two men put up my machan on the tree on which the vultures had been sitting and decided to remain there, while I felt I had just enough time to ascend the rest of the hill and look among the ruins.

Regaining the path, I hurried upwards, and reached the ruins just after 5 p.m. The walls of the fort had long since crumbled into decay, and a sea of lantana and thorny undergrowth covered the area as well as the old moat that lay outside. At this point, the remaining four men in the party elected to remain outside;

to await my return they ascended to the top-most branches of a tall fig-tree., the gnarled roots of which bit deep into the debris of the fort's wall.

Proceeding cautiously, I endeavoured to keep on top of the fallen wall, as far as it was negotiable, in order to maintain some elevation above the surrounding lantana, which was both impassable as well as dangerous to enter, as I would not be able to see the tiger in that undergrowth even were it but a yard away

Progress was most difficult and strenuous, and by the time I had reached the opposite end of the fort, I was breathing heavily from my exertions and bathed in perspiration. Here I faced the sun as the golden orb neared the western horizon.

Years ago I had been over the same fort, and I knew that about this spot were the almost-completely engulfed remains of walled enclosures, and what had been dungeons in the distant long ago. Because of these structures the wall at this point became impossible to follow. I was loath to step down into the lantana, but it soon became apparent that I would either have to do this and struggle through a distance of about one hundred yards to where the wall began again, or retrace my steps. Time was also against me; so to avoid delay I finally decided to risk the lantana, which I commenced to push my way through, as silently as I was able. But this soon turned out to be impossible, for the lantana twigs, covered with minute thorns, clung to my clothing at each step and made considerable noise as I broke my way through.

I knew I was now opposite the remains of the dungeons and enclosures, and that here, if anywhere in this deserted ruin, was where the tiger would most likely be hiding. At the same time, no doubt keyed up as I was by the unfavourableness of my position, my tensed nerves and senses signalled the proximity of danger. A sixth sense cried out that the tiger was near and on my trail, watching me for the moment of attack, which would take place very soon if I did not escape from the lantana. I had felt these warnings too often to ignore them, so while trebling my vigilance and looking in all directions, I pressed forward to higher ground.

Thirty yards more—twenty yards more—fifteen yards more—and then from the lantana to my left rose the snarling head of a tiger, its ears laid back in preparation for the spring, its jaws wide open to reveal the gleaming canines. My bullet crashed into the wide-open mouth, as the animal launched itself forward. Rushing blindly on to gain higher ground, I all but lost my eyes in the intervening lantana, the thorns tearing my flesh and clothing, while pandemonium broke loose behind me.

With the back of its head blown out, that tiger tried to get me, and when I had covered those remaining fifteen yards and spun around, it was but two yards away, with a great gaping red hole where half its skull had once been. Almost beside myself with terror, I crashed a second, third and fourth bullet into the beast and as, shattered, it toppled on its side, I sat on a piece of the ruin, shaken, sick and faint.

Ten minutes later I struggled to my feet, and avoiding the bloody mass before me, returned to the tree where I had left the four men, by completing the circuit of the remaining fort wall.

Hearing the four shots and the snarls of the tiger, they had concluded I had been killed, and were debating whether to come down from their tree and hasten back to their hamlet, or spend the rest of the night in its branches. It was quite obvious they had never expected to see me alive again.

Collecting them, we had hardly covered a furlong when we were met by Mac and the other two men. From where he was sitting, he too had heard my four shots and, like the staunch friend he was, had hurried forward to give any assistance I might need. As it was, seeing me tattered, scratched and bleeding from my rush through the lantana, his ruddy face drained to a chalky white and he ran forward to hold me, thinking I had been mauled.

Squatting there, I told him what had happened, while I puffed clouds of smoke from my cherished briar and received his warm congratulations. Indeed, I could not help remarking, as I smoked that soothing pipeful of tobacco, that I had never expected to smoke again, when I saw that terrible face, contorted with its lust to kill, but a few feet away.

Later that night we carried the tiger down, hoisted it on the car and took it to Chitaldroog town. As we had expected, it proved to be female and was undoubtedly the man-eater that had killed the boy. Its aggressiveness towards me also justified this conclusion. Early next morning, while skinning the animal, we were visited by the amildar, who wanted to see the devil that had killed his relative, the little girl at Hosdurga, by the district forest officer and other officials, and by hundreds of the inhabitants. It was late that evening before we could leave for Bangalore with the skins of the two tigers that had formed such an exceptional and unheard-of combination, as cattle-kitler and maneater hunting together.

Incidentally skinning the tigress revealed no sign of the reason for her having become a man-eater. As I have already said, this district had a long history of man-eaters behind it, extending for generations past, and I am of the opinion that this tigress came of man-eating stock. Such an explanation would also account for her mate, the big male that Mac had shot, being a normal cattle-lifter that had not touched human flesh.

The tigress had probably only met this male during the mating season that was just over—it lasts from November to January—and had not been with him long enough to infect him with her man-eating habits. Had she littered she would have undoubtedly have taught her cubs the taste for human flesh, just as she herself had been taught, and so have extended the generations of man-eaters of that district.

The third tiger, whose existence we had suspected, never materialised, for before leaving we left word with all the officials, as well as people, to inform us at once if a third tiger was heard of. This was because we felt there was always the remote possibility that the third tiger might also be the man-eater. But months passed and we received the glad tidings that all reports of man-eating had ceased throughout the district after the killing of that tigress on the summit of Togi-mutt'. Fred Todd, and the rest of her victims, had been avenged.

5

The Rogue-Elephant of Panapatti

He was a small animal, as rogue elephants go, standing about seven feet and a half in his socks. This could be gauged by the tracks of his forefoot, twice the circumference of which gives, to within a couple of inches, the height of an Indian elephant. But what he lacked in stature he made up for in courage, cold calculating cunning, and an implacable hatred of the human race, whom he had evidently made it his ambition to decimate, as and when the opportunity presented itself.

He had one tusk, about 18 inches long, while the other had been broken off short, by (it was said) the big leader of the herd inhabiting the banks of the Cauvery River and the jungle fastnesses that comprised the forest block of Wodapatti, in which was situated the cattle-pen of Panapatti, in the district of Salem. This youngster, before he became a rogue, had evidently been ambitious and was more than normally high-spirited, for he had thrust his unwelcome attentions upon the ladies of the herd under the very eyes of their lord and master. A warning scream of resentment and rage from the leader had had no salutary effect, and the youngster had offered battle when the tusker had attempted to drive him away.

This had led to a major encounter, in which years, experience and greater weight had told heavily in favour of the leader. The youngster had eventually bolted, battered and beaten, with vicious gashes in his sides, inflicted by the powerful tusks of the bigger male, while one of his own tusks had been snapped off short in the fray, no doubt to give him bad toothache for many days to come.

He had wandered in this condition, morose and surly, in the vicinity of the herd, but never daring to enter it, when one day, as he was walking down a forest cart-track, he had turned a corner to come suddenly face to face with a buffalo cart, laden with bamboos that had been felled for the contractor. A blind rage had seized him at that moment, together with a deep urge to get his own back on something. Madly he rushed at the cart, and the driver just escaped by jumping off and fleeing for life. But the unfortunate buffaloes were yoked to the heavily-laden vehicle and stood helpless to the onslaught.

The rogue—for rogue he had now become—proceeded to smash the cart to matchwood, before turning his attentions on the buffaloes. One he seized by its long, curving horn, and flung bodily down the embankment that bordered the track, where it was found next day with its horn torn out from the roots; one of its forelegs had suffered a compound fracture, and the broken, exposed bone had dug itself into the soft earth with the force of the fall, so that the weight of the animal effectively anchored it to the spot. The remaining buffalo it had gored with its one tusk, but this animal had bolted down the track, dragging the broken yoke of the cart behind it, and so escaped the fate of its less fortunate companion.

Thereafter the elephant steadily worsened his reputation, and many an unfortunate wayfarer to the river had gone to his death beneath its massive feet or, caught by that terrible trunk, had been beaten to pulp against the bole of a forest tree.

My first experience with this animal was by accident. I had gone down to Hogenaikal, on the banks of the Cauvery River and about four miles from Panapatti, for a week end's mahseer fishing, and to secure a crocodile if opportunity presented. As rumour had it, at that time the rogue was not in the locality, having crossed the river to the Coimbatore bank in wake of the elephant herd which had wandered there in search of fresh pasture.

In the evening of the second day, after having met with indifferent fishing, I had returned to the forest lodge for tea, when the call of a peacock close at hand had tempted me to go after the bird, which I hoped would make me a tasty roast for that night's dinner.

Slipping a couple of No. i shot into the breach of my shotgun, I cut diagonally across the forest to the glen where the peacock was calling. Reaching it, I stepped cautiously forward in an effort to locate my quarry, eventually arriving at the dry bed of the Chinar stream, a tributary of the Cauvery River, which it joined a mile further down.

My rubber-soled boots made no noise on the soft sand. I could hear the rustle of the peacock's feathers as it preened its tail somewhere behind the bushes on the opposite bank, and was just tiptoeing across the stream, when a shrill, trumpeting blast smote the silence, to be followed by the crashing bulk of the rogue as it broke cover fifty yards away and swiftly bore down on me.

Realising the futility of attempting to escape by running away—for elephants can cover ground at an astonishing speed and I had no chance of out-distancing him, because of the hampering soft sand and clinging thorny shrubs of the neighbouring jungle—I covered the curled trunk in the sights of my shotgun and fired both barrels at a range of about thirty yards.

The noise of the report and the stinging missiles stopped him momentarily and, while he screamed with rage and defiance, I fled up the path by which I had come, carrying my empty gun, at a pace I had never thought myself capable of attaining. Arriving at the Forest Bungalow, I seized my rifle and ran back again. But there was nothing to be seen on the deserted sands of the Chinar stream, and upon approaching the spot I found the rogue had swerved into the forest on the opposite side, where I did not care to follow him, as night was approaching.

The next day I had to return to Bangalore on business and could not possibly extend my stay, so I left the honours of the first round entirely to the rogue of Panapatti.

This creature, through his notoriety, had been declared as an undesirable or 'rogue' elephant by the government, and official notification had been broadcast by the Forest Department, both in print and locally by beat-of-drum, or 'tom-tom' as it is officially called, offering a government reward of Rs 500 (about £34) for its destruction.

An Indian gentleman of the locality then very bravely determined to put an end to the elephant's career and claim the reward. The details of his attempt—as I later pieced it together—were as follows.

Armed with a .500 double-barrelled black-powder Express rifle which had seen better days, he arrived at Panapatti and was told that the elephant was wandering in the adjacent Wodapatti Forest Block. The same Chinar stream, on the bed of which, near Hogenaikal I had nearly met my end beneath the monster's feet, curves gracefully past Panapatti and meanders through the forest, its north-western bank forming the boundary of the Wodapatti Reserve, and its opposite bank that of the Pennagram Block.

The Indian gentleman of whom I am speaking, having tried for two days without success to meet the rogue, spent the night of the third day in his tent about two miles within the Pennagram Block, away from the Chinar Stream and the Wodapatti

Range, out of which the elephant was said never to stray. But as a precaution he had his followers build a ring of camp fires around their two tents, and the men were given instructions to keep plenty of firewood in reserve for replenishing and stoking the fires during the night watches.

All then being peaceful, he apparently fell fast asleep; so, evidently, did his followers.

In the early hours of the morning the rogue came upon this peaceful scene. The fires had perhaps died low, with just their embers glowing. Normally, no elephant or any other animal will go anywhere near a fire. But the sight of the white tent and the urge to destroy proved too strong for this beast, for he carefully made his way through at a point where there was no fire and rushed upon the tent with a scream of rage.

The camp followers awoke at the pandemonium created and, realising the demon was upon them, scattered and fled in all directions. The unfortunate occupant of the white tent had no chance to use his time-worn Express. The structure fell about his ears and was trampled flat beneath the huge bulk of the elephant, which then proceeded to tear it to ribbons. It was while engaged in this congenial task that it came upon the hunter, alive or dead at that time, nobody knows. Curling its dreaded trunk around him, it carried him off in triumph to the clearing of a forest line which passed nearby. There it literally rubbed him into the ground beneath its huge feet, till nothing remained of the human body but a pulpy mass of bloody flesh and crushed bones, mixed with sand from the forest line. Finally, not liking the smell of blood, it tossed the bloody mass far away and returned to the fastnesses of the Wodapatti block.

As a result of this incident, the government reward was doubled to Rs 1000, while I determined to begin my second round against the elephant.

Arriving at Panapatti, I visited the scene of the recent tragedy, where I could not help wondering at the audacity of the blood-thirsty elephant in actually penetrating the circle of fires. The spot nearby, where it had rubbed its victim into the ground, was also clearly evident, although the remains had long since been demolished by vultures.

Returning to Panapatti, I requisitioned the aid of one of the cattlemen from the adjoining cattle-pen, who was also a fair tracker, to help me find the animal. Tracks there were aplenty across the sands of the Chinar stream, but the problem was to find and follow one that had been freshly made. This it was impossible to do, for the good reason that the elephant had evidently made off from the vicinity, and was either somewhere within the Wodapatti Block, or had wandered across the low hills to the main Cauvery River, which flowed, as I have stated, some four miles away.

The Wodapatti bank was clothed, for a couple of miles down the Chinar stream, with a species of tall flowering grass, whose roots subsist on sub-soil moisture and which attained a height of ten feet in places, topped by beautiful heads of flowering stems which somewhat resembled the flowering heads of cane-sugar, but were of greater length and much finer texture. In the early mornings, droplets of dew, which had gathered overnight on the fine strands of these flowering heads, glittered in the rays of the rising sun, giving a fairy-like appearance to the graceful fronds and a vision of beauty and peace which entirely belied the danger that threatened upon entering the grassy belt. The stems had grown to such height and thick profusion that one could not see more than a yard ahead, and to walk through the grass one had to part the stems with one hand, holding the rifle in the other. A herd of elephants might have lurked within, and nothing could have been seen of them until almost within touching distance. The tracks made by the rogue in his previous excursions were marked by crushed and bent stems, and even these were rapidly reassuming their upright positions.

The grass belt varied in width from 100 to 200 yards. As the hills at this point abutted the Chinar Stream, the jungle was represented by giant bamboo, traversing which was almost as dangerous as crossing the flowering grass. Fallen bamboos lay in profusion everywhere, their spiky ends impeding both advance and retreat. The tall boughs, clothed with their feathered leaves, curved gracefully overhead, bending and creaking to the forest breezes.

We spent four whole days searching for the elephant, laboriously traversing the grass belt and the bamboos, crossing the range of foodiills and descending their further slopes till the purling waters of the Cauvery River flowed past our feet as it hastened to the falls and cataracts at Hogenaikal, the great Mettur Dam some 35 miles downstream, then the eastern plain of Erode and the city of Trichinopoly, and finally the distant Bay of Bengal. In all this time, never a fresh track of the rogue did we see.

The afternoon of the fifth day found my guide and myself again on the banks of the Cauvery River, when I decided to follow the bank upstream in the hope of finding some trace of my quarry. We had advanced with considerable difficulty about three miles, stepping over the giant roots of the tall 'Muthee' trees that clothed the bank and ran down into the water for sustenance, interspersed with brakes of tall flowering-grass, when we came upon the fresh tracks of an elephant which had evidently crossed the river early that morning from the opposite bank of the Coimbatore District. Rough measurements revealed that they tallied with the spoor of the rogue.

Tracking now became easy, for we had a definite trail to follow, and the footprints and heavy bulk of the elephant had made a clear path through grass, bamboo and undergrowth.

The spoor led up and across a small foothill, near the top of which we came upon a heap of dung. Although quite fresh, this lacked that warmth to the touch which would have shown that it had been very recently cast. So we followed on, down into a deep valley. Here we found still fresher dung, but not warm to the touch, which showed that our quarry was yet some distance ahead.

FOOTHILLS

We struggled up the adjoining slope and across two more foothills, and then observed that the tracks suddenly slued round and made back in the general direction of the Cauvery River.

We were overcome by a fear that the animal had escaped us by returning across the Cauvery. Going forward as fast as possible, we came upon another heap of dung together with the mark of urine which had soaked into the ground. But this time minute traces of froth showed in the sand and the dung was warm to the touch. At last our quarry was not very far ahead, nor was the Cauvery River!

Our further progress turned almost into a race to reach the river at the same time as the elephant, and before it crossed out of rifle range. From fallen branches, oozing with freshly-flowing sap, we could observe that the pachyderm was grazing casually as it approached the river.

Finally, a sharp dip in the land and a murmur of sound told us that we had almost reached the river's bank, and soon the glint of water between tree-stems told us that we were there. Silently and cautiously we crept forward. The sand became soft. Then we noticed that the elephant, instead of crossing as we had feared, had changed its mind and walked upstream and across a grassy bank. Here it was apparent that the spoor was very recent, for the tender blades of grass were fast embedded in the moist ooze, from which bubbles of air burst before our eyes.

We had gone another 150 yards when we observed that a creek lay ahead, and as we came abreast of it we heard the noise of splashing and the hollow sound of air being blown through an elephant's trunk. Our quarry was having a bath.

Fortunately, the little breeze that blew was in our direction, and as we parted the intervening twigs and stems of grass, we saw an elephant lying on its side in the water, but facing away from us.

In this position, it was impossible to tell whether the animal was the rogue, or a wandering elephant from among the several herds that inhabited both banks of the river. So we settled down to watch.

After a further five minutes of snorting, blowing and splashing, the animal suddenly rose and began to walk in a leisurely way across the creek. In all this time it had not shown its head, nor had we been able to see whether it had two tusks, or a broken stump at one side.

The situation now called for early decision, as once the elephant reached the thick verdure clothing the opposite bank of the creek, it would be lost to view. So I snapped my thumb and finger twice in quick succession. The sound, infinitesimal as it must have been, penetrated the keen hearing of the elephant. With a swish and a swirl of water it spun around, and there before us stood the 'rogue of Panapatti', the stump of his broken left tusk clearly in view, while the right tusk, small as it was, curved viciously upwards. Within a second his small eyes located us, his trunk curled inwards, and with his head raised and his small tail sticking out ridiculously, screaming with triumph and hate, he charged across the intervening water, bent on yet another lustful killing.

My .405 spoke once, the heavy solid bullet speeding straight to its mark beneath the coiling trunk and into the throat. The animal stopped dead in its tracks, while a gout of blood spurted from the severed jugular. It turned sideways in an attempt to make off, when two more rounds both found their marks in vital places, one in the soft depression of the temple, and the other behind the huge ear as it flapped forward.

The great bulk stood still, then shivered as if stricken with terrible ague, and finally collapsed, as if pole-axed, in the shallow waters of the creek, which rapidly became reddened with blood, as the rays of the late afternoon sun vanished beneath the rim of the towering peak of Mount Ponachi Malai on the Coimbatore bank, sending streaks of crimson light into the orange sky.

6

The Man-Eater of Segur

The hamlet of Segur is situated at the foot of the north-eastern slopes of the well-known Nilgiri Mountains in south India, or 'Blue Mountains', which is what the word 'Nilgiri' literally means. On the summit of this lovely range stands the beautiful health resort of Ootacamund, at an average elevation of 7,500 feet above mean sea level. This 'Queen of Hill Stations', as it is affectionately termed, is the focal point of visitors from all the length and breadth of India. Ootacamund has a charm of its own, with a climate that allows the growth of all types of English flowers and vegetables to perfection. The all-prevailing scent of the towering eucalyptus ('blue-gum') trees, which is wafted across the station from the surrounding plantations, mingled with that of the fir and pine, makes memories of 'Ooty' unforgettable, and with its cool climate gives a welcome change to the visitor from the heat and enervating temperature of the sweltering plains far below.

A steep ghat-road, 12 miles in length, leaves Ootacamund, and after passing through graceful, rolling downs, where fox-hunting was once a pastime of the English residents—the local jackal taking the place of the fox—drops sharply downwards to Segur, at the foot of the range, where dense tropical forests prevail. The road is so steep in places as to be almost unusable, except to motor cars of fairly high power. At Segur the road bifurcates, one branch running north-westwards through dense forest, past the hamlet of Mahvanhalla and the village of Masinigudi, to meet the main trunk road, linking the cities of Bangalore and Mysore with Ootacamund, at the forest chowki of Tippakadu. The other bifurcation leads eastwards through equally dense forest, along the base of the Blue Mountains, to the forest bungalow of Anaikutty, nine miles away. Two perennial streams water this area, the Segur River and the Anaikutty River, both descending in silvery cascades from the Blue mountains; here their waters run through giant tropical forests to join those of the Moyar River, some fifteen miles away. The Moyar River, or 'Mysore Ditch', as it is known, forms the boundary between the native state of Mysore on the north, the district of Coimbatore on the north-east, and the Nilgiri Range with its foothills on the south, both Coimbatore and the Nilgiris forming part of the Province of Madras. The evergreen forests of the Malabar-Wynaad extend to the west and south-west.

All the areas mentioned are densely wooded, hold game preserves on the Mysore, Malabar, and Nilgiri sides, and are the habitat of large numbers of wild elephant, bison, tiger, panther, sambar, spotted-deer and other animals.

The forest-bungalow of Anaikutty is built on a knoll, past which run the swirling waters of the Anaikutty river. In summer it is an unhealthy place, full of malarial mosquito, and the origin of many fatal cases of 'black-water' fever. In the winter it is a paradise. The mornings are fresh and sunny, ideally suited to long hikes through the forest. The afternoons are moderately cool. The evenings chilly, while with nightfall an icy-cold wind descends from the mountain tops to take the place of the warmer air rising from the surrounding forests. The nights are then so in tensely cold that one is invariably confined to the bungalow itself, in all the rooms of which fireplaces have been provided. Here a truly Christmassy feeling prevails, before a blazing fire of forest logs, while the party discusses the latest stories of the 'abominable snowman', or ghost stories are related in hair-raising detail. Even within the compound of tins bungalow elephant and tiger and panther roam, their screams, roars and grants reminding the sleepy inmate, snugly tucked below double-blankets, with the glow of a fire by his bedside, that he is still in the midst of a tropical jungle.

These forests are a favourite resort of mine, and in them I have met with several little adventures that are still memorable after these many years.

To relate just one. Wild-dogs, which hunt in packs in India, varying in numbers from three to thirty, sometimes invade these forests from over the boundaries of Mysore and Coimbatore, where they are very numerous, more so in the latter district. These packs are very destructive to all forms of deer, particularly sambar and spotted-deer, which they hunt down inexorably, and tear limb from limb while still alive. On several occasions, both in these and other jungles, I have come across sambar actually being chased by these dogs. The method adopted is that, while a few dogs chase the animal, others break away in a flanking movement, to ran ahead of their quarry and ambush it as it dashes past them. When hunting, they emit a series of yelps in a very high pitch, resembling the whistling cry of a bird rather than that of a dog. The quarry is brought to earth after being attacked by these flankers, which bite out its eyes, disembowel it, hamstring or emasculate it, in their efforts to bring it down. I once saw a sambar pursued by wild-dogs, dash into a pool of water to try and protect itself. It had been disembowelled and trailed its intestines behind it for the distance of twenty feet. Sambar are extraordinarily hardy, and sometimes are literally eaten alive by these dogs, before being killed.

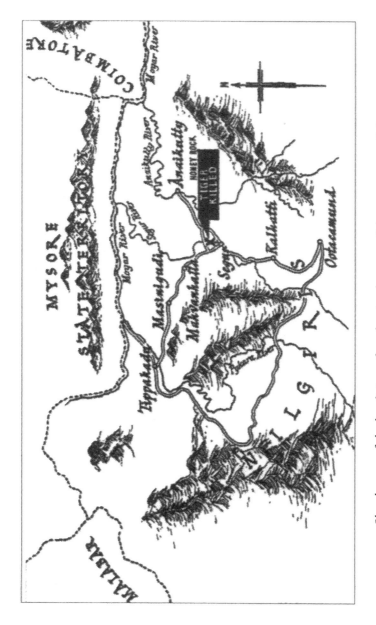

Sketch map of the localities referred to in the story of the man-eater of Segur.

One evening, at about 5 o'clock, I was a mile from the bungalow, interesting myself in an unusual species of ground orchid that sprouted from the earth in a spray of tiny star-shaped flowers. Suddenly I heard a medley of sounds whose origin I could not at first define. There were cries, yelps, and long-drawn bays, interspersed with grunts and Vhoofs that puzzled me. Then I knew that the noise was that of wild dogs, which seemed to be attacking a pig or a bear. Grabbing my rifle, I ran in the direction of the din. I may have covered a furlong, when around the corner dashed a tigress, encircled by half-a-dozen wild dogs. Concealing myself behind the trunk of a tree, I watched the unusual scene.

The dogs had spread themselves around the tigress, who was growling ferociously. Every now and again one would dash in from behind to bite her. She would then turn to attempt to rend asunder this puny aggressor, when a couple of others would rush in from another direction. In this way she was kept going continually, and I could see she was fast becoming spent.

All this time the dogs were making a tremendous noise, the reason for which I soon came to know, when, in a lull in the fray, I heard the whistling cry of the main pack, galloping to the assistance of their advance part}'. The tigress must have also heard the sound, for in sudden, renewed fury, she charged two of the dogs, one of which she caught a tremendous blow on its back with her paw, cracking its spine with the sharp report of a broken twig. The other just managed to leap out of danger. The tigress then followed up her momentary advantage by bounding away, to be immediately followed by the five remaining dogs. They were just out of sight when the main pack streamed by, in which I counted twenty-three dogs, as they galloped past me without the slightest interest in my presence. Soon the sounds of pursuit died away, and all that remained was the one dead dog.

During the affair I had been too interested, and too lost in admiration at the courage of the dogs, to fire at either the tigress or her attackers.

Next morning I sent out scouts to try to discover the result of the incident. They returned about noon, bringing a few fragments of tiger-skin, to report that the dogs had finally cornered their exhausted quarry about five miles away and had literally torn the tigress to pieces. As far as they could gather, five dogs had been killed in the final battle, after which the victors had eaten the tigress, and even the greater portions of their own dead companions.

Three distinct tribes of natives inhabit these areas. There are the Badagas, descendants of long-ago invaders from the state of Mysore, themselves fleeing from Mahommedan conquerors from the north. These Badagas have now become rich; they own lands, vast herds of cattle and semi-wild buffaloes, *with* tremendously long, curved horns. Next come the Kesavas, the greatest in numbers but laziest in disposition, who work under the Badagas as herdsmen and tillers of the soil. Lastly, come the Karumbas, comparatively few in number, the original inhabitants of the land and now entirely jungle-men; they live on wild hone); roots, hunting and the trapping of small animals and birds. These Karumbas make excellent trackers, and like the Sholagas of the Coimbatore District and Pujarees of Salem, are true children of nature, who are born and live in the forests till the day of their death.

Having given the reader a little idea of the country in which the adventure took place, I shall lose no further time in telling the story of the 'Man-eater of Segur'.

This tiger was reported to have come originally from the jungles of the Silent Valley Forest Block in the District of Malabar-Wynaad, below the extreme opposite, or south western face, of the Blue Mountains. This area is infested with elephants, of which it holds the record for 'rogues', and with bison. As a rule it does not hold many tiger. A few human kills took place in the Silent Valley and then ceased entirely, to recommence at Gudalur, some twenty7 miles from Tippakadu, at Masinigudi, and finally in all the areas between Segur and Anaikutty. How and why the tiger came so far from its place of origin, encircling the greater portion of the Nilgiri Mountains in doing so, nobody knows.

It was midsummer and the tiger had been particularly active, killing at Segur and, within a week, at Anaikutty, when I arrived. The last victim had been a Kesava herdsman, tending his herd of semi-wild buffaloes some two miles from Anaikutty along the lower reaches of the river, as it wended its way towards the Moyar. In this instance, the man-eater had stalked and attacked the man, completely ignoring the surrounding grazing buffaloes. It had killed him, and was perhaps carrying him away, when the buffaloes had become aware of its presence.

These animals, as I have already stated, are only semi-domesticated, and extremely dangerous to a stranger, especially if he happens to be dressed in the unusual mode—to them—of a European, when they frequently charge on sight. Seeing the tiger, they had evidently attacked him en masse, and succeeded in driving him off, leaving the dead man where he had been dropped.

That night, neither buffaloes nor herdsman returned to the kraal, so early the next morning a search party set out to discover the reason for their absence. It did not take them long to find the dead herdsman, surrounded by his herd of placidly grazing buffaloes, which had effectively prevented the tiger from returning to its prey. An examination of the corpse, the pug-marks of the tiger, and the pursuing hooves of the charging buffaloes, revealed the sequence of happenings as I have related them.

The kill that had taken place a week earlier at Segur had been that of a woman, as she went down to the Segur River with her water-pot to fetch the daily supply of water for her family. In this case the tiger had succeeded in carrying off its victim, the only evidence of the occurrence being the mute testimony of the broken water-pot, the pugs of the tiger in the soft mud that bordered the river, a few drops of blood, the torn saree, and a few strands of human hair that had become entangled in the bushes as the tiger made off with its prey.

I visited both localities and by careful measurement and examination of the pugs, which were very clear on the river bank at Segur, determined that the tiger was a smallish-sized male of considerably less than adult age.

Reports had it that the tiger very frequently traversed the ten miles of forest road between Segur and Anaikutty, his pugs being seen, along this track, especially in the vicinity of both places. As a preliminary, I therefore decided to sit up along this road at differently selected places, and without wearying the reader with details, put this plan into practice, spending thus a whole week, alternately in the vicinity of Segur and Anaikutty, without seeing any signs of the tiger.

The seventh night I spent on a tree a mile-and-a-half from Segur. Returning the next morning to the Anaikutty forest bungalow, where I had established my headquarters, I was informed that a Karumba, who had left the previous morning to gather wild honey from the combs of the giant rockbee that abound by the hundred in the region of a place called 'Honey Rock', about four miles from the lower foothills of the Nilgiris, had not yet returned.

Assembling a group of twenty persons as a search party, I accompanied them to this wild and densely wooded spot. Splitting the party into four groups of five men each, as protection against possible attack by the man-eater, we searched till noon, when one of the men discovered the body of the dead Karumba lying in a nala, and brought me the news. I went to the spot and found the man had been killed by being bitten through the throat. Beside him lay his empty kerosine-tin, in which he had been gathering honey, all of which had spilt on the ground to form a feast for a colony of black-ants, which covered the tin in a black mass.

Thinking at first that the tiger had killed him, and wondering why it had not devoured him in that quiet, secluded spot, we cast around for tracks, but soon discovered that the killer had been a female sloth-bear, accompanied by its cub. The human-like imprints of the mother's feet, and the smaller impressions of the cub's, were clearly to be seen in the soft sand that formed the bed of the nala.

Evidently the she-bear had been asleep with its cub, or perhaps about to cross the nala, when the Karumba, in his search for honey, had suddenly come upon it. The sloth-bear has a very uncertain temperament at the best of times, being poor of sight and hearing, so that humans have often been able to approach them very closely before being discovered, when in the fright and excitement of the moment, they will attack without any provocation. Undoubtedly this is what happened, when the she-bear, surprised, frightened and irritated, and in defence of her young which she fancied was in danger, had rushed at the Karumba, bitten him through the throat, severing his jugular, and then made off as fast as she could.

I did not wish to spend time in hunting a bear which, after all, had only killed in defence of its cub, and was for returning to the bungalow at Anaikutty when the four Karumbas that were included in the party, urged me to track down and shoot the animal, which they felt would be a menace to them when they, in turn, came to the same place for honey. More to please them than because I had any heart in the venture, I therefore sent the rest of the party back and followed these four men on the trail of the she-bear.

The tracks led along the nullah and then joined a stream, down which Mrs Bruin and her baby had ambled for some distance before breaking back into the jungle. Thence she had climbed upwards towards the many rocks and caves that gave them shelter, where hundreds of rock-beehives hung from every conceivable rock-projection in long, black masses, sometimes attaining a length of over five feet, a width of a yard, and a thickness of over a foot.

The ground we were now traversing was hard and stony, and to my unskilled eyes presented no trace of the bears' passing. But the Karumbas were seldom at fault, and their powers of tracking really worth witnessing during the long and tiring walk that followed. For more than two hours they led me uphill and down dale, and across deep valleys and stony ridges. An overturned rock or stone, a displaced leaf, or the slightest marks of scraping or digging, showed them where the bears had travelled.

At last we approached the mouth of a cave, high up over a projecting rock from which hung twenty-three separate rock-beehives. This cave they declared, was the home of the she-bear and her cub.

Standing ten yards from the entrance, and to one side, I instructed the men to hurl stones into the interior, which they did with unabated vigour for quite twenty minutes. But not a sound did we hear. Then the Karumbas made a torch of grasses, which we ignited and threw into the cave, but still nothing happened. Finally they made five similar torches. Lighting one of these, I followed the Karumba that carried it into the cave, while the remaining three Karumbas came behind us, carrying the four spare grass torches.

The cave was comparatively small inside and was obviously empty, the occupant and her youngster having left at hearing our approach, if not before. But I was glad of this, because, as I have said, I had no quarrel with this animal, and would have regretted having to shoot it and leave the baby an orphan.

We had lit our third torch, and were just about to leave, when one of the Karumbas came upon an interesting curiosity of the Indian forest, of which I had heard but never seen, and the existence of which I consequently never believed.

He found in a corner what the natives call 'bear's bread', or 'Karadi roti', as it is named in Tamil. This was a roughly circular mass, about ten inches across, an inch thick, and of a dirty blackish-yellow, sticky consistency. Female bears are reported to seek out the fruits of the 'Jack' tree, a large fruit with a rough, thorny exterior; wild 'Wood-apple' fruit, the size of large tennis balls and with hard shells; and pieces of honeycomb, including bees, comb and honey. Each of these ingredients is first eaten by the she-bear in turn, the whole being then vomited in the cave in a mass, which the she-bear allows to harden into a cake, as reserve food for her young.

Due possibly to its long hair, the bear is marvellously impervious to the stings of the rock-bee, which prove fatal to a human being if suffered in large numbers. It can climb trees and rocks with astounding ability in search of wild fruit and honeycombs. A cave, inhabited by a she-bear with her young, is reported to contain sometimes a dozen such cakes. In ~~this~~ *this* case we had found only one, but in as much as I had never come across or seen one before, I was immensely interested. As evidence of the wholesomeness of this 'bread', the four Karumbas offered it to me for immediate consumption, but I declined with thanks. They then divided it equally between themselves, and ate it with evident gusto.

We were now sitting at the entrance of the cave. Whether the flames of the torch, the smoke, or the sound of human voices disturbed them, I do not know, but suddenly a few black objects buzzed around us, and as we sprang to our feet to make off, the rock-bees from the hive immediately above, grossly disturbed and angry, descended upon us in an avalanche.

It was every man for himself, and as I grabbed my rifle and sprinted down the hillside, the agile Karumbas out distanced me very quickly. What I lacked in speed I made up, however, by being clothed, the bees being able to register some twenty stings on my neck and hands and other exposed parts, as compared with about forty that I counted on each of the bare skins of the Karumbas, when we slowed up half-a-mile away. It was indeed a comical ending to a tragic but interesting morning, and we returned to Anaikutty a far wiser, but very sore and smarting party.

I set out at 8 p.m. that night, motoring slowly to Segur in my Studebaker, a Karumba acting as assistant by my side and flashing the beams of my 'sealed-beam' spotlight along the jungle on both sides. Meeting nothing, we continued for six miles along the north-western road, past Mahvanhalla and Masinigudi, and finally the four miles to the forest chowki at Tippakadu. Here we allowed an hour to pass before returning, this time encountering, three miles from Tippakadu, a herd of bison along the roadside.

These animals crashed away as the car approached closer. Between Masinigudi and Segur we met several spotted-deer, and just after taking the turn to Anaikutty a large bull elephant in the centre of the road, his tusks gleaming sharply white in the powerful beams of the spot light. A gentle toot of the horn sufficed to send him scurrying on his way, and finally we reached the Anaikutty bungalow without seeing a trace of the man-eater.

The following morning dawned bright and fine, and I set out with my Karumba guide across the forest towards the Moyar River, nine miles to the north. Again we encountered no trace of the tiger, but came across the pugs of an exceptionally large forest-panther as the land began to dip sharply to the basin of the Moyar. Judging by its tracks, it was indeed a big animal, approaching the size of a small tigress, and would have made a fine trophy, had I the time to pursue it. We returned to the bungalow in the late afternoon, tired and somewhat disappointed, after our long and fruitless walk.

Again that night we motored to Tippakadu and back, encountering only a solitary sambar, when returning, at the river crossing before the Anaikutty forest bungalow.

With dawn I undertook another hike with my Karumba, this time in a south-easterly direction and towards the Nilgiris. We found a dead cow-bison in the bush four miles away, an examination of the carcase revealing that the animal had died of rinderpest. The Forest Department had reported some two months earlier that this epidemic had spread from the cattle of the Badagas, whose herds it afflicted in a contagious and epidemic form, to the wild animals, especially bison, and here lay proof of the statement.

That afternoon a report came in from Mahvanhalla that the tiger had taken a woman near the bridge by which the main road to Tippakadu crosses the Mahvanhalla Stream before it joins the Segur River. Motoring to the spot I was shown the place where, the previous evening, the tiger, which had been lurking on the banks of the stream, had attacked the woman, who had been among the herdsmen watering the large number of mixed cattle and buffaloes kraaled at Mahvanhalla.

Apparently nobody had actually witnessed the incident, the woman having been a little apart from the rest of the party assembled near the bridge and hidden by the bend the little stream takes just before it passes under the road. She had screamed shrilly and silence had followed. The remaining graziers, five in number, had hastened to Mahvanhalla, gathered reinforcements in the form of six others, including the husband of the unfortunate woman, and returned to the spot to look for her. They had found the basket she had been carrying, and close by in the soft earth, the pug-marks of a tiger; then the whole party had returned to Mahvanhalla. At dawn the next day, the four men who now reported themselves had set forth by footpath to cover the ten miles to Anaikutty and report the incident to me, it having become known that I was in the area to shoot the tiger.

We went to the place where the woman had been attacked, and with the expert help of my Karumba tracker were soon able to pick up the trail of the tiger and its victim. Before following I dismissed the party from Mahvanhalla, together with the bereaved husband, who made me promise faithfully that I would bring back at least a few bones of his beloved spouse to satisfy the requirements of a cremation ceremony.

Almost without faltering, my Karumba guide followed what was to me the completely invisible trail left by the tiger. The man-eater was evidently making towards a high hill, an out-spur of the Nilgiri Range, that ran parallel to the road on the west at a distance of about two miles. Years ago I had partly climbed this very hill in search of a good bison head, and knew its middle slopes were covered with a sea of long spear-grass which gradually thinned out as the higher, and more rocky, levels were reached. In that area, I felt we had little chance of finding the tiger or its prey.

Nevertheless my stout little guide continued faultlessly and within a mile of the foot of the hill came across the woman's saree, caught in the undergrowth. Shortly afterwards the tiger appeared to have changed its mind, in that its trail veered off to the right, parallel to the hill, which now was quite near, and back again towards the bed of the Mahvanhalla Stream. Still following, we eventually reached the stream, which here ran through a deep valley. Scattered bamboo-clumps grew in increasing numbers down this declivity, and the shrill squeal of vultures and the heavy flapping of their wings soon heralded the close of our search. The remains of the woman lay below a clump of bamboo, eaten by the tiger, and the vultures had finished what had been left over from his feast. We found the head lying apart, the eyes picked out of their sockets by the great birds, which had also devoured most of the flesh from the face. This ghastly remnant, together with her hands and feet, her glass bangles and silver anklets, we gathered together and wrapped in grass, and in fulfilment of my promise, the Karumba very reluctantly carried the bundle to her husband. Sitting up at the spot seemed a waste of time, as the tiger would not return to such scattered remnants.

That night I continued my hunting by car but without success, and next day procured a young buffalo, which I tied close to the bend in the stream at Mahvanhalla, where the woman had been attacked. The chances of the tiger visiting the same spot being remote, I decided not to sit up over the live buffalo, but to await a kill, should it occur.

In this surmise I was wrong, for before noon next day runners came to Anaikutty to report that the buffalo had been killed and partly eaten by a tiger. By 3 p.m. my machan was fixed, and I sat overlooking the dead bait, at a height of some fifteen feet.

A large red-martin, a big species of mongoose that inhabits the lower slopes of the Nilgiris, was the first visitor to put in an appearance at the kill. He came at about 5.30 p.m., at first nibbled cautiously, and then began to gobble chunks of the raw meat. By 6 o'clock he had filled himself to bursting-point, and made off to pass the night in dreamless contentment, or with a heavy attack of indigestion.

As dusk fell the shadowy forms of three jackals slunk forward. With the greatest temerity they approached the dead animal, sniffed it while glancing around apprehensively, and made off in frightened rushes, only to return each time, as hunger and the demands of a voracious appetite urged them on. At about the fourth attempt they finally settled down to eat, but had hardly taken a few mouthfuls when there was a rush and a scamper and they were gone.

This was surely the coming of the tiger, I thought, and sure enough a slinking, grey shape flitted into the open and cautiously shambled up to the kill. No tiger would so shamefacedly approach his own kill, however, and the hyaena—for hyaena it was—began all over again the cautious and frightened approaches of his smaller cousins, the jackals.

Several times he sniffed at the meat, the while he glanced furtively to right and left. Several times he shambled away, to scurry around in a wide circle and see if the coast was clear, before cautiously slinking up again to take a hasty mouthful. Then off he went in another wide circle to make sure that the rightful owner of the kill was not in the vicinity to catch him red-handed. This continued for quite half-an-hour, before the hyaena settled down to a serious meal.

He had been eating for ten minutes when a tiger called nearby, '*A-oongh, Aungh-ha, Ugha-ugh, O-o-o-n-o-o-n*', was four times repeated in the silent night air, and the hyaena whisked away as if by magic and did not return.

I sat in readiness, momentarily expecting the appearance of the king of the jungle. But the hours dragged on and he did not come. Whatever may have been the reason, that tiger gave the kill a wide berth that night, and the false dawn found me shivering with the intense cold that had now set in despite the summer season. I remained till day light to descend from my machan, cramped and stiff, thoroughly disgusted and disappointed with the world at large and with the tiger in particular. What caused him to approach so close to his kill that night without actually putting in an appearance will ever remain a mystery.

I rested the next day and followed my usual nightly procedure of motoring along the road to Tippakadu and back, but without seeing any sign of the tiger. This time a small panther jumped off a roadside culvert exactly at the turning point on the road to Anaikutty, and crouched in the ditch, its bright eyes gazing into the spotlight as the car passed by. I let the little brute alone, to pass its days in happiness in the beautiful forests where it rightly belonged.

The next week proved uneventful, and I began to think of giving up the chase and returning to Bangalore, but eventually I decided to wait three more days before departing. One of these three days passed uneventfully, when, at midday the second day, a Badaga boy, the son of a rich cattle-owner at Segur, was carried away by the tiger while taking the midday meal to his father, who was with the cattle, and other Kesava herdsmen.

I was soon at the spot with my Karumbas, to follow up the trail. The tiger had carried the boy across the Segur River and into the jungle to the north. Again we followed, without delay, and this time found the body hidden in a nala and only half-eaten. Unfortunately, the father arrived at the scene, and wanted to remove the body, and an hour was lost in argument to persuade him to let it remain and give me a chance of sitting up.

In the vicinity of the body there was no suitable tree or rock in which to conceal myself, and eventually it was decided to move the corpse some fifty feet towards a bamboo clump, on the top of which an unstable machan was erected. To reach this, I had to climb up the notches of a cut bamboo stem, only to find the machan one of the worst I had ever sat on in my life. It swayed alarmingly with every current of wind, and my slightest movement caused the bamboos to creak ominously below me. Besides, I did not have a good view of the body, which was over thirty yards away The bamboo stems growing around me completely obstructed any view at a close range.

The beginning of my vigil was most uninteresting, and no living thing put in an appearance beyond a peacock, which alighted higher up the nullah bank from the place where the corpse was lying. From there it walked slowly downwards, till it suddenly caught sight of the prone, human form in the nullah where we had left it, when with a great flapping of wings it sailed away above my head, its flowing tail glinting a greenish-red in the rays of the setting sun, for all the world like a comet flapping through the forest.

At 9 p.m. I became aware of the presence of the tiger by the low moan he emitted from near the spot where he had originally left the corpse. I cursed myself for having shifted it, but realised that this had had to be done, as there was absolutely no shelter for me at that spot.

Finding his kill had been moved, the tiger then growled several times. After all, we had shifted it a bare fifty feet, and from where he stood the tiger would undoubtedly see it in its new position and come towards it; or so I hoped. But moving the kill had been fatal, raising within the tiger a deep suspicion as to why the man it had left dead, and had partly eaten, had now moved away. It is extraordinary how very cautious every man-eater becomes by practice, whether a tiger or a panther, and cowardly too. Invariably, it will only attack a solitary person, and that, too, after prolonged and painstaking stalking, having assured itself that no other human being is in the immediate vicinity. I believe there is hardly any case on record where a man-eater has attacked a group of people, while many instances exist where timely interference, or aid by a determined friend or relative, has caused a man-eater to leave his victim and flee in absolute terror. These animals seem also to possess an astute sixth sense and be able to differentiate between an unarmed human being and an armed man deliberately pursuing them, for in most cases, only when cornered will they venture to attack the latter, while they go out of their way to stalk and attack the unarmed man.

This particular tiger was definitely possessed of a very acute sixth sense, for it guessed something was amiss. Instead of openly approaching its kill, as I had hoped it would, it then began to circle the whole area, plaintively moaning at intervals, as if in just complaint against the meaness of fate at having moved the kill. Around and around it travelled for quite an hour, till it finally decided that the kill was forbidden fruit, and the last I heard was its plaintive moaning receding southwards, as it made for the sheltering hills.

This last episode, with its attendant failure, caused me to redouble my determination to bag this most astute animal, and to postpone my departure, if need be, for another fortnight, to enable me to do so.

Gossip with the Karumbas now suggested that the tiger might be met at nights along the many cart-tracks that branched into the forest from Anaikutty, Segur and Mahvanhalla, rather than along the main roads on which I had been motoring for several nights. As these cart tracks were unmotorable, I hired a bullock cart for the next week, and determined to spend each night in it meandering along every possible track in the vicinity of the three places. The driver of this cart, a Kesava, was an unusually doughty fellow, and my two Karumba scouts were to accompany me to suggest the most likely tracks.

The next three nights we spent in this fashion, encountering only sambar and spotted-deer, and on the third night, an elephant, which gave us some anxious moments. It was where the track crossed the Anaikutty River, two miles from the village, that we first met him. He had been standing under a mighty 'Muthee' tree, as motionless as a rock, and quite unnoticed by us. In the cart we carried the car-battery, which I had detached together with the 'sealedbeam' spotlight, to be used in emergency only. For ordinary illumination, and for picking up eyes in the jungle, we were using two torches, a seven-cell and a five-cell respectively.

As I was saying, we were crossing the river, and the cart was about midway in the stream, the bulls struggling valiantly to pull the huge wheels through the soft sand, when the elephant, alarmed and annoyed by the torches, let forth a piercing scream, like the last trump of doom, and came splashing at us through the water. Switching on the 'sealed-beam', I caught him in its brilliant rays about thirty yards away The bright beam brought him to a halt, when he commenced stamping his feet in the water and swinging his great bulk and trunk from side to side, undecided whether to charge or to make off. We then shouted in unison, and focussed all lights on him, and with a paring scream of rage he swirled around and shuffled off into the black forest, a very angry and indignant elephant indeed.

We continued these bullock-cart prowls for the next three nights, but without success.

On the morning of the seventh day, the tiger killed the son of the forest guard stationed at Anaikutty, a lad aged eighteen years. At 9 a.m., and in bright sunlight, he had left his hut in the village and gone a short distance up the path leading to the river and to the bungalow where I lay sleeping after my nights in the cart. He had gone to call his dog, which was in the habit of wandering between the village and the bungalow, less than a mile away, because of some scraps which I daily gave it after each meal. That boy was never seen alive again.

His father, the forest guard, thinking he was with me at the bungalow, took his absence for granted. When noon came, and it was time for the midday meal, the youth had not yet appeared and the guard decided to come to the bungalow and fetch him. By the roadside, within a furlong of the river, he came across his son's cap. This alarmed him, and he called aloud to the boy. Receiving no answer, he ran the remaining distance to the bungalow and awoke me, to tell me what he had found.

Feeling something had befallen the lad, I picked up the rifle and accompanied the anxious father to the spot where the cap was still lying. Looking around, we found his slipper under a bush ten yards away and realised that the worst had happened. Remaining at the spot, I told the now-weeping guard to hurry back to the village and summon the Karumba trackers.

Within a quarter-hour these men had joined me and we started on the trail.

The boy appeared to have struggled and had probably cried aloud, although none had been there to hear him, for within a few yards of where we found the slipper, the tiger had apparently laid him down and bitten him savagely. This was made clear by the sudden spurts of blood that smeared the dried grass for the area of quite a square yard. The tiger had then proceeded with its prey, leaving a trail of blood on the ground, which gradually petered out as the blood began to coagulate.

The river here turned north-west and we found that the tiger was making in its direction. Pressing forward, we soon reached the thick jungle that clothed the river-banks, where the blood-trail once again became evident in the occasional red smear that marked the leaves of the undergrowth as the tiger, holding its prey in its mouth, had pushed through.

In the soft mud of the river-bank we saw the fresh pug-marks of the killer, which passed across the shallow water to the opposite bank. Here it led up the slope to the shelter of a clump of jungle-plum bushes, before which we found the lad's remains. He had been almost half-devoured and was a ghastly sight. The reason for the sudden spurts of blood on the trail we had followed now became apparent. The boy had obviously been still alive when carried off by the tiger, as we had already surmised, and must have screamed and struggled in an effort to get free. Annoyed, the tiger had thrown him down and dealt the boy a smashing blow across the skull with its forepaw. The forehead had been crushed inwards, like a squashed egg-shell, while the sharp talons had half-torn the scalp away, leaving the bare bone of the skull exposed to view. One of the eyes had also been gouged out by a claw, and hung from its socket.

The grief of that poor father was truly heart-rending to watch, as he prostrated himself at the feet of his only son, kissed the poor mangled remains, and called aloud to heaven and earth for vengeance, while heaping dust, that he scratched from the dry ground, on to his own head. Shaking him roughly to bring him to his senses, and telling him earnestly that the more noise he made and the more time he wasted correspondingly lessened our chances of shooting the tiger, we succeeded in reducing his cries to a whimper.

A medium-sized 'Jumlum' tree overshadowed the plum-bush beneath which the boy lay, and on this tree I determined to erect my machan. I sent the father and the two Karumbas back to the bungalow, instructing the latter to bring my portable 'charpoy5 machan, and pending their return climbed up into the 'Jumlum' tree, both for my own protection, and to get a shot if the tiger should suddenly put in an appearance.

The two Karumbas were back in under an hour with the machan, which they securely and efficiently tied in the lower branches of the 'Jumlum' tree at the usual height of a little over fifteen feet. They had also brought my water-bottle, gun-torch and blanket, as instructed, and soon after noon I climbed into the machan in high hopes of securing a shot.

Evening came, and nightfall, without a sign of the tiger. Then followed a sudden rain-storm, such as sometimes occurs in the midst of a dry summer in India. Lightning flashes illuminated the forest as bright as day, vividly revealing the corpse beneath the plum-tree below; thunder crashed, reverberating against the adjacent hills; and the rain literally descended in torrents, preceded by a sharp shower of hailstones.

Within a minute I was soaked to the skin, and as the downpour continued, before my very eyes the river rose with the mass of water that rushed down from the surrounding hills, till I judged it to be unfordable.

This dreadful state of affairs continued till well past midnight, when the rain died down to a thin, cold drizzle. Then a horribly chill wind set in, blowing down from the Nilgiris to the sodden forest. The drizzle finally ceased, the wind continued and, as evaporation began in my soaking clothes and blankets, the cold became intense and unbearable.

Gladly would I have faced a dozen man-eaters and returned to the bungalow, but this was impossible owing to the swollen river, which still remained unfordable. The waters swirled by, carrying with them uprooted tree-trunks, stripped branches, and debris of all kinds, including dead logs that had been lying for years along the river bank. To attempt a crossing of that raging torrent, in pitch darkness, would have been to invite death by drowning, if not by a blow across the head from a racing tree-trunk.

To add to my difficulties, the acute cold, the exposure, the lack of proper sleep and my now generally exhausted condition, brought on a sharp attack of malaria. The onset of the attack was in the usual form of ague, which caused my teeth to chatter like castanets, followed within an hour by high fever to the verge of delirium. I lost all interest in shooting and the tiger, and how I passed the remainder of that never-to-be-forgotten night without falling off the machan, I shall never know.

It was past 8 o'clock next morning before my Karumbas returned, to find me almost unconscious and still in a high fever. Somehow they got me across the river and to the bungalow, where I spent the next forty-eight hours in bed in the grip of successive attacks of malarial chills and fever, which only abated on the third day with the assiduous use of paludrine.

How I did not contract pneumonia as an after-effect of this terrible experience is a question to which only Providence knows the answer.

On the third day, when I began to take a little more interest in life, my men told me that the tiger had returned, either during or after the raging storm, and removed its victim while I was huddled, so ill, in the tree above it. This gave me an added reason for gratitude to Providence, for had I fallen off that tree in delirium, I might easily have become a fresh victim.

I took it easy for the next two days to give myself a chance of recovering completely from my bout of fever, and also to await news of a fresh kill, which was bound to occur, sooner or later. The third day I spent in procuring three buffalo baits, tying one each at Anaikutty, Segur and Mahvanhalla. They were all alive the following morning, so on the next day I resumed my peregrinations, roaming the forest around Anaikutty in the morning in the hope of meeting the tiger accidentally, and driving by car to Tippakadu and back by night.

Two days later, the run of bad luck I had been experiencing over the past three weeks suddenly changed for the better. That morning, for a change, I decided to follow the course of the Segur River for some miles downstream; driving with my Karumbas to Segur village, I left the car at a large banana plantation and began to put this plan into effect.

Hardly a mile downstream is a swampy area, much inhabited by bison in years gone by, and still locally known as 'Bison Swamp'.

A half-mile beyond this, a large patch of dense bamboo jungle covers both banks of the stream. These bamboos have always been a favourite haunt of elephant and sambar, tiger occasionally passing through on their way down from the hills.

It was 8.30 a.m., and we had just entered the bamboos, when a sambar doe belled loudly from the opposite bank, to be taken up almost immediately by the hoarser cry of a stag. The Karumbas and I sank to the ground among the rushes that grew profusely along the river edge at this spot. The two sambar repeated their calls in quick succession, and it was obvious that something had alarmed them.

At first I thought they had seen or winded us, but I dismissed the idea with the realisation that what breeze existed was blowing upstream, from the sambar to us. Also, they could not have spotted us, being, as they were, some distance within the bamboos, from where we were quite out of sight. Our progress had been very silent and cautious, so the only conclusion to be drawn from the continued strident calls of the sambar was that they had seen or winded a tiger or panther, as no other human beings would be about in such a lonely place, due to the panic created by the man-eater.

We lay in the rushes for almost ten minutes when, with a loud clatter over the loose stones in the river-bed, a sambar stag, closely followed by a doe, dashed across, to disappear among the bamboos on the same bank as that on which we were hiding.

Not a move came from any of us as the anxious moments passed and then, silently, gracefully and boldly, a tiger stepped out of cover from the opposite bamboos and glided down the steeply declining bank to the river's edge. Without hesitation he walked into the river, ignored the cobbled stones, and when the water had reached his chest, he stopped and commenced lapping.

Taking careful aim, I fired behind his left shoulder. He sprang backwards, emitting a coughing-grunt, and then rolled over on his side, facing away from me and towards the bank from which he had just come. Running forwards out of concealment, I advanced some forty yards, from where I could just see a part of the side of his face, the rest having sunk below the water. Here I waited quite fifteen minutes, to put in another shot if need be, but it proved unnecessary, for the tiger was dead.

I have mentioned that I had taken careful measurements of the man-eater's pugs, which I compared with those of the specimen now before me, to find they corresponded exactly. Thus I knew that at last, after many tiring efforts and exasperating failures, I had shot the man-eater of Segur.

The reason for his man-eating propensity also became apparent, in that the animal had only one eye. The remaining eyeball had shrunk to nothing. When skinning this tiger I took particular trouble to investigate the cause of the loss of that eye, and upon digging out what remained of the organ with a knife, I found a gunshot slug embedded in the socket.

Here was clear reason why the animal had become a man-eater. Someone, in all probability a poacher armed with a muzzle-loader, had fired at the animal's face, in the far-away Silent Valley of the Malabar-Wynaad. A slug had entered the eye and blinded him. Desperate, in pain, and hampered by the loss of his eye, the tiger had found it difficult to hunt his normal prey, and so had taken his revenge upon the species that had been responsible for the loss of his eye.

7

The Man-Eater of Yemmaydoddi

Yemmaydoddi is an area of forest in the Kadur District of Mysore in southern India. It is bordered by a ridge of foothills, the highest of which is named Hogar Khan, that form the eastern spurs of the great mountain range known as the Baba Budans, which reach a height of 6,500 feet. A magnificent lake, called the 'Madak', entirely surrounded by forest-clad hills, forms the southern limit of this area, from which a narrow water-channel, paralleled by an equally narrow forest road, runs for ten miles north-east wards, till the former joins a smaller lake about three miles north of the little town of Birur.

This area is rich in game, and still richer in vast herds of cattle that are driven into the forest by day to graze, and driven back each evening to Birur.

Small wonder it is, then, that the surroundings abound with tiger, that come there in the first instance as game-killers, to feed on the plentiful sambar, spotted-deer and wild pig, but sooner or later become cattle-lifters, because the cattle are so much easier to kill and because of the complete complacency and indifference

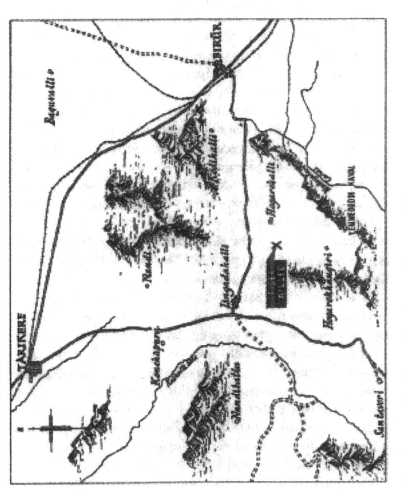

Sketch map of localities referred to in the story of the man-eater of Yemmaydoddi.

with which the local herdsmen look after their charges. It is no exaggeration to say that hardly a day passes without the loss of a fine cow or bull in the jaws of a tiger, while the panther's destruction of calves, goats and village dogs on the outskirts of Birur is almost as common.

Actually, these smaller carnivores are fewer in number than their bigger cousins, and confine themselves to the outskirts of the town itself, well out of the tiger area, because of their fear of the larger animal to whom they themselves sometimes fall prey.

Early in 1946 a small male tiger appeared in this locality with habits distinctly its own. It began with minor killings of calves and goats, snatched in the evenings from returning herds, near the outskirts of Birur, and its depredations were at first taken for those of a panther, except for the characteristic breaking of the neck in the case of the larger calves. This method of killing is almost exclusively followed by tiger, and sometimes by the larger species of forest panther, known as 'Thendu' in Hindustani, so that there was appreciable cause for mistake in identifying the marauder as one of the latter, till on one occasion a frightened herdsman actually witnessed the killing of a young cow, where-after the question was no longer in doubt.

This young animal rapidly grew to adulthood in the area, miraculously escaping the shots of various shikarees, both indigenous and foreign, and grew in cunning and daring too, till in eighteen months it became a major menace to the cattle-grazers, killing twice, and occasionally thrice a week, and invariably selecting a particularly fine specimen on each occasion.

Towards the end of 1948, I accompanied a party of friends to Yemmaydoddi, with the object of procuring a trophy for one of them, Alfie Robertson, who was shortly due to return to England. I had received news of the tiger on several occasions and felt sure it would be a fairly easy matter for my companion to bag the animal, provided we camped at Birur a few days till receiving news of a kill.

We motored from Bangalore, the distance being 134 miles. Unfortunately I was detained at my office and we left late in the evening. The roads were execrable, and we met with an accident near a place called Tiptur, 86 miles from Bangalore. We were using my friend's car and he was driving. The rear wheel went over a deceptively flat stone, which stood up on its edge when the wheel passed over one end of it, the other cutting a nine-inch slit in the petrol tank, which was at the rear of the car. Eight gallons of gasolene thereupon poured on to the road, and the vehicle came to a stop.

We had no spare petrol, but were carrying a Primus Stove, for which we had brought two bottles of paraffin oil. Passing one end of the rubber lead of the foot pump into a bottle of paraffin, we contrived to fit the remaining end on to the pipe leading into the carburettor after having first started a syphon-feed. Thus we managed to cover the short remaining distance to Tiptur. Here we awoke the only tinker in town, unbuckled the fuel tank and managed to patch up the rent with the side of a paraffin tin which I found outside some sleeping inhabitant's house.

Next came the major problem of fuel for the onward journey. We pushed the car to the one petrol station in the town, only to be informed that the supply of gas had been exhausted the previous day and would not be replenished till noon the next day, at the earliest.

It seemed that we were doomed to a prolonged halt at Tiptur. There were one or two lorries in the town. We awoke the sleeping drivers and offered them fabulous prices for just one gallon of petrol to carry us the sixteen miles to the next town of Arsikere, where was a Burmah Shell petrol pump at which we were bound to be able to get a fresh supply. But one and all pleaded they themselves had run out of fuel, and were awaiting the expected fresh stock at noon next day.

The situation was disheartening, till I decided on adopting desperate measures. It was about 3.30 a.m., and scruples and conscience, like the town of Tiptur, had long since fallen asleep. Calling to Alfie to bring the paraffin tin, from which we had cut the patch for our fuel-tank, and carrying the rubber-lead of the foot-pump myself, we commenced a stealthy stalk through the silent streets of Tiptur. In a lane we spotted a battered 'A' Model Ford. Instructing Alfie to keep careful watch against the owner awakening. I crept forward on the off-side of the vehicle. Reaching the bonnet, I removed the fuel-tank cover behind the engine, slipped one end of the rubber tube into the tank, and syphoned a little over a quart of the precious fuel into the tin, which I balanced between my knees. A second trip procured us another quart. Mixing the fuel with the re maining bottle of paraffin oil, we made off hastily to Arsikere, where we obtained a fresh supply.

As a result, we did not arrive at our destination, the small town of Birur, until about 7.30 in the morning. We passed through the town and had gone about two miles towards the forest, when we came upon an open field in which a number of vultures were crowded. My friend took a photograph, while I got down to investigate the cause of this assembly, and was agreeably surprised to find a half-grown bullock, killed by a panther, right up against the hedge that bordered the road we had just traversed.

There was no doubt that the kill had been made by a panther, as the fang marks on the throat of the dead animal showed where it had been strangled. The vertebrae of the neck were intact and had not been broken, which would have been the case had the killer been a tiger. Besides, the underportion of the animal had been eaten, while the entrails were still inside the carcases, conclusively proving a panther to have been the miscreant. For a tiger is a clean feeder, and before beginning a meal makes an opening in the rear portion of its kill, through which it removes the entrails and stomach to a distance of ten feet, so that its meal shall not be polluted with excreta.

We were highly delighted at this early stroke of luck, and after protecting the kill from the vultures with branches broken at a distance from the hedge, I constructed a hide in the hedge itself, overlooking the kill at pointblank range. We made a good job of this construction, and Alfie felt himself more than compensated for the trouble we had experienced with his car the night before, in the certainty of bagging the panther when it returned to its kill late that evening.

We then moved on some distance, ate, and slept in preparation for the night's adventure. By 5 p.m., were turned to the kill and our hide-out, removing the covering which had effectively kept the vultures from the dead animal. Alfie then sat himself inside the hide, complete with rifle, torch, blanket and water-bottle, and I was in the act of driving back to Birur in the car, when a breathless herdsman ran up to inform us that one of his large milch cows had just been killed by a ~~deer~~ *tiger*, hardly half-an-hour earlier and not a mile away.

I gave the decision to Alfie. Would he prefer a panther as a certainty, or a tiger as a chance? In keeping with what would have been my own decision, he chose to make an attempt on the tiger. We accordingly bundled the paraphernalia out of the hide and into the car, drove swiftly up the road for half-a-mile till the herdsman told us to stop, brought the things out again, and then hastened after him into the forest and to the kill.

We did not have far to walk, and within three furlongs came upon the dead animal, a fine black milking cow. The neck had been distinctly broken and bubbles of froth were still coming from the nose. But the tiger had not eaten a morsel, evidently having been disturbed by the herdsman, or perhaps by the buffaloes, which had been grazing along with the cattle.

It was now 6 p.m. and rapidly growing dark. Unfortunately, there was no tree at this spot, and a few minutes' search made it evident we would either have to abandon the kill or risk a ground shot at the tiger when it returned.

Alfie was too keen even to hear of abandoning the kill, so with the help of the herdsman I broke a few branches from adjoining bushes, and made a very rough hide, into which we all clambered shortly after 6.30 p.m.

It was almost dark by now, and within fifteen minutes the outline of the dead cow, twenty-five yards away, faded into obscurity. Although moonless, the stars diffused sufficient light to enable us to see in the immediate vicinity, but the kill itself was just out of range.

An hour passed, and then about half-a-mile away I heard the weird cry of the solitary jackal. Much has .been written and many theories propounded about this strange phenomenon of the forests the lone jackal. Jackals usually wander in packs near the outskirts of towns and villages, the precincts of which they enter at night in search of offal. Their chorus cry, headed by a leader, is distinctive, familiar to the people of India, and sounds something like : *'Ooooooooh! Ooo-where? Ooowhere? Ooo-where-where-where ? 'Here! Here! Here! Here! Here! Heee-re! Heeee-re! Heee-jah! Heee-yah! Heee-ee-ee-yah! Here-Here-Here-Here-Heeeee-yah. yah! yah! yah.'*

The lone jackal, however, although a jackal of the same species in every sense of the word, adopts a very different call. His solitary, long-drawn, *'Ba-loo-ah! Baa-oooo-ah!'* had earned him a reputation, coupled with endless superstitions, fables and jungle-lore. But from this maze of conjecture two theories stand out. The first is that this jackal accompanies a tiger or panther, generally the former, which it leads to a kill by its weird cry, claiming as its share of the strange partnership a bite at the remains after the rightful owner has gorged its fill. The second theory is that the lone jackal attaches itself to a particular carnivore, which it follows at a very safe distance, most tenaciously, in order to make certain of regular meals at what is left over from kills every time his patron feeds. Whichever of the two theories is correct, the presence and cry of a lone jackal is a certain indication of the proximity of a tiger or panther, a fact of which I have had personal corroboration in many forest areas of India.

Therefore, the cry of the lone jackal told us that night, in as definite a way as if we had seen the tiger itself, that the cattle-slayer was approaching. About ten minutes elapsed and then we heard a distinct '*Ugha-ugh! Ugh!*' in the direction of, and beyond, the kill. The tiger had arrived! Softly I nudged Alfie's leg, but he was all attention. Time passed, and we heard a slight crackle in the scrub followed by a faint thud and dragging sound.

Alfie depressed the torch switch and a bright beam of light flared out. Unfortunately, with the uncertain back ground, he misjudged the spot where the kill was lying, and shone a little too far to the left. The warning was enough for the tiger, and with a guttural '*Wrr-oof! Wrroof*' it sprang back into the shelter of the undergrowth.

We remained an hour longer, but I knew it was time wasted, and that the tiger would not return. At the end of this time we heard a faint '*A-oongh! Aungh-ha! O-o-on-o-o-n!*' as the tiger crossed a ridge over a mile away, leaving us to ourselves.

Ruefully we packed up and returned to the car, only to find that Alfie had mislaid the switch-key. While searching, the night bus, carrying passengers from the town of Lingadhalli to Birur, passed us. Then Alfie found the key, and we followed in the wake of the bus.

Arriving at the spot where we had constructed our hideout for the panther, we were surprised to see, reflected in the glow of the headlights of the bus before us, the eyes of the leopard which had now returned and was devouring its kill. At the same time the driver of the bus saw the eyes, and brought the ponderous vehicle to a halt with a screech of brakes, and a cloud of suffocating dust which enveloped us behind.

Alfie and I got down, walked abreast of the bus and located the panther sneaking away half-across the intervening field. He fired and the animal sprang into the air with a sharp '*Arrr-aarh*! and then streaked across the field like greased lightning.

Too late we realised that we had done the wrong ~~riling~~ THING. Alfie should have got back again in our hideout and I should have driven away in the wake of the bus. The leopard would undoubtedly have returned to its kill within minutes of the departure of the two vehicles, and given Alfie an easy shot. As matters stood, I had not counselled correctly, and we had now a wounded leopard on our hands.

But it was no use crying over spilt milk, so we returned to Birur, to spend the night at the Travellers' Bungalow Next morning found us back at the spot, and after casting around I found a faint blood-trail which began to make itself evident only at the extreme end of the field, increasing as we entered the dense undergrowth. Here we were confronted with a tough proposition. The leopard had evidently been hit in the flank, and it had taken time for the blood to flow down the animal's side and drip to the ground, which is why it only appeared as a blood-trail at the end of the field. Thereafter it had dripped freely, while the animal had crawled into the densest undergrowth, consisting of lantana and 'wait-a-bit' shrubs, where it was impossible to follow except on hands and knees. A time-worn wild pig trail led through this undergrowth, and the leopard had passed along it, as was evident by the copious blood-trail he left.

On hands and knees, and pushing my cocked .405 Win Chester before me as I progressed, I crawled in the wake of the wounded beast with Alfie bringing up the rear, as a safeguard against a flank attack, or one from behind. We had progressed about seventy-five yards in this fashion when, without warning, the leopard, which had been lying up at the next bend in the trail, saw fit to launch his attack. There was hardly room for a miss, and I hit him almost at muzzle-length, the soft-nosed bullet smashing his skull and completely removing the rear segment of the brain pan. He died in front of me, the fluid from his brain oozing from his shattered skull.

We remained at Birur a full ten days, but in all this time only one further kill occurred, and that on the forenoon of the seventh day at a place six miles down the Yemmaydoddi channel. By the time that word of the incident was brought to us and we arrived at the spot, it was late evening and we found that vultures had completely demolished the kill, no precaution having been taken to hide it with leaves. A tree overlooked the remains at about forty yards distance, and Alfie sat in a crotch till midnight, but the tiger did not put in an appearance.

Thereafter nothing happened, as I have said, and on the morning of the eleventh day we left for Bangalore.

Time passed. Then one dark night along the road from Lingadhalli to Birur motored a quartette of' 'Car-shikaris'—people who shoot from their car with the aid of spotlights, never so much as setting foot to the ground when passing through the forests. Of tracking, the science of big-game shooting, and the beauties of the jungle and Mother Nature, they know nothing and care less. For them, the highest form of sport lies in casting intense beams of light from their sealed-beam spotlights into the bordering forest and discharging a volley of rifle and gunshots at whatever eyes might catch and reflect the brilliance of their sealed beams. As to what animal they fire at, male, female or young, they do not care, for they are filled only with the lust to kill or wound. Needless to say, such activities are against all existing regulations, but they often take place nevertheless.

And so it transpired that, when about four miles from Birur, they picked up the large fiery white eyes of a tiger as it crested a bank that bordered the road.

Two shots rang out and the tiger sprang away, its lower jaw smashed at the extremity by a rifle bullet, while the other shot had gone wide. Needless to say the 'car shikaris' did not stop to investigate, nor did they return next morning to trail the wounded beast and put it out of its misery. They merely went on their way, seeking for other eyes at which to fire.

The wounded tiger must have suffered intense agony for the next two months, nor could it eat properly. Being unable to maintain a death-grip on its prey with a badly-healed broken lower-jaw, it was unable to procure its usual food in the form of game or cattle.

One day, about three months later, it attempted to secure a goat from a herd that had been driven to graze in the forest. With infinite caution it stalked the herd, and had just sprung upon a fat nanny, to kill her with a powerful blow from its paws, instead of the usual neck-breaking process with the jaw, when the audacious herdsman, standing close by, flung his staff. The chance aim proved true in this instance, and the staff caught the tiger a flanking blow. Enraged, it charged at the herdsman, the paw-blow substitute again proving eminently successful in almost completely scalping the unfortunate man while still alive. His scream of terror and agony was cut short by another powerful blow of the forepaw, which this time crushed the man's skull as if it had been an egg.

The man collapsed, leaving the tiger the choice of two victims to eat, the goat or a human being. It hesitated over the carcase of the latter, and licked the blood that oozed from the smashed skull. As if to make a fair comparison it then went across to the nanny, which it seized by the neck and after a moment began to carry away into the jungle thickets. But within a few paces, and for no accountable reason, it stopped, dropped the nanny, walked across to the dead herdsman, and seizing him by a shoulder, disappeared into the all-concealing fastnesses of the surrounding forest.

The dreaded man-eater of Yemmaydoddi was thus created, and his reign of stark terror had commenced. Thereafter, deaths attributable to this beast occurred within an area of about 250 square miles, ranging from Birur, Lingadhalli and up to Bhagavadkatte on the north, across to Santaveri on the Baba Budan Mountains on the west, and southwards past the Ironkere Lake to Sakrepatna and back to Birur.

While human kills followed each other with alarmingly increasing regularity, they were spaced along a definite beat and had the distinctive mark that every victim had been killed by a powerful blow of the paw and not die by usual fatal jaw grip. Further, the fact that the tiger was unable to use its lower jaw effectively was amply evident through examination of the various corpses, to none of which was it the man-eater's custom to return for a second meal. The flesh had been scraped from them in a peculiar way, obviously by the upper-jaw working alone on the strips of human flesh which this animal would lay bare with its powerful claws to facilitate the difficult task of eating.

With the advent of the man-eater, the activities of the erstwhile very energetic cattle-killing tiger which had been operating along the Yemmaydoddi and Lingadhalli routes, ceased abruptly, leaving room for the conclusion that it was this cattle-lifter, and none other, that had now developed into a man-eater. The story of the 'car-shikaris' did not become known for some time, till one *of* them, in a 160 Nine Man-Eaters and One Rogue moment of boastful hilarity, revealed that they had fired at and wounded a tiger on the Birur-Lingadhalli Road. A subsequent piecing together of these facts brought the story to light as we now know it.

As I have said, the man-eater followed an almost well-defined beat, killing at the outskirts of villages and hamlets bordering the places I have named, and in regular succession. These facts I gathered upon reading the reports that appeared in the Press regarding the beast's activities, and by marking off on my forest map the names of these places and the dates on which people had been killed.

The centre of this region, which the tiger had chosen as a regular beat, comprised the rocky and heavily-forested slopes of the foot-hill range, topped by the hill called Hogar Khan, some 4,500 feet in height. I concluded that these fastnesses, almost without population, sheltered the tiger, that from them it made forays into the more populous areas in a series of almost regular calls. A study of the dates of past killings revealed that the animal almost regularly returned along its rounds every third or fourth month. The total number of killings had by this time reached twenty-seven.

In making my attempt to shoot this animal, I decided to operate at the village of Hogarehalli, which lay almost midway between Birur and Lingadhalli, and was only three miles and a half from the base of Mount Hogar Khan itself through downwardly sloping scrub jungle. I selected this area primarily because I was fairly well-acquainted with the geography of the surrounding forest, and was fairly well-known to the inhabitants, from whom I could expect reasonable cooperation. Further, the village of Hogarehalli was, as I have said, near to the foothills of Hogar Khan, where I was sure the tiger had its headquarters. Most important of all, this village had not escaped losing a life every time the tiger passed on his rounds. In other words it was almost a certain call for him.

I arrived at Hogarehalli a full fortnight before the close of the three-month cycle, that is within two to six weeks of the next projected visit. Thus, I gave myself plenty of time to make inquiries into the details and nature of the various killings, and to arrive at a plan of circumventing this brute if possible.

The village itself is fairly large and although not very heavily populated, contains houses of a permanent nature, constructed from stone of reddish hue which abounds in the vicinity, occurring in the form of flakes and varying in size from the palm of one's hand to an area of several square feet. Hogarehalli is also old; it dates from distant times and possesses two ancient and solidly-built temples. It is bounded on the west, south-west and north-west by the dense scrub leading to Hogar Khan, and on the south by a large and beautiful lake that abounds with geese, wild duck and teal in the winter months, to the south of which a track leads to the Yemmaydoddi water-channel about three miles away To the south-east lies a belt of dense plantations of coconut and banana trees, interspersed with the tall slim stems of the areca-nut, the whole being thickly matted below by growths of the betel-vine, the leaves of which are liberally chewed by Indians throughout the peninsula. This area consists of very moist land, naturally low-lying and irrigated by a channel from the lake to the south of the village. Southward of Hogarehalli lie a few scattered rice fields, and then south-eastwards and eastwards and northwards fields of dry crops, fed only by the monsoon rains, extending up to the Birur-Lingadhalli road, about a mile and half away.

As you may have guessed by now, the majority of kills occurred in the scrub-belt to the west, south-west and north-west, while two had taken place in the heart of the coconut plantation itself, one of the victims being a cousin of the owner. The remaining and more open areas had been avoided by the man-eater. Furthermore, the kills had taken place in the late afternoon in the majority of cases, as the inhabitants had, since the killings commenced, cultivated the healthy habit of securing themselves indoors before sundown. The tiger's pug-marks had shown, on several occasions, that he had entered the outskirts of the village in early morning, but that the stoudy-built houses and solid wooden doors had prevented him, at least so far, from effecting any nocturnal entries.

It was difficult to formulate a plan of action in these circumstances. I knew that once the tiger killed he would move on and not visit Hogarehalli again for another three or four months. At the same time, it was humanly impossible for me to anticipate where the next man would be attacked and killed. The only remaining and obvious line of action, therefore, was for me to attempt to attract the tiger to myself by acting as bait, a procedure which, you may be quite well assured, I felt most reluctant to follow. Nevertheless, it appeared to be the only way

Since my arrival at Hogarehalli a week had passed in obtaining all these details, studying the circumstances in which the various kills had taken place and visiting the spots where they had actually occurred. The time was now fast approaching when the man-eater's next visit fell due.

I found that the victims in the scrub area to the west had been either woodcutters or herdsmen grazing cattle. Not one of the cattle had been harmed by the man-eater, although an occasional wandering panther had taken its toll. An idea then occurred to me which, I flattered myself, was quite ingenious. Selecting a tree about half a mile inside this scrub, I arranged for a chair to be tied within its branches about fifteen feet from the ground and out of range of the tiger's leap. I then procured a stout piece of wood, about six feet in length and three inches in diameter, one end of which I suspended from a branch by a stout cord while the other end rested, at an angle, against a branch of the tree below me. To this end I tied another piece of string, which I passed through a loop on to the front portion of my shoe. It was thus possible for me to remain comfortably seated in a chair, armed and prepared, while by merely moving my foot up and down on its heel, I would cause the piece of wood suspended below to strike against the branch it rested upon, emulating the sound made by a woodcutter, although, of course, considerably less in volume. When one foot became tired, I could change the string to the other foot. I even left this string long enough to operate by hand, when, by increasing the length of the pull, I could increase the swing of the wood and consequently the noise of the blows. Above my head, as shelter from the sun, I arranged a canopy of the leaves of the tree itself, without cutting them. It was also comforting to know that I could smoke, eat, drink, cough and move about in my chair without any need for cramped concealment. In fact, as I was acting as bait myself, the more I advertised my presence, the greater chance would there be of the tiger attempting to stalk or attack me.

The patel or headman of Hogarehalli village, Moodlagiri Gowda, gave me his fullest co-operation. I explained my plan to him and stressed that from the time I started operating from my perch, it would be his business, at all costs, to see that nobody entered the scrub jungle, or the coconut plantation, thus ensuring that the tiger had no bait to attack but myself. This he promised to do, and forthwith broadcast to the village, and to the surrounding areas, under threat of dire consequences, that nobody was to be about after midday, especially in the direction of the scrub jungle and plantation. There was enough hay and dried grass around the village on which to feed the cattle for a fortnight to three weeks, by which time I hoped the tiger would have put in an appearance. The patel's instructions were all the more popular because nobody wished to the beneath the paws of the tiger, and because it provided the villagers with the attractive prospect of being completely idle for the next three weeks.

Precisely on the tenth day after my arrival at Hogarehalli, I began to put my plan to the test. After an early lunch I arrived at the tree shortly before n a.m. armed with water-bottle, sandwiches and pipe, and of course my .405, and my first day's vigil commenced. Moving my foot to create the tapping sound was, I soon discovered, a monotonous and tiring pastime, added to which the reflected rays of the noon-day sun caused me great discomfort and proved extremely tiring to the eyes, gazing as I must, through the shimmering heat haze, at the scrub jungle around me. I remained on my perch till sundown and continued to do so for the next week, without hearing or seeing any indication of the tiger's return. By this time I had completely familiarised myself with the position of every large bush within my range of vision, and had mentally mapped out the various lines of approach, consistent with available cover, the tiger was likely to take in stalking me on my tree, that is, when and if he returned.

After the first unproductive week, and to relieve the deadly monotony I had experienced, I purchased a couple of cheap novels from the small bookstall at Birur Railway Station, which I read while sitting on my perch, automatically operating the string that pulled the tapping wood, and relying on my hearing to tell me of anything that was happening while I read. Thus I reached the end of the second week, still without any indication of tlie tiger's return.

It will be appreciated that by this time I was growing impatient; I was, in fact, very fed up with my forced inactivity. I racked my brains to think of some better plan but failed to arrive at any conclusion offering a more likely line of action than the one I was following.

We were now in the fourth month, and the return of the tiger was due at any time, provided of course he was still following his beat. I had arranged with the deputy commissioner at Chikmagalur, the headquarters town of the district, to keep me posted of all human kills in the area through his subordinate, the amildar at Kadur, which was only four miles from Birur. A runner was to be despatched to me as soon as any news was received of a kill, and sure enough, two days later the runner arrived from the amildar, telling me the tiger had killed at a hamlet on the Chikmagalur-Sakrepatna road four days earlier. The very next day the runner came again, to inform me of the slaying of a cowherd on the northern shores of the Ironkere Lake. This was five miles from the Madak Lake, which in turn was about nine miles from Hogarehalli.

Reports so far had been satisfactory, inasmuch as they definitely indicated that the tiger was still following his regular beat and was only some fourteen miles away at the time of the last killing, two days before the news had reached me. I could therefore expect that by this time the tiger was very near to the outskirts of Hogarehalli, if not already there, and as the morrow would make the third day since he had eaten, there was every hope that he would be eagerly looking for a fresh victim.

That evening I told Moodlagiri Gowda to warn the inhabitants of Hogarehalli and the neighbourhood that the killer was in the vicinity, and to keep away from the scrub area and the plantation at all costs.

The next morning found me seated in my accustomed place even earlier than usual. This time I had not brought a novel, but concentrated on banging the piece of wood as loudly as I could, coughing, and moving about on the branch of the tree so as to show myself as much as possible. In returning to the village that evening I took the greatest precautions against a surprise attack, but another two days passed and nothing happened. Nor did I receive any word regarding further kills.

It now occurred to me that the tiger might have returned to his fastnesses in the Hogar Khan ridge, or perhaps bypassed Hogarehalli and gone in a north-westerly direction to Lingadhalli and Bagavadkatte, or even westwards to Santaveri.

As the weather was comparatively warm and a half-moon had risen, I determined to spend the entire afternoons and nights of the next two days in the tree, in the hope that I might thus be afforded an opportunity of attracting the tiger which undoubtedly would also be on the move after dark. This would place a still greater strain on me, tired out as I was with fifteen days of fruitless sitting. Nevertheless, I determined to undertake the ordeal in a desperate attempt at success.

The next forenoon found me back again, this time with a basket containing my dinner, a flask of hot tea, a blanket, water-bottle, torch and other accoutrements that accompany the night-watcher who spends long, cramped hours on a tree. I also brought three tablets of Benzedrine to make sure that I did not fall asleep.

I repeated the same ordeal of tapping all afternoon, and kept it up until late at night. The jungle was inordinately silent except for the call of a horned owl, and the faraway bark of a Kakar or jungle sheep. The moon set by 1.30 a.m. and it became pitch dark and also very cold. Around 3 o'clock I felt sleepy and swallowed two out of the three tablets of Benzedrine. Half-an-hour later I heard a rustle, and then the excited cackle of a hyaena as he winded or saw me. '*Ha! Ha! Ha! Ha! Ha!*

What-have-we-here? Ha! Ha! he commented, and then slunk on his way in the darkness.

Again silence and darkness, till the pale glow of the false dawn heralded one hour to sunrise. That hour passed, and then, '*Whe-e-e-ew! Kuck-kaya-kaya-khuck*,*m*' crowed the grey jungle cock, greeting the rising sun, as I dropped wearily from my perch, to struggle back to Hogarehalli and snatch four hours of sleep.

Eleven a.m. found me back again on the tree to continue the tiresome watch. I had come to the conclusion that I could not stand much more of it. The hot afternoon passed as usual, the '*Tok-tok-tok-tok*' of a green barbet, and the '*Ko-el! Ko-yel*' of the Indian Kweel, which is related to the cuckoo family, being the only sounds. Evening approached, and a spurfowl, picking among the dried leaves below a nearby bush cried '*Kukurruka-wack. Kukurruka-wack*' There was the excited chatter of a group of birds coloquially known as the 'Seven-sisters' as they prepared to roost for the night, and as the sun sank below the slopes of Hogar Khan, a peacock issued his farewell note, '*Mia-a-oo- Ah-oo-Aaow-Ah-h-o-o-Tar-h-oo.*'

Then the birds of the night took up the cry. '*Chyeece-Chyeece!*' chirped the nightjars, as they flitted overhead, to alter their call to '*Chuckoo-chuckoo-chuckoo*', when they perched on the ground or branches of trees nearby.

Ten o'clock came, and, shortly afterwards a series of calls—'*Aiow! Aiow! Aiow!*'—from a herd of spotted deer in alarm. '*Aiow! Aiow!*' they repeated persistently, in warning.

Undoubtedly a carnivore was on the move, and had been seen or winded by the watchful hinds, but whether a panther or ordinary tiger, or the man-eater itself, remained the question to be answered. I tapped louder and more vigorously with the wood, hoping the tiger would not ponder as to how this mysterious woodcutter came to be operating by night.

The minutes dragged on, and then there came abruptly the strident belling-cry of an alarmed sambar stag not half-a-mile away: '*Ponk!-Whee-onk!-Whee-onk!*' he repeated, moving up towards Hogar Khan.

Then deathly silence reigned again! Continuing the tapping, I scanned every bush that was visible in the half-moon, mentally revising the various lines of cover I anticipated the tiger might take in stalking the tree. Nothing moved along any of these, and all was still, except for one last '*Ponk !*' from the sambar, at a distance.

The strange feeling that something would occur at any moment came over me, and I felt that I was being watched, yet not a sound or crackle disturbed the stillness. Tapping away, I coughed, then moved and finally stood up from my seat, coughing and spitting in true Indian fashion. Yet not a sound, and then, like a bolt from the blue, he came!

'*Woof! woof!*' he roared, and an enormous grey mass, as large as a Shetland pony on wings, appeared as if by magic from behind a bush barely ten yards away, to charge at the trunk of the tree and reach the crotch below me.

A great grey head appeared only three yards directly below me; I depressed the torch switch and fired between the glaring eyes. With the explosion of the rifle the tiger fell backwards to earth, emitting a nerve-shattering roar. I put in a second shot. He acknowledged this, too, with a further roar, and the next second he was gone. From the scrub a hundred yards away I heard a last '*Wrrr-uf!*' and then complete silence.

I knew that neither of my shots had missed, but cursed myself, nevertheless, at not having dropped the animal with, at least, my second shot. Nevertheless I was certain it had been severely wounded and could not go very far. I allowed myself to doze for the rest of the night, and with the rising sun warily returned to Hogarehalli, to organise plans for following up the wounded beast.

Moodlagiri Gowda rallied splendidly, and while I had a short rest, followed by hot tea, toast and bacon, arranged with the owner of a buffalo herd to drive his animals through the bush in the wake of the wounded tiger in the hope that it would be induced to reveal its whereabouts when the buffaloes came near.

By 9 a.m., I was back at my tree, accompanied by Moodlagiri, two scouts, fifteen buffaloes and their owner. First I ascended to the top of the tree, and tried to locate the tiger, but nothing could be seen. At the foot of the tree, splashed against the bark, were flecks of blood from his face or head, as my first bullet hit him. Behind the bush, where he had retreated, we picked up a copious blood-trail, showing my second shot had also taken effect.

Thereafter we drove the buffaloes slowly in the direction the retreating tiger had taken, spreading them out as far as possible into a rough line. I followed the buffaloes, the two scouts keeping immediately behind me. Moodlagiri and the owner of the buffaloes remained in the tree where I had sat.

We had covered about 200 yards when we heard a deep growl. At the same time the line of buffaloes stopped, and lowered their heads, horns extended, in the direction from which the growl had come.

A tree grew a little to my left, and I whispered to one of the scouts to climb it and see if he could locate the tiger. This he did, but signalled back to me that he could see nothing. The buffaloes had meantime backed from the spot, nor could we get them to go forward. Leaving them there, and the scout still up the tree he had ascended, the remaining scout and I tiptoed back to Moodlagiri and instructed him to return to the village and try to collect some of the village dogs to help us. This he agreed to do, but it was a full hour and a half before he returned, accompanied by two mongrels only saying that these were all he could succeed in collecting. We now set the dogs on the buffaloes to cause them to move forward, and so gained twenty-five yards, when the tiger set up a horrible growling. The buffaloes immediately came to a standstill, while the curs began yapping vociferously

Creeping forward for shelter behind the two foremost buffaloes, I endeavoured to peer between their legs in an attempt to penetrate the undergrowth and catch a glimpse of the tiger, but could see nothing. I then attempted to prod the animals forward, but one of them turned on me suddenly, and I narrowly escaped the sweep of the long horns.

My position was awkward in the extreme, with a wounded tiger before me that might charge at any moment, and nervous buffaloes around, that would defend themselves with their horns in a united stampede against the tiger, or myself, whichever provoked them first. Retreating a few steps, I signalled to the scout, who was still in the tree, to descend. With his and the other scouts' help, I then began throwing stones over the buffaloes into the undergrowth at the point from which the growls had come. This action was greeted with a fresh outburst of growling, but nothing we could do would induce the tiger to break cover and show himself. Nor would he retreat, and this fact indicated that he was in a bad condition.

Further stoning proving useless, I withdrew the two scouts, leaving the buffaloes where they were, and with their help, and accompanied by the two curs, made a wide detour of the jungle, to come up at the rear of the tiger and about 300 yards beyond it. From here we advanced very slowly, the scouts under my instructions climbing every tree and point of vantage as we crept forward in an endeavour to see the tiger. Thus we covered some 200 yards, when one of the scouts signalled he could see something from the branch into which he had climbed. Descending, he whispered he had glimpsed a white and brown object beneath a bush about fifty yards away and roughly half-way to where the buffaloes were standing.

Climbing into the branch with him, he indicated a clump of bushes, at which I first stared in vain before I saw an indistinct brown and white patch just beyond the clump. Aiming at this object, I fired, and the tiger, mistaking the direction of our approach, charged the buffaloes with a series of short roars. The nearest was taken by surprise as the tiger leapt on him. The remainder got together and rushed forward with lowered horns. Meanwhile, the buffalo which had been attacked bellowed with pain and fear and endeavoured to shake his adversary off. The tiger remained perched on the buffalo, snarling and growling vociferously.

From my point of vantage in the tree the scene was clear to me, but I dared not risk a shot for fear of killing the buffalo, or one of the herd that was fast approaching.

And then the remaining buffaloes reached the spot and the scene became a medley of tossing horns and struggling brown bodies. Finding his position precarious the tiger leapt off the buffalo he was straddling and rushed back to cover, behind a bush only twenty-five yards away. I could clearly see him, crouched and watching the buffaloes. A single shot behind the left shoulder gave him his quietus. Later, on examining the tiger, I found that my first bullet of the night before had struck his right cheek, some two inches below and to the right of his eye, passing through his flesh and shattering his cheek-bone. My second shot had cut through his belly, and in passing out had formed a gaping hole through which his entrails were trailing. My third and recent shot had penetrated his heart. The broken jaw, smashed by the 'car shikaris' months ago, had healed badly, thus explaining why the animal had been unable to bite properly and had turned man-eater in consequence.

The attacked buffalo had been badly mauled by the powerful claws, but not bitten. Compensation satisfied the owner; I am certain the animal recovered from the wound, as buffaloes are invariably much hardier than cattle and can survive severe physical injuries.

Thus ended the career of 'The Yemmaydoddi Man-Eater', and while the district was well rid of a murderous and unrelenting killer, it must be remembered that the irresponsible and unsporting shot from the 'car shikaris' was the root cause of all the trouble, and to their discredit must be laid the twenty-nine innocent human lives that were lost.

8

The Killer of Jalahalli

This is not the story of a man-eating tiger, nor even of a man-eating panther, but of an ordinary leopard of very average size, who fought bravely in defence of its own life, fought cleverly and effectively, killing three persons and mauling eleven others in the process, dying gamely at last, undefeated and after days of suffering.

In 1938, prior to the outbreak of Second World War, the village of Jalahalli, situated barely seven miles north-west of Bangalore, near the road to Tumkur, was an unimportant hamlet, perhaps boasting 150 houses, some of which were made of brick and others of thatch. As the city of Bangalore is the headquarters of the government of Mysore, the Forest Department of that state, which is rich in forests of both evergreen and monsoon varieties, had its headquarters in Bangalore. The systematic loss and destruction of various forms of natural forest woods by insect and other pests was then engaging the close attention of the government, and a plantation of forest seedlings had been set within a mile of Jalahalli, covering about four square miles of land, in which sandalwood, rosewood, red rosewood and other trees had been grown in natural array, in order to study the action of the various insect pests (which had also been introduced), in close reach of the laboratories at Bangalore. These plants had grown to an average height of ten feet, while the usual undergrowth of spear-grass, lantana, and occasional wait-a-bit thorn thickly carpeted the ground, to form dense thickets that had become the home of innumerable snakes, quite a number of rabbits, an occasional pea-fowl, and of course partridge and quail in considerable quantity.

Into this area one day strayed a wandering leopard from the rocky hills of Magadi, twenty miles away. It began its sojourn by living on the rabbits, rats and other small inmates of the forest plantation, but soon learned that it had a ready larder in the nearby hamlet of Jalahalli, in the form of goats and village dogs, which it began to eat with irksome regularity.

All went well till one day the leopard destroyed a goat belonging to the fat police-daffedar (or sergeant) of Jalahalli. This act the official held to be an affront to his dignity and rank, and he swore to avenge it with the death of the leopard.

The native police force had been armed with service .303 rifles, from which the magazines were removed, so that only one round could be fired at a time. This had been done as a precautionary measure against over-enthusiastic policemen firing round after round into mobs during local riots, which are sometimes common at relatively slight provocation.

So the daffedar sat up in a tree over his dead goat, armed with a single-shot service .303. Along came the panther at sundown, quite unsuspectingly, to receive a wound in its left foreleg, for the daffedar's aim had become unaccountably unsteady due to equally unaccountably shaky hands.

The panther bounded away with a grunt, the fat daffedar shivered through the night in his tree, descended next morning, examined the ground for blood but found none, and concluded that he had very fortunately missed the leopard. Anyhow, he figured that it had been taught a lesson and would leave his goats severely alone in future.

This happened on a Friday night. The next day, Saturday, passed uneventfully, and that evening the villagers decided on conducting a large-scale rabbit beat the following morning. Yards and yards of two-foot high rabbit-net were laid along the edge of the Forest Department plantation, and around some three acres of casurina trees that adjoined it. The beat next morning was to be conducted by about a hundred villagers, accompanied by dogs and armed with short wooden clubs. The rabbits would run into the nets, and while struggling to get free, would be clubbed to death.

All went according to plan till the casurina clump was reached, where, to the surprise and horror of all nearby, out jumped a leopard instead of a harmless rabbit. It rushed the ring of beaters in the near vicinity, and in less time than it takes to write, had mauled six of them in various degrees of intensity from a scratch or two to a regular bite, or a deep raking from the razor-sharp claws.

The beaters scattered in every direction and the panther returned to the casurinas.

Nearby lived Hughey Plunkett and his mother. He had been a hunter of considerable repute in his days, having shot a round dozen tigers, and perhaps twice that number of panthers, in the forest areas of Diguvametta in the Kurnool District of the Madras Presidency. The dispersed beaters approached him with news of the leopard, and appealed for help. Hughey had been spending a late morning in bed, and was in pyjamas. He had not heard about the incident of the police daffedar's wounding the leopard, and scarcely credited the possibility of such an animal having strayed to within seven miles of the city of Bangalore. Anyhow, to appease the worrying villagers he slipped an L.G. and a ball cartridge into the respective barrels of his 12 bore shotgun, and accompanied them to the casurina belt.

Here he saw the mauled beaters and realised for the first time that a panther was actually in the vicinity

A careful stalk through the casurinas commenced, a small crowd of half-a-dozen men following in a knot at his rear. Hughey had passed more than half-way through the trees when the panther made the mistake of showing itself by darting from one patch of cover to the other. A quick left and right from Hughey bowled him over, and the animal lay twitching on its side.

Hughey dashed up, trailed by his followers, and then made the mistake which cost him his life. He touched the now still form with his foot.. The animal came to life, galvanised into action. It sprang upon Plunkett, fastened its fangs into his upper right arm, so that he could not use his weapon, while its hind claws raked him into streaming red ribbons. The men around scattered, only one of them attempting to beat off the animal with his ridiculous rabbit club. The panther then left Hughey and sprang upon this man, whom, together with four others, it clawed and bit before rushing back to the sheltering casurinas, leaving its own blood-trail behind.

The scene of carnage can well be imagined, with Plunkett as its centre. It took quite sixty minutes for the men to pull themselves together and carry Hughey, who had fainted and whose right arm hung on by a mere strip of sinew, back to his farmhouse. He bled profusely during this journey and I wondered, when following the trail two days later, that a human being could lose so much blood and still live.

Mrs Plunkett, with commendable presence of mind, bundled him into their car, together with four of the more severely wounded men, and headed for the Bowring Hospital in Bangalore. The remaining seven mauled villagers were taken to the Victoria Hospital, also at Bangalore.

Blood transfusion was given to Hughey and an effort made to save his arm, but when gangrenous symptoms set in the following day it was amputated. The shock and loss of blood proved too great for him, and he died the next day in a delirium of fever.

All this had happened on a Sunday morning. That same afternoon a wandering goat-herd observed the blood-trail of the leopard as it entered the outskirts of the Forest Department plantation, having left the casurina trees, and informed two brothers living in the village of Jalahalli, named Kalaiah and Papaiah respectively.

Next morning—Monday—these two brothers very pluckily, albeit foolishly, determined to follow-up the leopard on their own. The elder brother, Kalaiah, owned a hammer .12 bore of old design. The younger brother, Papaiah, had a single-barrelled muzzle-loader.

Loading up, these two brave men, shoulder to shoulder, followed the blood-spoor into the undergrowth of the plantation.

Wandering along like this they became separated, and in a twinkling the leopard pounced upon Kalaiah, throwing him to the ground and biting through bladder and testicles with savage ferocity. The force of the pounce had knocked the .12 bore from his hands, and as he lay screaming with the animal on top of him, his younger brother rushed to the rescue, discharging his muzzle-loader into the panther as it lay on top of Kalaiah. How he did not also shoot his brother remains a mystery.

The leopard, now still further wounded, left Kalaiah and pounced on Papaiah, who fell on his face, the fangs tearing through his back into his lung, while the talons of the hindfeet raked the unfortunate man's buttocks and the backs of his thighs. The animal then made off.

I was eating lunch that day when a man appeared at my door in a lather of sweat to give me the news. Hastily, I grabbed rifle, shotgun and torch and jumped into the car, my wife, not to be outdone at the last moment, determining to come with me. As I turned out of the gate of our bungalow on to the main road, I met Eric Newcombe of the local police force, who was on his way to visit me. Telling him what had happened and making my apologies, I endeavoured to get away, but Eric refused to be excluded from the party and piled into the car also.

It did not take us long to reach Jalahalli, and the sight that met us there was ludicrous in the extreme. Every inhabitant, from the youngest to the oldest, had come out. A vast concourse had approached the edge of the plantation in order to catch a glimpse of the leopard, if possible. These had all taken to the branches of trees for personal safety, until the trees in the vicinity literally bent almost to breaking-point with the load of humanity they carried. But nobody had gone forward to rescue Kalaiah and Papaiah, who still lay in the plantation where they had fallen four hours earlier, feebly shouting for help.

The first thing was obviously to succour these men, so we recruited a dozen carriers and entered the bush. Kalaiah we found in a very bad way and in extreme agony. Bubbles of blood were oozing from Papaiah's punctured lung.

We conveyed them to the car, and I had started the engine to carry them to hospital, when a villager dashed up, with quite the longest spear I had ever seen in my life (of what practical use it is impossible to say, being upwards of twelve feet in length) and the news that he had just seen the panther slink into a big bush 300 yards away, where we could easily shoot it if we would only go with him.

I am aware that what happened hereafter was my own fault, in that I failed in my duty of first conveying the injured men to hospital. I plead, however, that the excitement of the situation and the temptation of this easy opportunity to bag the panther overcame my better judgement and caused me to go after the animal. Eric Newcombe insisted in accompanying me, so I handed him my .12 bore shotgun, loaded with L.G. in the left barrel and a lethal cartridge in the right, together with a few spare shells, while I retained the .405 rifle for my own use. This again was another mistake, as future events proved. I should have armed myself with the shotgun instead. We were accompanied only by the individual with the exaggerated spear, the remainder of our party having melted away. My wife brought up the rear, as a spectator, at a distance.

We approached to within twenty-five yards of the big patch of scrub not one particular bush as had been stated by the spearman into which the panther was seen to have crawled, and I told Eric to move over about thirty yards to my right, so as to avoid each other's line of fire, while completely covering the animal's every possible escape from the vicinity. I then instructed the spear-holder to stone the scrub, which he did very thoroughly for about twenty minutes. However, we heard and saw nothing. I confess that I then became very doubtful whether the panther was in the neighbourhood at all. A little later Eric called out that he could see right into the scrub and that the panther was not there.

By this time some bolder spirits from the crowd had joined us. One of them was accompanied by a dog, which we tried to induce to enter the scrub, in the hope that its sense of smell would locate the leopard. But the dog refused to have anything to do with this proposition, and remained on the outskirts, barking at the undergrowth.

This made me revise my opinion with regard to the panther being absent. Eric had by this time, however, become impatient and approached to within a few yards of the scrub, which he then commenced to stone on his own account. Nothing happened when his first few stones fell.

Then he threw a large one, which evidently landed directly on, or very near, the panther. There was a loud *'Augh! Augh!'* and like a streak of yellow light the beast shot from out of the scrub. He had no time to raise the shotgun, but nervous reaction evidently compelled him to press his trigger-finger and thus probably save his life. The gun went off, blowing a hole in the ground before him and undoubtedly scaring the panther considerably. The next second it landed upon him, sweeping the gun out of his grasp, while Eric and panther, in close embrace, rolled down a short steep bank of khud and into the long spear-grass that clothed a small adjacent nullah.

All this time Eric was shouting to me to shoot and the leopard growled horribly. I could only see the violent agitation of the spear-grass. I rushed forward, afraid of risking a shot from my heavy rifle at such close quarters, which would pierce both the leopard and Eric, tangled up as they were together.

Then the panther left Newcombe and sprang into the lantana bordering the khud. I fired, and as subsequent events proved, scored but a furrowing wound along the top of the beast's neck.

I expected Eric to lie prone after that encounter but was gratified to see him spring to his feet and race in the opposite direction, at really marathon speed. I have often chided him on his running abilities since that day, and it is, with him, a very sore point. He had been bitten right through his side, one of the ribs being cracked by a fang, while his thighs and arms were badly lacerated by the sharp and powerful claws.

We called it a day then and went to the Bowring Hospital, the seats of the car being soaked with human blood by the time we got the three wounded men there. The rest of that evening was spent in writing statements for the police, and in answering innumerable questions, some of which were inane.

Poor Kalaiah died that night in extreme pain. His brother Papaiah recovered after a month, having narrowly missed succumbing to the injury to his lung. Eric Newcombe, due to the intervention of Providence and a good constitution, did not run even the slightest temperature and made a complete recovery in a fortnight.

The next day, Tuesday, saw several hunters after the wounded animal. There was Lloydsworth of the Tobacco Factory, a famed shikari who had shot many tigers and panthers, and Beck, an equally renowned shot and big game hunter. Never a trace could we find, however. All blood-trail had petered out, and the panther had vanished, seemingly into thin air.

That evening it killed a herdsboy, aged about twelve years, who had ventured too near the spot where, unknown to him, the beast was lying. Incidentally, this spot was over a mile from the locality where the earlier incidents had taken place. The boy was killed outright; the panther had seized his throat and bitten through the jugular and wind-pipe.

The morning of the fifth day, Wednesday, found me at the spot where the herdsboy had been killed. We made every endeavour to follow the wounded animal which, although very severely hit, had ceased bleeding by this time, due to the congealing of the blood, at least externally. I floundered about in the dense grass and lantana, which grew thicker as the ground sloped into a hollow. Half-way down this slope the leopard heard or saw me coming, and began to growl its warning against further approach. This was fortunate, for otherwise I might not be here to tell you this story. The undergrowth being almost impenetrable, I called a halt to further advance, which would have been suicidal and decided to await events, which I was almost certain would end in a day or two with the death of the panther from its many major wounds.

Later that day occurred an amusing incident. The police had turned out in force from Bangalore. Some thirty' of them, armed with single-shot service rifles, had been crowded into a police-van, which was protected all around by expanded metal meshing against stoning by mobs during times of riot. The driver of this improvised armoured car had been instructed to scour the plantation till the enemy was located and brought to book by the riflemen. This he proceeded to do to the best of his ability, but, not knowing where he was going in the long spear-grass and tangled undergrowth, he eventually succeeded in half-capsizing the vehicle in a concealed, overgrown ditch. The driver and men were imprisoned inside and shouted lustily for help. None of them would venture out, for was there not a man-killing leopard loose that would kill and eat the first to alight?

Hearing cries at a distance, we approached the spot and released the imprisoned representatives of the law, who then managed to set their vehicle back on its wheels and return to their barracks, hardly any the worse for their adventure. Before leaving, they stated they had heard growls in the undergrowth, but this I put down to a bad attack of mass nerves.

I had made it a point to be at the plantation daily from 7 a.m. till sunset, and at about noon on the sixth day, which was Thursday, I saw vultures gathering in the sky. Watching them through my binoculars, I saw them alight in the midst of the small valley that divided the plantation, the same one, in fact, as that into which I had tried to force my way the previous day.

I knew these sagacious birds had found something dead. It was either the panther itself, or something that had been killed by the panther. Cautiously I forced myself through the dense lantana and clinging wait-a-bit thorn, expecting any moment to hear the guttural coughs of the leopard as it charged at me. Nothing happened, however, and at last, lacerated by the thorns, I reached the valley. I had gone about fifty yards when four vultures rose from the ground with a heavy flapping of wings. Advancing, I came on a small pool of water, with the panther lying dead beside it, in the act of drinking.

The unfortunate animal had bled internally a great deal and suffered the pangs of thirst and fever. The exertion of crawling to water and drinking must have increased the bleeding, for it had vomited a great gout of thick blood into the water before dying, and this stained half the pool a clouded crimson. The vultures had just settled upon my arrival and fortunately had had no time to destroy the skin.

Going back to Jalahalli, I soon found the men to carry the dead animal to my car, lashed to a pole. I took it to Yesvantapur Police Station to make an official report. Here I was delayed for three hours while awaiting the arrival of the necessary officials, much to my annoyance, as I feared the skin might spoil from not being removed from the carcase.

At last I was given permission to take away the dead animal, which you may be sure I lost no time in doing. While skinning, I had ample opportunity to piece together the sequence of facts that had resulted in the death of three persons, and the several maulings.

The wound in the leopard's left foreleg, which had been inflicted by the .303 bullet of the fat police daifedar, was crawling with worms and completely gangrenous. Hughey Plunkett's shotgun ball had passed completely through the animal, cutting through the stomach without inflicting an immediately fatal wound. A single L.G. pellet from the other barrel was imbedded in the bone of the forehead, and had evidently stunned the animal completely, allowing Plunkett to walk up and touch it. Five slugs from Papaiah's musket were embedded in its side, but all too far back to cause immediate effect. Lastly, my own thoroughly ineffective rifle shot, as the beast bounded away from Newcombe, had scored but a deep furrow across the back of the animal's neck.

I produced this skin at court, in support of a claim for government assistance by Kalaiah's family for the loss of their breadwinner, and the gift of a plot of land for their sustenance. I am glad to record that, in the course of time, the dead man's daring was recognised.

With the advent of Second World War, Jalahalli underwent a radical change. The Forest Department plantation and the casurina trees were cut down and thousands of buildings appeared, first to house Italian prisoners of war, then as one of the largest hospital bases for the projected invasion of Burma and Malay and latterly to house Air Force personnel, being one of the main training bases in India for her rapidly expanding air arm.

The skin of this panther now adorns the hall of my bungalow. I cannot help but record the deep admiration and respect in which I hold this beast. For while others killed in stealth, taking their victims unawares, this leopard fought cleanly and courageously in defence of its own life, against great odds, though it was severely wounded.

9

The Hermit of Devarayandurga

He was called 'the hermit', because in many ways he resembled one, both in the choice of his abode, and in his eccentric habits.

For he was an unusual tiger. Although no man-eater, and never once accredited with eating human flesh, he was of a particularly ferocious disposition and very hostile to the human race. He killed three people—two men and a woman—within the short space of five days, and all on the impulse of the moment and out of sheer aggressiveness. Further, his habits were unlike those of a tiger, in that he ate goats and village dogs, which tigers rarely do, especially dogs. And then again, he suddenly appeared in the scrub-jungles clothing the hill of Devarayandurga, six miles from the town of Tumkur and within fifty miles of the city of Bangalore. Devarayandurga had not held a tiger for many a decade, being the home only of a few wild-pig and pea fowl. The area did not boast a regular forest, but was covered with very ordinary scrub-jungle of lantana bushes and wait-a-bit thorn. Moreover, the hilltop was very rocky, and held a few small caves. In these an occasional small panther was known to take up residence, ousting the previous occupant, usually a porcupine, by the simple expedient of devouring it. But the caves hardly provided sufficient shelter, let alone a safe hiding place, for a large animal like a tiger. The whole area was but an island scrub among flat, cultivated fields, which no normal tiger would ever risk crossing either by day or night.

But this is exactly what 'the hermit' did, for cross these fields it must have done, to reach the doubtful and scanty shelter provided by Devarayandurga hillock.

At first no one knew that a tiger had appeared. The few villages that are scattered in the area began to suffer the loss of an unusual number of goats and dogs, and the loss was ascribed to a panther, till the tiger's pug-marks were picked up one morning traversing a ploughed field near one of these villages. Within the next two days a large cow was killed that had been left out to graze all-night within the hitherto safe outskirts of the village. The owner of this cow, an old woman, was very attached to the animal, and when she heard next morning that it had been killed, she proceeded to the spot, a quarter of a mile distant, where she squatted down beside her dead protege and commenced to weep and wail aloud, calling heaven to witness the great sorrow she felt, and the loss she had suffered, with the death of her beloved cow. The other members of the small family had accompanied the old lady to the spot, and had sat around a while in silent sympathy, to listen to her weeping and wailing. But they soon grew tired of it, besides having other things to do, and one by one they returned to the village, leaving the old woman alone beside her dead cow, still weeping with unabated vigour.

It was now 11 a.m., and a bright sun shone down on the scene. No ordinary tiger would have returned to its kill at such a time, in that glare and heat, and to a place disturbed by such noisy wailing, but 'the hermit' was not an ordinary tiger. This tiger did return and saw the old woman beside the kill, rocking herself to and fro while she cried aloud. The beast concluded that this noise was intolerable and must be stopped. So out it sprang on the old woman, and with a simple blow of a paw put an abrupt end to her life. It then dragged the cow some yards away and ate a hearty meal. The body of the old woman was untouched, and her existence apparently forgotten by the tiger. When she did not return by 4 p.m., her family, judging that she must have exhausted herself with weeping and fallen asleep, came to the spot to take her home, when great was their surprise and horror to find she had been killed, while the tiger had made a hearty meal of the dead cow and returned into the brushwood. Rushing pell-mell back to the village, they spread the sad news. Soon the headman, armed with a muzzle-loader, and accompanied by two dozen stalwarts carrying a miscellany of handweapons, came to the spot. They then attempted to follow the tiger's trail, but not for long, for the animal had entered the dense scrub quite close at hand. Being too afraid to enter the brushwood, they commenced to shout lustily and throw stones, and the headman discharged two musket shots into the air. Nothing happened and they turned back in order to carry the body to the village, when out rushed the tiger and pounced on the last man of the party, the unfortunate headman, and incidentally the only member of the group to carry a firearm. He was dead before he became aware of what had happened.

The party' broke and fled to the village, and only late next morning did they return in great force to recover the two corpses, both of which had been untouched during the night. The tiger, however, had made a further meal of the cow.

For the next two days consternation reigned supreme. On the third morning, a traveller approached the village from Tumkur, driving before him two donkeys laden with a variety of goods. A mile down the road from the village the tiger pounced on the leading donkey, which collapsed beneath its attacker. The second donkey stood still, while the traveller, with a scream of terror, ran down the road whence he had come. His action appeared to provoke this extraordinary tiger, for it chased and killed him, and then returned to the dead donkey, which it carried away and ate. Both in chasing the man, and on its return, it had passed the second donkey, which it did not even touch. The body of the man remained uneaten.

These incidents, occurring so close to Bangalore, were headlined in the local Press; next morning I left for Devarayandurga by car, reaching the spot in just over two hours.

Questioning the frightened villagers, I was told the story as I have just recounted it. The weather being dry and the roads dusty, all pug-marks had disappeared by this time, and for a short while I was disinclined to believe that the marauder was a tiger, thinking it more likely to be a large and strangely-aggressive panther. Th^ men who had accompanied the headman, however, and had witnessed his attack and death, assured me that it was indeed a tiger. Nevertheless, knowing how prone the villager is to exaggeration, I was still in doubt.

After a short lunch, I spent the afternoon, accompanied by an obviously nervous guide, in scouring the surrounding area, poking among the caves and tiring myself out completely in looking for 'the hermit'; but never a trace, nor a pug-mark, did I come across.

At 4 p.m. I returned to the village, and with great difficulty procured a half-grown bull as bait, no buffaloes being available in this area. This bait I tied about three-quarters of a mile from the village, at a spot where the road was crossed by an extremely rocky and thorny nullah. It was now close on 6 o'clock, and as there was no time to erect a machan, I decided to spend the night at the Travellers' Bungalow at Tumkur, six miles away and return next morning, by which time I hoped the tiger would have killed the bait.

This I did, waking at 5 a.m. and reaching the spot where I had tied the bait by about 5.30. It was just growing light when I stopped the car a half-mile down the road, so as not to disturb 'the hermit', if he had made a kill. Approaching the spot cautiously, I found my bait had disappeared. Closer examination revealed the animal had been killed and the tethering rope severed, apparently by deliberate, and very vigorous tugging on the part of the slayer. Pug-marks were also visible, and these showed, first, that the killer was a tigress and not a tiger after all, and second, that this was an adult animal and large for a tigress. Remembering the stories I had been told of the peculiar nature of this animal and her disposition to attack suddenly, I followed the drag very cautiously, scanning the area ahead and on all sides most carefully at each step, looking behind me, too, every little while. Progress was thus very slow, but the drag was clearly visible nevertheless, and in 150 yards I came upon my dead bait. The tigress, apparently, had moved off.

The young bull had been killed in the usual tiger fashion, its neck being broken. The tigress had then carried it to the place where it now lay, when she had sucked the blood from the jugular, as was evident by the deep fang-marks in the throat and the dried blood on the surface. She may then have left the kill and returned later in the night, or settled down to a feed right away. The tail of the bait had been bitten off where it joined the body, and left at a distance of about ten feet; this is a habit normal to most tigers, and generally to big panthers also. Finally, the stomach and entrails had been neatly removed to a distance of again about ten feet, but not near where the tail had been left. The tigress had then begun her meal in the usual tiger fashion from the hindquarters, eating about half the bait.

From all these facts it was therefore apparent that the tigress was not, after all, the very strange and eccentric animal she was reported to be. She just appeared to be a particularly bad-tempered female.

Hoping that she might return, I climbed a scraggy tree that grew about twenty yards away, and was the only cover available for my purpose. Here I remained till 9.30 a.m. No tigress appeared, but on the contrary the sharp-eyed vultures, from their soaring flight above, spotted the kill, and I soon heard the rattling sound of the wind against their wing-feathers, as they plumeted to earth for the anticipated feast.

To save the kill from being consumed, I was therefore compelled to descend and cover it with branches broken from the adjacent bushes, afterwards returning to the car and making for the village. Here I procured the services of four men and came back to the tree, where I instructed them to put up my portable charpoy-machan, which I had brought with me in the car. By noon all was ready. One of the men then suggested that, as 'the hermit' was particularly fond of goats, I would considerably increase my chances of bagging her if I tied a live goat in the vicinity. The bleating of the goat, he said, would surely draw her to the spot, even if she had decided to abandon the half-eaten bull. Thinking there was something in the idea, I motored back to the village and soon returned with a half-grown goat of the size that usually bleat vociferously.

After some biscuits and tea, I ascended the machan after instructing the men to tie the goat only when I had taken my place; thus the goat would feel it was alone and bleat loudly as soon as they were gone. It was about 2 p.m. before the men finally departed, and very shortly afterwards the goat began to bleat in really grand style.

This it kept up intermittently till about 5.45 in the evening, when I heard the tigress approaching by the low, moaning sound she occasionally emitted. The goat heard this too, stopped its bleating, and faced the direction of the sound while its state of stark terror was pitifully visible as it trembled violently from head to foot.

Most unfortunately the tigress was approaching from behind me. Though my charpoy-machan provided ample room for me to turn around, the trunk of the tree itself and a clump of exceptionally heavy wild-plum bushes that grew nearby completely obstructed my line of vision. Moreover, the ground sloped steadily downwards from the direction in which the tigress was corning, and this probably caused her to spot my machan while she was still some distance away being on a level with her eyes from the higher ground down which she was approaching.

Or it might have been the extraordinary sixth sense, with which I have noticed some carnivora are particularly gifted, that put her on her guard. Whatever it was, that tigress sensed something suspicious in the surroundings and that danger lurked nearby, for she gave vent to a shattering, snarling roar and began

to encircle the whole area repeatedly roaring and snarling every little while. The unfortunate goat almost died with fright, and the last I could see of it as darkness fell was a huddled, trembling patch crouching close to the ground.

That extraordinary tigress made the night hideous with her roars until 9 p.m., when, with a final snarl, she walked away. Thereafter nothing happened, except for a sharp drop in temperature towards the early hours of the morning, when it became intensely miserably cold. My teeth chattered in the tree, while those of the goat chattered below me, to a slower rhythm, but more audible—or so I believed.

Dawn found us both exhausted after a sleepless night in the freezing cold. The goat was, moreover, so hoarse after its vigorous bleating of the night before, followed by the exposure, that although it opened its mouth in an effort to make some noise, no sound was forthcoming.

I spent two hours at midday looking for the tigress, without finding a trace. I then selected another tree, this time of a leafy variety and overlooked by no rising ground, where I erected my machan, into which I ascended by 4 p.m., with another goat tethered below me. But this goat was as insensitive or as callous as the one of the night before had been sensitive and nervous; for with the departure of the villager who had tethered it, it settled placidly down on the ground to chew heaven knows what, which it continued to do until darkness hid it from view.

This time I had clad myself more warmly, and by midnight, closely wrapped in my blanket, I fell into a deep and dreamless slumber, to awaken at dawn to see that most placid of goats still chewing, again heaven knows what, as if there was not a single carnivore in the whole, wide world.

Again I searched for the tigress at noon, and again I failed; and again by 3 p.m. I was up in my machan, this time with a young bull as bait below me.

It was 7 o'clock and almost dark, when unexpectedly a party of villagers, carrying a lighted lantern, came from the village to tell me that the tigress had killed another cow only half-an-hour earlier, near the bund (or embankment) of a small tank, a furlong from the village, but in the opposite direction, and was engaged at that very moment in eating it.

Considering it a waste of time to remain, I therefore descended and, instructing the men to leave the bait where it was on the off-chance of the tigress passing in that direction later in the night, hastened after them towards the village and the tank. Once we reached the village I instructed them to extinguish the lantern. I then took only one of them as guide and advanced towards the tank. My companion whispered that the cow had been killed on the left of the road, hardly food, fifty yards from the verge and just a furlong from the village.

It was pitch dark by now, and, with the villager close behind me, and walking down the centre of the road, I switched on the torch which was mounted on my rifle, and began to direct it to my left.

There was a snarl and a woof, and then two large, red-white orbs shone back at me from a distance I judged to be within 200 yards and at a slightly higher level. I was puzzled by this last factor, till the villager whispered that the tigress was standing on top of the bund of the small tank.

Walking along silently in my rubber shoes, with the villager following bare-footed behind, we made no noise whatever. Meanwhile the tigress stared back at the light. In this way I advanced down the road for more than 100 yards, till I reached the place where the tank-bund joined it. We then turned left, and commenced the slight ascent to the top of the bund.

The tigress was now about 100 yards away and began to growl. I stopped, and was in the act of raising my rifle to my shoulder for a shot, when her courage gave way, and she turned tail and bolted along the top of the bund in three or four leaps, after which she descended to the right on the far side of the tank and was lost to view.

We then walked along the top of the embankment, shining the torchlight down into the tangle of scrub. A large, solitary banyan-tree grew there, and great was our surprise when the eyes of the tigress reappeared at a fork in the tree, quite fifteen feet or more above the ground and level with the top of the tank-bund on which I was standing. It was surprising, because tigers generally do not climb trees to such heights, especially when followed by torchlight.

I could now make out her form clearly, squatting dog-like in the crotch of the tree. Taking careful aim between the shining orbs, I fired. There was a loud thud as the tigress hit the earth, followed by a coughing grunt and then silence.

We walked along the tank-bund for some distance, shining the torchlight into the tangle of bushes below the bund to our right, but not another sound did we hear. Knowing that my bullet had struck 'the hermit', I decided to get some sleep and return next morning. Accordingly we retraced our steps to the village and to the spot where I had left the car, a mile away and beyond where my bait was secured. At Tumkur I ate a light dinner, washed down with some strong tea and a pipe-load of tobacco, after which I turned in for the night with the highest hopes of being able to pick up the tigress in the morning.

I was back at the village at day-break and, collecting my assistant of the night before, we were soon ON the tank-bund, from which we very cautiously descended the sloping ground to the foot of the solitary banyan tree, in which the tigress had been sitting when I fired my shot.

Our attention was immediately arrested by blood splashed over a wide area where the animal had hit the ground in falling off the tree. Looking about, we then found a segment of bone, about a square inch in area, in which a part of the lead of my 405 bullet was imbedded.

By the sharp claw-marks on the tree-trunk we saw the way in which this extraordinary tigress had pulled her great weight up the tree to attain the fork. My companion soon climbed up nimbly to the same place, and found a few drops of blood in the fork itself.

We then began very cautiously to follow the blood-trail from the banyan tree, and it was soon apparent that the tigress had been hit in the head and was severely hurt. The blood-spoor zig-zagged about aimlessly, going in a narrow circle and recrossing itself several times. She was obviously in a stunned condition, or perhaps blinded, and did not know what she was doing or where she was going.

Frequently we came on large pools of clotted blood, and finally to a spot where the tigress had fallen, or probably lain on the ground for part of the night. The whole circle, roughly ten feet in diameter, was red with blood. When she had moved away, evidently in the early hours of the morning, bleeding had almost stopped, and only an occasional drop marked thereafter a wayward path into the dense undergrowth of lantana, grass and wait-a-bit thorn, that clothed the foot of the embankment.

First of all, we encircled this belt of undergrowth, right to the end of the long embankment some 200 yards away, and back again along its upper end, but there was no blood-trail in any direction, or trace of the tigress having left this cover. She was obviously, therefore, somewhere in this belt of dense undergrowth, which, as I have just said, was about 200 yards long and varied in width from about seventy-five yards to barely ten. But was she dead or alive? That was the question, and on the answer depended the lives and limbs of my companion and myself.

Returning to the spot where the last drop of blood indicated the place at which the tigress had entered the undergrowth, we then began systematically to beat the area. My companion and I, standing close together, hurled stone after stone into the massed vegetation, but only complete silence and stillness greeted our efforts.

We progressed in this fashion along the edge of the belt of undergrowth. In hopes of getting the tigress to show herself, I fired five rounds in all into the lantana, but without response from the tigress. About three-quarters of the way along this belt, a low tree, a dozen feet in height, stood out from the surrounding bushes. My companion slipped towards this, and began to climb it with the view to obtaining a better view, when, without warning, out came the tigress with a single roar and scrambled up behind him.

The man screamed with fright, while from my position, barely twenty yards away, I fired three rounds into the tawny form before it toppled backwards into the lantana. 'The hermit' was dead at last.

The tigress, as I had judged, was an old female with blunted fangs. Her age had probably forced her to seek easier living in the proximity of man, where there would be goats, dogs and cattle for easy killing. Hunger and old age probably accounted for her quick and vicious temper, but lack of courage, and an inborn aversion to man, had prevented her from actually becoming a man-eater, although I have little doubt that she would have eventually turned into one had she been allowed to continue her career unchecked. Incidentally, my bullet of the night before had struck her on the bridge of the nose, but rather high up,

172 / Nine Man-Eaters and One Rogue

removing the piece of bone we had found, but at the same time not entering the head of the animal deep enough to kill it. Indeed, it had actually richochetted off, carrying the piece of bone with it, so that it was just possible the old 'hermit' might have recovered after all, despite the vast quantity of blood she had lost, had she not disclosed herself by attacking my companion as he climbed the tree.

10

Byra, the Poojaree

He wore only a lungoti when I met him, a strip of cloth some three inches wide that passed between the thighs and connected, before and behind, to a piece of filthy knotted string that encircled the waist; but he was a gentleman to his fingertips, and he was, and is, my friend.

Twenty-five long years have passed since first I met Byra, and it happened this way.

The false dawn was lighting the eastern sky above the hills that encircle the little forest bungalow of Muthur, nestling at the foot of the lofty hill of Muthurmalai, that caused the winding jungle stream known as the Chinar River to alter its leisurely course through the dense jungle in a sharp southerly bend to complete the last seven miles of its journey through the wilds, before it joined the Cauvery River in rocky cataracts at Hogenaikal. It was midsummer, and the Chinar was at that time bone dry.

I had come out early and was padding noiselessly down the golden sands of the Chinar in the hope of surprising a bear, large numbers of which were accustomed, at that time of the year, to visit the banks of the river and gorge their fill on the luscious, purple, but somewhat astringent fruit of the 'Jumlum' tree, which grew to profusion in the locality. If not a bear, I hoped to meet a panther on his way home after a night-long hunt. These animals, I knew, favoured closely skirting the undergrowth along the banks of the river on their look-out for prey that might cross the stream. Deer, in the way of sambar, jungle-sheep and the beautiful chital were fairly plentiful in those bygone days, but such graceful quarry were not my objective that morning.

I had gone about a mile from the bungalow, and the light of the false-dawn was rapidly fading into that renewed period of darkness before the real dawn was to be heralded by the cry of the jungle-cock and the raucous call of pea-fowl, when I suddenly heard a surreptitious but distinct rustle from a clump of henna bushes that grew by the stream to my left.

That day I carried no torch, so cautiously approached the henna to within about ten feet and stopped. Then immediately before me I noticed that a large hole, about three feet in diameter and equally deep, had been dug, into which about a foot of water had trickled through the dry sands by sub-soil percolation. This, I knew, was the work of a poacher, to attract parched deer to quench their thirst, when a well-delivered ball or hail of slugs from a muzzle-loader would end their existence. And the noise I had heard had undoubtedly been made by the poacher himself, perhaps upon seeing me, or perhaps just stirring in his sleep after a night-long vigil.

Calling out in Tamil for the man to come out or I would shoot, I at first received no answer. Upon advancing a few paces, a diminutive figure stood up from the undergrowth and, stepping forward on to the river sand, prostrated itself before me, touching the earth with its forehead in three distinct salutes.

Telling him to stand up, I asked who he was. 'Byra, a Poojaree', came the simple answer. 'Where is your gun?' I demanded. 'Gun, what gun? How can a poor, simple man like me own a gun? I can't even shoot, master. I am a traveller and lost my way last night, and being very tired, fell asleep in these bushes. Your honour, by calling out just now, awoke me, and you ask for my gun! I have never even seen such a thing.' 'Pick it up and bring it here,' I ordered. He hesitated a few seconds, then stooped down and brought forth an ancient matchlock, some feet in length, with a butt hardly three inches across at the widest point.

And that is how I met Byra, the Poojaree, and my friend for twenty-five years, who has taught me most of all I now know about the jungle and its wild, carefree, fierce, but lovable and most wonderful fauna.

'What have you shot?' I asked him. 'Nothing,' he replied. 'No animal came to the water last night.' 'What did you shoot?' I demanded in a sterner tone. Bidding me to follow, he walked diagonally upstream towards the opposite bank. I saw a dark heap lying on the river sand, which, upon approach, turned out to be a sambar-doe, a great gaping hole in her neck, from which the blood had flowed to stain the fair white sands.

I looked at Byra witheringly, anger and indignation in my glance. 'Master, we are hungry,' he said simply, 'and if I do not hunt we cannot eat, and if we do not eat, we shall Die.'

Squatting on the sands a few yards away, I invited Byra to sit beside me, and taking out some pipe-tobacco from my pouch, handed it to him. Receiving the tobacco from me on to the palm of his hand, he sniffed it suspiciously, and then, beaming with pleasure and satisfaction, introduced the lot into his system, by the simple process of tilting back his head and pouring it down his mouth. The next few minutes were spent in silence, Byra being too busy chewing my tobacco!

'Master will not tell the forest-guard about my gun,' he then ventured anxiously. 'It is my only way of living, and if the guard knows, he will come and take it away. Also I will be sent to jail, and my wife and four children will starve.'

Here was a pretty conundrum for my solution. My duty as a forest licence-holder was to hand over poachers to the authorities. Indeed the terms of the licence actually authorised me to help in arresting such individuals. Moreover, my conscience urged me to have no sympathy for this rascal, who was ruthlessly murdering female deer by the most unsporting method of slaughtering them when they came to slake their burning thirst during the hot summer months. And yet, there was something likeable about the little fellow, and the degree of confidence he was now beginning to bestow upon me after our short acquaintance. Or perhaps my strong tobacco had induced this trust.

Avoiding the question and a direct answer, I asked him where he lived. 'We have no homes, no hut, no fields' he replied. All day we wander in the forest in search of beehives. If we find one, we are lucky, for we gather the precious honey which we take to market at the village of Pennagram, seven miles away. For a small pot of honey we may get one rupee. With this we shall buy ragi (a foodgrain), which may perhaps feed us for four days. If we don't find honey, we may be able to catch an "Oodumbu" (a large snake-lizard). This is even greater luck, for not only will we eat the "oodumbu", whose flesh is very good for our strength, but we shall sell its tail to the native doctor at Pennagram. He is a wonderful man, that doctor is. He cooks the tail and mixes with it some wonderful medicine. Then he mashes the whole thing into a fine powder, which he divides into paper packets and sells at eight annas a packet. These packets are sold to lovers, and are very efficacious. If a man sprinkles just a pinch of this powder on to the left shoulder of the girl he loves, she will not be able to resist him.'

Here he looked at me sideways. 'If your honour cannot capture the heart of the lady you love,' he continued confidentially, 'I will get some of this powder for you from this native doctor, free of charge, as he is a great friend of mine, and, moreover, beholden to me for the continued supply of oodumbu's tails. All you have to do is to sprinkle a little of it on the left shoulder of the mem-sahib you love, and she is yours, forever and ever.'

Hastily telling him that I was not so much in love just then as to have to resort to oodumbu's tails, I bade him to continue about himself.

'Sometimes, when we are very hungry, we dig for the roots of the jungle yam, which in these parts grows as a creeper with a three-pronged leaf. These yams, or roots, when roasted in a fire, or boiled with salt-water and currypowder, are very tasty and good to eat. At night my wife and children and I sleep in a hole that we have dug in the banks of the Annaibiddahalla River, a small tributary of the Chinar River, as you may know, Sir. In the hot weather I go shooting, like I have done tonight. At such times my wife or one of the children, by turns, remain awake all night, to give the alarm should elephants approach, when they will then leave the hole and scramble up the bank or the big tree that grows beside our shelter. For these elephants are very dangerous and sometimes attack us. Only a year ago one of them pulled a Poojaree woman out of a similar shelter, while she was asleep, and trampled her to pulp. Should we shoot anything, we eat some of the meat, and dry some by smoking. The rest we sell at Pennagram and perhaps get fifteen rupees for it. With the money we can purchase enough grain to feed the family for a whole month. Knowing this,' he concluded, coyly, 'I am sure you, the Maharaj, will not divulge the fact of my possessing the matchlock to the forest-guard. Incidentally, it belonged to my father, and his father before him, who, we are told, purchased it in those days for thirty rupees.'

The rascal then looked at me winningly, a happy smile about the corners of his mouth, although there was an anxious look in his eyes. My sense of duty as a licence holder vanished; I strangled my conscience then and there and replied in a voice which I tried unsuccessfully to make non-committal, but it was distinctly sheepish instead, 'No, Byra, I shall not tell, I promise you.'

He sprang to his feet and prostrated himself before me, his forehead again touching the ground three times in the only form of salutation the Poojarees know. 'I thank you from my heart, master, and on behalf of my family,' he said simply. 'Henceforward we are yours to command.'

Having extracted a promise from Byra to call at the forest lodge later that day, as I wished to question him about the presence and movement of carnivora in the locality, I went my way, assiduously avoiding a second glance at the murdered sambar-doe, for fear my conscience should come to life again and cause me to regret my hasty promise to this plausible advenmrer.

True to his word, Byra turned up at about ten that morning, and close questioning disclosed that just two nights earlier a tiger had passed within five feet of him when sitting up for sambar at a spot about two miles downstream, called Aremanwoddu, where another tributary joined the Chinar. He said that this animal lived in the locality, was an old tiger, and that: his beat was very restricted, probably due to his age.

Then he related an unusual story, to the effect that a month earlier he had been in hiding close to this very spot, when a Chital had appeared, which he had successfully accounted for with a single shot from his matchlock. It had been a bright moonlit night, and the chital having fallen in its tracks, Byra had reloaded his musket and was preparing to spend the rest of the night in sleep, when a large tiger had walked out of the undergrowth, passed the dead chital, stopped, sniffed at it, and finally calmly picked it up and walked off with the prize. Byra had not dared to dispute ownership with the tiger, in consideration of the fact that he was armed with a muzzle-loader, which took a considerable time to reload.

I had no live bait with me at the time, and to procure a heifer meant sending to Pennagram, and probably a delay till the next day So I decided to sit that night with Byra on the banks of Aremanwoddu, after telling him definitely that, at least as long as he was in my company, no deer poaching of any sort would be condoned.

By 6 p.m. we were seated in an excellent and very comfortable hide that Byra had set up in the rushes clothing the confluence of the two jungle streams. The nights were warm and Byra wore nothing more than his lungoti. It was a lesson in patience I learned that day, for from the time Byra had first squatted in the rushes, he never moved as much as his forearm that whole long night. Nothing came that night, and by 2 a.m. I became impatient and finally fell asleep, to awake at dawn with Byra still squatting immovably beside me.

Seeing my disappointment, he offered to accompany me on a tracking venture later in the morning. So after returning to the bungalow for a bath and breakfast, we were back again at Aremanwoddu shortly before 9 a.m. With Byra in front we walked upstream, and had gone perhaps half a mile when we came upon the tracks of a large male tiger that had crossed the sand during the night and was making up the rocky incline of the Panapatti Ridge, a little over a mile away. The ground was too dry for tracking, but Byra said he thought he knew some likely spots where the tiger might be lying up.

So we continued, crossing ridge after ridge, exploring the little valleys of undergrowth and dense bamboo that lay between. Once we heard the rumbling sound produced by the digestive process taking place in the cavernous stomach of an elephant. Giving the spot where he was resting a wide berth, we continued our peregrination, climbing upwards continuously to the Panapatti Ridge.

We had now reached shrub-jungle level, and outcrops of rocky boulders appeared on all sides. Byra said that the tiger lived in one of the many caves that existed among the huge, piled rocks, as did bears too. Handicapped by the stony, sun-baked earth that did not show tracks of any kind, I was for turning back, but my companion had become really interested by now, and advocated pushing on, over and across the ridge.

Streaming with sweat from exposure to the mercilessly blazing sun, we at last reached the summit and began to descend the opposite slope. On this face the ridge was even more boulder-strewn than was the one we had just climbed At last we came to a series of massive rocks, forming many caves. Byra advocated that I sit in the meagre shade offered by an overhanging rock, while he explored the vicinity. I gladly assented and sat down to cool-off with a smoke, while my companion slipped away amidst the sea of boulders.

Within ten minutes he was back, saying excitedly that he had smelt the tiger and was sure it was hiding in one of the caves close by. By this time I was distinctly disgruntled and incredulous, and told Byra, in a few terse words, to cut out the bluff. He looked at me with amazement, and then I could see condescending pity written plainly across his pudgy countenance. 'Come and see for yourself' he said shortly, and without waiting for my reply, moved off the way he had come.

Following with my rifle, we approached a number of cavernous openings between piled boulders. Creeping within twenty yards of the nearest one, Byra halted and beckoned me to approach silently. 'Can you smell it,' he whispered. I sniffed carefully, but could smell nothing. There was certainly no odour such as one gets in a zoo or animal circus. I shook my head to indicate a negative reply. Stealing some distance closer, Byra halted again. 'Surely you can smell it now?' I exercised my olfactory organ to its utmost, and thought I could detect a peculiar odour, which for want of a better term I can only describe as 'greenish'—that very indefinable smell of slightly decaying vegetable matter. Only after many years have I now learned to associate this smell as that of a passing tiger.

Byra looked upwards, scanning the five distinct openings that now showed between the huge boulders. He studied them in silence for a while, and then, indicating the fourth in line from us—and almost the most unlikely in my opinion—whispered, 'I think the tiger is in there.'

I looked at him in evident disbelief, but ignoring my incredulity, he beckoned me to follow him, till at last, by working our way forward soundlessly, and with infinite caution, we reached a stony ledge immethately below the opening he had indicated, which was just above the tops of our heads. Standing on tiptoe to peer in, I saw nothing, and then the very next second, soundlessly and as if by magic, appeared the massive head of a tiger, mild surprise written on its countenance.

My bullet struck it fairly between the eyes at a range of perhaps eight feet. The tiger slid forward in a queer gliding motion, and came to rest level with our faces, his massive head in repose between his forepaws, his yellow-green eyes half-closed with the approach of death, and the drip, drip, drip of a thin, dark-red blood-stream that spouted from the hole in his forehead.

That was the first of my very many experiences of Byra's knowledge of jungle-lore. To say that I was immensely pleased at having discovered him would have been to put it very mildly, and as the years rolled by and our mutual confidence in each other increased, I have never regretted that occasion in the far distant past when I lulled my conscience to sleep.

I shall now tell just two of the many adventures we have experienced together, namely that of the bears of Talvadi, in which Byra so nobly offered his life for mine, and the story of the man-eating tiger of Mundachipallam.

Talvadi is the name given to the wide valley, through the centre of which trickles the mountain stream known by the same name. It is situated some eleven miles north of the spot where I first met Byra, and is quite one of the wildest spots of the Salem North Forest Division.

The Talvadi River takes its rise in the forest plateau of Aiyur, whence it dips sharply into a mountainous gorge, locally known as Toluvabetta gorge, but rechristened by me as 'Spider Valley', because of the species of enormous red and yellow spiders that weave their monstrous webs across the narrow jungle trail. These webs are somewhat oval in shape and sometimes reach a width of over twenty feet. In the centre hangs the spider itself, often nine inches from leg-tip to leg-tip. Despite its size, it is a very agile creature and extremely ferocious, and its prey—the large night moths and beautiful butterflies and insects of the forest stand no chance of escape once they become entangled in the huge web. These spiders are equally cannibalistic, and will not tolerate the presence of another member of their tribe within their own web. I have sometimes amused myself by transporting one of these fierce creatures at the end of a stick to the web of another of its kind, when a battle-royal immediately ensues, often lasting half an hour, but always ending in the death of one or other creature, whose blood is then thoroughly sucked by the victor, till the loathsome insect is so gorged that it can only just crawl back to the centre of its web.

The Talvadi Stream passes down this gorge and then bifurcates, the lesser portion flowing southwards, bordered by the towering peak of Mount Gutherrain and the small hamlet of Kempekarai, to join the Chinar River in the stream of Annaibiddahalla. This area was once the stamping ground of the notorious rogue-elephant of Kempekarai, which killed seven humans, two or three cattle, smashed half-a-dozen bullock-carts and overturned a three-ton lorry loaded with cut bamboos. However, that is another story. The main portion of the stream flows westwards for some miles and, bordering the forest-block of Manchi, then turns south-westwards, crossing the forest-road leading from Anchetty to Muthur and Pennagram in the afore-mentioned valley of Talvadi.

As may be imagined, all this area is densely wooded, clothed on its higher reaches by miles upon miles of towering bamboo, and towards the lower levels by primeval forest, interspersed with rocky stretches, till it finally flows into the Cauvery River near the fishing village of Biligundlu. The whole area, from source to estuary, forms the home of herds of wild-elephant, a few bison, and invariably a tiger or two, which use the line of the stream as a regular beat. The Talvadi Valley itself, abounding in rocks and very long grass, is the habitat of large panthers, many bear, and wild pig, sambar, barking deer, and more pea-fowl than I have met anywhere else.

My Story begins at the time when Byra had sent word to me, in a letter written by the postmaster of Pennagram, that a panther of exceptional size had taken up its abode in the valley and was regularly killing cattle all along the Muthur-Anchetty road from the ~~nth to~~ the ~~isth~~ mile stone. The letter asserted ~~me~~ ~~that~~ the panther was of enormous proportions, 'much bigger than ordinary tiger'.

Having some five days to spare, I motored by the shortcut road through the forest from Denkanikota to Anchetty and past Talvadi Valley to Muthur, where I met Byra. From there we returned to the 15th milestone, which was right in the valley itself. The road was really execrable, with many streams to be crossed, ruts made by cart-wheels, and interspersed with boulders galore, taxing the car and its springs severely. After pitching camp, we went down to the nearest cattle-patti, some three-quarters of a mile distant, where I was able to hear for myself about the depredations of this panther. The story told was that it generally attacked the herds on their homeward journey to the pens about 5.30 p.m., and that it would select the largest cow among the stragglers for its victim. Several herdsmen had actually seen the animal and attempted to drive it from its kills, only to be met with snarls and a show of ferocity quite exceptional for a panther. The animal was not known to live in any particular spot, but as I have said, ranged for about four miles along the road.

It was difficult to persuade these herdsmen to sell me live baits, as although they realised the slaying of the panther would benefit them directly, their caste and religious obsessions were such as to oppose absolutely the practice of deliberately sacrificing a life in this way. Albeit, by various methods I finally succeeded in purchasing two three-quarter grown animals, one of which I secured on the bank of the river itself, about a mile downstream from the road, and the second not far from the 14th milestone.

There was now nothing to be done but wait, and as I did not deem it wise to disturb the countryside by shooting the pea-fowl and jungle-fowl that abounded, I contented myself by strolling in the forest in other directions, both morning and evening, in the hope of accidentally meeting the panther or perhaps a wandering tiger from the Cauvery.

As luck would have it, I received news at about 7 p.m. on the third day that the panther had that very evening killed a cow belonging to another cattle-patti three miles away, as the herd was returning home. A runner had been sent to inform me as soon as the loss was discovered, which had accounted for the passage of time.

Grabbing rifle, torch and overcoat, Byra and I hastened to the spot, and when still some furlongs away I extinguished my torch, creeping forward in the wake of the herdsman who had brought us the news, Byra following at my rear. A half-moon was just raising its silver crescent above the ragged line of jungle hills that formed the eastern horizon, when we turned a sharp bend in the cattle-track and came upon a panther, crouched behind the dead bullock that lay across the track.

I had armed myself with my .12 shot-gun for work at close-quarters, while Byra, behind me, carried the Winchester, but before I could raise the gun the panther bounded off the carcase and into the undergrowth beyond.

Hastily whispering to Byra and the herdsman to return slowly the way we had come, talking to each other in a normal tone to give the panther the impression we had departed, I dived behind a wild plum-bush that grew some twenty paces away, hoping the animal would return.

The panther did not take long to advertise its presence, for within a few minutes I heard its sawing call from the forest before me. The sound gradually receded in the direction Byra and the herdsman had taken, by which I interpreted that it was following them at a distance, probably to ensure that they had really departed. Afterwards there was tense silence, unbroken by any sound for perhaps the best part of an hour. And then, as if from nowhere, and unheralded by even the faintest rustle of dried leaves or crackle of broken twig, appeared an enormous panther, standing over its kill, but still looking suspiciously down the track we had just traversed.

Aiming behind the shoulder as best I could in the halflight, the roar of the gun was followed by the panther leaping almost a yard into the air. Without touching earth again it convulsed itself into a spring and was gone before I could fire the second barrel. Its departure was heralded by the unmistakably low, rasping grunts of a wounded panther. Waiting for a few minutes, till the sound died away, and realising that nothing further could be accomplished that night, I retraced my steps to the cattle-patti and to camp.

By dawn next morning, Byra and I were at the place of my encounter. Casting about where the animal had disappeared, it did not take long for Byra to detect a blood-trail on the leaves of the undergrowth through which the animal had dashed away. Heartened by the fact that at least some of my L.G. pellets had found their mark, I took the lead, this time armed with the rifle, Byra following close behind and guiding me on the trail. In this formation, it was my business to keep a sharp lookout for the animal, and deal with it should it charge, while Byra, in the slightly safer position behind me, could concentrate on his tracking.

Within the first 100 yards we came to a spot where the animal had lain down, as revealed by the crimson stain that covered the grass and the unmistakable outline of the body. From here the animal had slithered down the banks of a narrow nullah, densely overgrown with bushes on both sides, where following up became terribly difficult and hazardous.

As we tiptoed forward, with many a halt to listen, I scanned each bush before me, striving to penetrate its recesses for a glimmer of the spotted hide, alive or dead now, we did not know. I strove to pierce with my eyes the rank undergrowth of jungle-grass that grew between the bushes, and to look behind the boles of trees and rocks that fortunately were few in number just there. We had advanced a comparatively few paces in this way when suddenly, from out of a hole in the ground before me, rose a shaggy black shape, a smaller similar shape tumbling off beside it. Wehad stumbled upon a mother-bear with her young, asleep in the hole she had dug overnight in the bed of the nullah, in her assiduous search for roots!

I could see the white V mark on her chest distinctly as she half-rose to her feet, surprise and then fury showing in her beady, black eyes. Down she went on all fours again, to come straight at us. Thrusting the muzzle of the Winchester almost into her mouth, I pressed the trigger. Then occurred that all-important moment, which balances the life or ignominious death of the hunter: a misfire !

The she-bear closed her jaws on the muzzle, and with one sweep of her long-toed forepaw wrested the weapon from my grasp, so that it hung ludicrously from her mouth for a moment before she dropped it to the ground. Involuntarily I had stumbled backwards, and as the bear rose to her feet to attack my face—which is the part of a human anatomy always first bitten by these animals—Byra attempted the supreme sacrifice.

Nimbly throwing himself between me and the infuriated beast, he shouted at the top of his lungs in a last-minute attempt to divert its further onslaught. He was successful only to the extent that it turned its attention upon him. seemingly to forget my existence for the moment.

As he ducked his head in the very nick of time, the bear buried its fangs in Byra's right shoulder, while the long talons of its forefeet tore at his chest, sides and back. Byra went down with the bear on top of him. I sprang for the fallen rifle. Working the under-lever to eject the misfired cartridge, I found to my horror that, with the force of its fall, the action of the rifle had jammed. All this took only a few seconds. Byra screamed in agony, while the bear growled savagely. Stumbling forward and using the rifle as a cudgel, I smote with the butt-end with all my might at the back of the animal's head. Fortunately my aim was true, for the bear released Byra and like lightning grabbed the rifle in its mouth, this time by the butt, again tearing the weapon from my grasp. It then started to bite the stock savagely. By an act of Providence the cub, which during all this time had remained in the background, a surprised and obviously terrified witness, at this juncture let out a series of frightened whimpers and yelps. As if by magic the attention of the irascible mother became focussed on her baby, for she dropped the rifle and ran to its side. There she sniffed it over to assure herself that all was well, and as suddenly as this unwelcome pair had appeared on the scene, they disappeared, a few last whimperings from the now reassured youngster forming the last notes to that unforgettable scene of horror, from which it took me days to recover.

Byra, was on his hands and knees, streaming with blood and evidently in great pain. Going across to him, I removed my coat and shirt, tearing the latter into strips and attempting to bind up the more serious of his wounds and to stem the bleeding. Then, hoisting him on my back and carrying my damaged rifle, I staggered back to the cattlepatti, where I placed him on a charpoy. Four herdsmen carried him to my camp, where I poured raw iodine into the wounds. Camp was struck and in a few moments my car was jolting the fifteen miles to the village of Pennagram, where at the dispensary rough first aid was rendered. By this time the poor man was faint with the loss of blood and almost unconscious. Replacing him in the car, I covered the sixty-one miles to the town of Salem, where there was a first-class hospital, in almost record time.

Penicillin was unknown in those far-off days, and the first week that Byra spent in hospital, hovering between life and death, with me at his side, was an anxious time. But his sturdy constitution won through and after the first few days the doctors definitely pronounced him out of danger. I returned to Pennagram, where Byra's wife and children had come and were anxiously awaiting news. Giving them some financial help, I also received a surprise when I was presented with the worm-eaten skin of the panther, which I had quite forgotten in the excitement and pressure of subsequent events. It appeared that the sight of vultures on a carcase had attracted some of the herdsmen of the cattlepatti at Taivadi, who had found the body of the animal within 200 yards *from.* ⋇ where the adventure with the bear had occurred. It was stated to have been an outsize specimen, but as I have said, the skin was worm-eaten and beyond preserving.

Returning to Salem, I left sufficient money to cover Byra's treatment, expenses and final return to his native haunts at Muthur, but it was over two months before he could go back to his family with a slight permanent limp in his right leg due to the shortening of a damaged muscle, and with many permanent scars on his body as reminder of the incident.

My rifle needed a new stock, and to this day, six inches from the muzzle, it bears the marks of the she-bear's teeth. Thus ended the adventure which formed the blood brotherhood, so to speak, between Byra and myself, founded on his attempted cheerful sacrifice and almost literal fulfilment of the words 'greater love than this hath no man, than that he should lay down his life for another.'

Many years passed after this occurrence to the occasion of my next story, that of the man-eating tiger of Mundachipallam.

Mundachipallam or to give it its literal Tamil translation, the hollow, or stream, of Mundachi is nothing more than a rivulet skirting the base of the Ghat section, half way between the 2,000 foot high plateau occupied by the village of Pennagram and the bed of the Cauvery River, only some 700 feet above sea-level. This stream crosses the Ghat Road, which drops steeply from Pennagram to the Cauvery River at a point just about four miles from the destination of the road where stands the fishing hamlet of Ootaimalai above the famed waterfalls of Hogenaikal. The Forest Department has constmcted a well on the banks of Mundachipallam, beside the road, to facilitate the watering of cattle, especially buffaloes and bullocks, drawing heavily-laden ~~carts~~ of timber and bamboo, before they begin the remaining six miles of steep ascent to Pennagram.

This little well, surrounded as it is by dense jungle, except for the narrow ribbon of road and the small width of Mundachipallam, which cross at right angles, is the spot where my story begins and, strangely enough, ends, though only after many deaths, and the narrow escape of Ranga, my shikari.

It was early morning, about 7.30 a.m., and droplets of dew twinkled on the grass like myriads of diamonds cast far and wide, as they met, scintillated, and reflected the rays of the newly-risen sun, filtering through the leafy branches of the giant 'muthee' trees and the tall straight stems of the wild-cotton trees that bordered the shallow banks of Mundachipallam.

One man and two women, carrying round bamboo baskets, laden with river fish netted during the night on the Cauvery River, approached the well and laid down their heavy burdens on the low parapet wall that encircles it. The man unwound a thin fibre rope, coiled around his waist, and slipping one end of it over the narrow neck of a rounded brass lotah, carried by one of the women, let the receptacle down the well, from which he presently withdrew a supply of cold, fresh water. In accordance with the normal village custom, where a man comes before a woman, he began to pour the contents down his throat in a steady silvery stream, not allowing his lips to touch the mouth of the vessel, for to do so was considered unhygienic.

The fish were being taken to market at Pennagram, and this was the last water available before tackling the stiff climb to their destination. After drinking his fill, the man returned the lotah to the well and twice refilled it, for the benefit of the two maidens who accompanied him. They were in their twenties and wore nothing above their waists beyond the last fold of their graceful sarees, which passed diagonally across one shoulder. Their smooth dark skins glistened with sweat despite the coolness of early morning, due to the heavy load of fish they had carried for four miles from the big river.

After drinking, the party sat down for a few minutes, each member producing a small cloth bag, from which were taken some 'betel' leaves, broken sections of areca-nut and semi-liquid 'chunam' or lime of paste-like consistency. Some sections of nut were placed in an open leaf, which was liberally smeared with the chunam, and then chewed with evident relish. In a few minutes the mouths of all the members exuded blood-red saliva, which was freely expectorated thereafter in all directions.

Just then, rustling and crackling was heard from the undergrowth bordering the well. These sounds ceased and began again at intervals. There was no other sound.

The trio conjectured among themselves as to the cause of these sounds, and reached the conclusion that it was some member of the deer family, probably injured by gunshot wounds or wild-dogs or some other animal, and struggling to get to its feet. Urged on by the hope of obtaining easy meat, and undoubtedly in order to impress the females of the party, the man got up and, with a stone in his hand, walked into the jungle.

The noise had momentarily ceased, and he penetrated further to try to find the cause of the disturbance. Rounding a babul tree that grew in the midst of a clump of bushes, he was petrified when he almost walked into a pair of tigers, probably engaged in the act of mating.

Now a normal tiger is a beast with which very wide liberties may be taken. When once out fishing, I was surprised by a tiger that broke cover hardly fifteen paces away; it was difficult to tell which of us was more alarmed by the presence of the other at the time. Anyhow, that tiger simply sheered off the way he had come, and although unarmed at the time, curiosity and natural excitement urged me to follow it, to ascertain if possible the presence of a kill. But it just kept running before me like any village cur, till I eventually lost it among the many bushes that grew around.

But there are certain moments with tigers when even they demand privacy. Or it may have been the urge to show off to the female of the species, an urge which I have known affect otherwise quiet men in a very surprising manner. Anyhow, this tiger definitely resented the intrusion and with a short roar he was upon the unfortunate fish-seller, burying his fangs through the back of his neck and almost severing the spinal column. Not a sound escaped the man as he fell to earth, the tiger still growling over him. The two women had heard the short roar and, recognising the sound as that of a tiger, fled the way they had come to Ootaimalai. The victim was not eaten on this occasion, the effort having been but a gesture of annoyance at being disturbed at the wrong moment, but it had taught that particular tiger the obvious helplessness of a human being.

Some weeks later, a woodcutter, carrying his burden from the forest, encountered the same tiger on turning a bend in the path. Again that short roar, followed by the deadly spring, and another man lay dead, killed for no reason at all. Again the tiger did not eat.

Two months passed, and a party of women had gone into the forest to gather the fruit of wild tamarind trees that grew in profusion throughout the valley. One of them had strayed a little away from the rest. She had stooped down to lift the basket to her head, when, looking up, she met the glaring eyes of the great cat. A single shrill scream escaped her before that short roar sounded for the third time and the cruel fangs buried themselves in her throat. This time the jugular was severed and the salty blood spouted into the tiger's mouth; thus was born the man-eating tiger of Mundachipallam. The woman was dragged away to some bushes and there devoured, except for her skull, the palms of her hands, and the soles of her feet.

Three more deliberate kills followed in quick succession, one at the 7th milestone of the road itself, the other by the banks of the Chinar River near to its confluence with the Cauvery, and the third but a mile from the village of Ootaimalai itself. In all three cases the victims were eaten, or partly eaten.

It was this last kill that caused the greatest consternation, leading the villagers of Ootaimalai to come in deputation to Pennagram to beg the authorities to take some action to rid them of the menace that now threatened their very village. Ranga, my shikari, was there at the time and promised them that he would persuade me to help, and having made the promise, travelled the hundred odd miles to Bangalore by bus, arriving late in the evening to present his report.

Now a few words about Ranga will not be amiss at this stage. Strangely enough, I had also met him at Muthur, where I had met Byra some years earlier. Ranga was the hired driver of a buffalo-cart, used to haul cut bamboo from the forest to Pennagram. He had initiative, however, and in his spare time was given to poaching, like Byra, with a matchlock that he hired for the occasion. He was a very different man from Byra, however, in both physical and personal attributes. For he was tall and powerful compared with Byra's somewhat puny build, and showed a forceful and distinctly positive character in all his undertakings. He had spent a year in jail for the attempted murder of his first wife, whom he had stabbed in the neck in a jealous quarrel. After returning from jail he had married again, and at the time I first met him had three children. Not being content, he later took one more wife and now had a dozen children in all, and was a grandfather besides. He had better organising capacity than Byra and got things done when required. I have known him to thrash a recalcitrant native thoroughly for not obeying instructions. He has also a lucrative side to his character, trade in liquor illicitly distilled in the forest from Babulbark and other ingredients. I have sampled some of his produce and can tell you it is the nearest approach to liquid fire that I have known. Lastly, he is a far more dishonest man than Byra and given to petty pilfering, especially of .12 bore cartridges. He despises Byra, whom he looks down upon as a semi-savage. Secretly, I think he is jealous of my affection for the little Poojaree. But Ranga is a brave man, staunch and reliable in the face of danger, who certainly fears no jungle animal or forest-spook, as do the vast majority of other native shikaris.

Unfortunately, Ranga came at a time when I was very busy and could not possibly leave the station for another fortnight. So I sent him back* to Pennagram with a number of addressed envelopes and instructions to write to me every second day, regardless of events.

My inability to answer Ranga's first summons was perhaps indirectly responsible for two fresh tragedies that occurred before I was able at last to pick Ranga up in my car at Pennagram, motor down to Muthur for Byra, and arrive at Ootaimalai, where I was joined by a third henchman, an old associate named Sowree. This Sowree, like Ranga, was quite a versatile fellow, and had himself spent three months in jail for shooting and killing a wild elephant with his muzzle-loader while on a poaching trip. The elephant was a half-grown cow and had approached the hide in which Sowree lay concealed. Fearing that it might really tread upon him, Sowree had aimed his musket behind its left ear. The solid ball had only too effectively done its work, and the elephant dropped in its tracks. Unfortunately for him, he was caught red-handed. I had been shooting on the Coimbatore bank at the time, and had seen and photographed the elephant, which incidentally was how I met Sowree.

I was extremely fortunate in being able to obtain the services of these three men, as in their varied spheres and capabilities, they presented a vast store of jungle experience and ability. Byra at once volunteered to scout around the neighbouring forest, and along the Coimbatore bank, in an effort to ascertain the immediate whereabouts of the tiger. This I emphatically forbade him to do, as being suicidal. We finally compromised by agreeing that he should be accompanied by Sowree, armed with my .12 bore gun, and another man who, very surprisingly, bore the name of Lucas and was a 'Watcher' in the employ of the Government Fisheries Department. Ranga was given the job of obtaining three baits and tying them out in likely spots. The usual difficulty in obtaining animals was met, but the resourceful Ranga quickly overcame it by threats and other expedients, of which I was not supposed to know.

The first of the three baits was tied a mile up the Chinar River from where it joined the Cauvery and the second some three miles further on, where Mundachipallam met the Chinar. The third was tethered within 100 yards of the well where the first tragedy had occurred. On alternative days, Byra and his party would scour the forests on one bank of the Cauvery, while I, with a local guide, combed the opposite bank. Ranga, as I have said, attended to the feeding and watering of the baits.

In this way we spent four days, while nothing happened. Tiger pugs were discovered at several localities, but they were not fresh, and nobody could tell with certainty whether they belonged to the man-eater or some other animal.

There was no possibility of driving the man-killer to cattle-killing to avoid starvation, by prohibiting the villagers from entering the forests or using the road to Pennagram. To begin with, considerable traffic existed along this road, as it formed a main artery to the many hamlets lying on the opposite bank of the

Cauvery In addition, the forests, particularly on the Coimbatore side, were plentifully stocked with game, to which the tiger could always turn in necessity.

In the meantime I endeavoured by every possible means to spread the news of my presence and purpose to all surrounding hamlets, in order that I might hear of any fresh kill with the least possible delay. There was then some hope, with Byra's expert help, of being able to track the animal to where it was lying up, or perhaps even to its lair. Beating was out of the question, even if there had been volunteers for the task, of which there were none, as we were dealing with a very bold and clever animal, who would as likely as not add one more victim to his list from among the beaters themselves.

Early in the morning of the fifth day, I received news that a man had been killed at Panapatti cattle-pen, some four miles away, late that previous evening. He had gone out of his hut for 100 yards to call his dog, which was missing, and had not been heard of again. We hurried to the spot and Byra was successful in discovering the spot at which the man had been attacked: the great splayed-out pugs of the tiger were soon clearly visible across the sandy bed of the Chinar River as he had dragged his victim across and through the intervening reeds to the borders of the sloping bamboo forest beyond. Here we discovered the remains, almost totally devoured.

No trees were available, except for a mighty clump of bamboo that grew some thirty feet from the remains. Inside this I instructed Byra to make me a suitable hide by the simple expedient of removing some eight or nine of the stout bamboo stems, cutting through them about four feet from the ground and again at the ground level, and then taking out the intervening four-foot lengths. The upper parts of the bamboo stems being in the centre of the clump, would not fall to earth, so entangled were the tops with the fronds of neighbouring stems and those of other clumps.

After completing his work, Byra had succeeded in making a sort of hollow cave for me in the midst of the clump. Seated in the middle of this I knew I would be quite safe from attack by the tiger, either from behind or from either side, as he could not get at me owing to the numerous intervening stems. The only way he could reach me was from in front, and this I felt quite capable of countering provided I kept myself awake throughout the night. The faithful Poojaree persisted in his wish to sit with me, till I was compelled to order him peremptorily to go. I would, indeed, have been glad of his company, but the space we had cleared in the midst of the bamboo-clump offered only restricted accommodation to one individual. To cut more steins to increase this space meant that we were reaching the outskirts of the clump and the unsupported bamboo stems would then fall to earth, not only causing much disturbance by the crash, but littering the surroundings with debris, which might quite possibly frighten the tiger away.

The night would be dark, with no moon, so I took the precaution of clamping my spare shooting light to my shotgun, which I carried into the hide with me, in addition to the Winchester, with its own lighting arrangement. Being in the midst of the bamboo, I knew I was almost completely sheltered from the dew and the cold jungle air, and fairly safe from snakes or so I thought.

I was in position by 1 p.m., and sent my followers away, Byra still protesting, with instructions to call to me from the bed of the Chinar next morning before approaching. With their departure I was left to my own devices for the next seventeen hours.

You will appreciate that from my position in the midst of the bamboo-clump my view was entirely restricted on all sides except for the narrow lane of jungle right in front of me, with the human cadaver in the foreground. Much as I would have preferred a wider range of vision, I knew I would be thankful once the hours of darkness fell, as the more I could see by day the more I would be exposed to the man-eater after dark, when the tables would be turned and he could see while I could not.

The human remains, being hidden from the sky by the canopy of overhanging bamboos, were not troubled by vultures. Flies, however, covered it in hordes and the stench soon began to get painfully noticeable.

I will not burden you with descriptions of the sounds of a jungle evening and the close of a jungle day, beyond mentioning that they were practically all present on that occasion and offered sweet accord to my jungle-loving ears.

Nothing happened before darkness set in, which it did both earnestly and rapidly, till I was left in Stygian blackness, intensified by the additional shadows cast by the towering bamboo stems above me. It was so dark that I could not see my own hands as they rested on my lap; I would have to feel for the trigger and the torch switch, and indeed, everything. All that was visible was the luminous dial of my wristwatch showing that it was a quarter to eight. Ten long hours before daylight came.

I knew that during this time I would have to strain myself to the utmost in pitting my poor, human, and town-bred skill against that of the king of the jungles, at which he was a past-master, with decades of skilful ancestors behind him; namely, at listening and hearing. For I could not see an inch before me, while he could see clearly. Nor could I smell him at all, but neither could he smell me. For success I would have to depend entirely on my hearing the sound of his soft approach, and I well knew from long experience how soundless the approach of a cautious tiger can be. I would have to remain absolutely silent myself; worse, the slightest movement or sound from me would betray my presence to those ever-acute ears, and once he knew I was there, only one of two possible things could happen. Either his courage would fail him and he would desert the kill, or he would attack me by a sudden pounce through the opening in front of me, before I was aware of his coming. I certainly had no wish to become the next item on his menu.

Therefore, I could do nothing but sit absolutely and completely still. Mosquitoes found their way even inside that clump, and tortured me acutely. Once some cold creeping thing passed across my lap. It had length but no legs and was undoubtedly a snake. Movement at that time meant a bite and, if it was a poisonous snake, possibly death. With extreme difficulty I controlled my twitching nerves, and the snake glided away. I could just sense its rustle as it slipped between the intervening bamboo stems and was gone.

By and by my throat began to tickle and I had an over-powering desire to cough. I counted sheep to divert my thoughts from this urge till it eventually died away.

At 10.25 p.m. I heard a distinct sound in the jungle behind me. A faint rustle, then all was still. The minutes dragged by. Then it came again, on my right and in line with the very clump where I was sitting. Heavy breathing was clearly audible. A very faint grunt, silence, another grunt, and then the quick rush of a heavy soft body before me. Was it on the kill, or was it staring me in the face from the inky darkness, perhaps even at that instant drawing the powerful hindlegs below the supple belly to catapult itself upon me? And I could not see even the end of my own nose.

I had already cocked my rifle, and had slowly raised the muzzle, finger on trigger, to meet the coming onslaught at point-blank range. The perspiration poured down my face in sheer terror, and my whole body trembled with nervous suppression.

I depressed the torch switch and the brilliant beam blazed out upon a large hyaena, standing above the kill, growling to find out it was a dead man that lay there. He stared blankly at the light for seconds and was gone. I could have laughed aloud with relief and the thought that I was safe once more at least for the present.

Anyhow, my position had been temporarily revealed and I could only hope the man-eater was not in the vicinity to become aware of it. Hastily I took advantage of the disturbance to swallow a mouthful of hot, refreshing tea from the flask I had brought, and quickly move my cramped limbs before resettling myself for the remainder of my vigil. I was in Stygian darkness again, but considerably refreshed and relieved of the morbid nervous tension that had threatened to overcome me a few minutes before.

At ten minutes to twelve I heard the moan of a tiger in the distance. This was repeated again at intervals of five to ten minutes, the last being at twelve-twenty, and from a spot I judged to be a quarter of a mile away. It was difficult to gauge the exact distance of sound in this densely wooded locality, but I thanked Providence and my lucky stars that the tiger had decided on making a noisy approach rather than the silent one I had dreaded.

A quarter of an hour slipped by without further sign. In the meantime the usual mid-nightly jungle-breeze had sprung up, to cause the bamboo stems to groan and creek against each other weirdly. This aroused a fresh and sminous thought in my mind. Supposing one of the several cut bamboo stems, balancing upright above my head, was to become dislodged and slip downwards under its own weight. The cut end would impale me to the ground, like some rare beetle in a collector's box. The thought was not very pleasant and for a moment it eclipsed even the thought of the man-eater and its proximity

And then I heard the crack of a bone on the cadaver lying in the darkness before me. Slowly I lifted the rifle to shoulder-level, steadied it and depressed the torch-switch for the second time that night. But nothing happened. I depressed the switch again and again, but still nothing happened. Undoubtedly the bulb had burnt out or some connection had come loose. I had now the choice of sitting very still till the tiger fed and departed, or changing my rifle for the smooth bore and attempting a shot. I quickly decided to use the gun. Ever so gently I lowered the rifle to ground level and then groped silently in the dark for the .12 bore. Finding it, I drew it towards me and then began manoeuvring the weapon to shoulder-level. I could only hope that the tiger was looking away from me, or was too engrossed in his meal to notice all the movement that was going on in the midst of the bamboo-clump. And then misfortune befell me. Slightly, but quite distinctly, the muzzle of the gun came into contact with a bamboo stem and there was an audible knock.

The sounds of feeding stopped abruptly, followed by a deep-chested and rumbling growl. Hastily I got the gun into position and pressed the switch of the new torch. Luckily it did not fail, and the beam burst forth to show clearly a huge striped form as it sprang off the cadaver and behind the bamboo clump next to mine. From there a succession of earth-shaking roars rent the silence, as the man-eater demonstrated in no uncertain manner his displeasure at being disturbed, and his discovery of a human being in the near vicinity.

Keeping the torch alight, and a sharp lookout for his sudden attack, with one hand I groped for the spare bulb I always carried in my pocket. I extracted it and kept it on my lap. Still working with one hand, I unscrewed the cover of the torch on my rifle, extracted the faulty bulb and substituted the new one. Fortunately, the torch was one of those focussed by adjustment from the rear and not the front end, and as the rifle torch was now functioning again, I extinguished that on the smooth bore, though I kept the gun ready across my knees for any further eventuality.

The tiger was still demonstrating, but had moved to a position in my rear. I knew I was safe enough, except from a frontal attack. To guard against this I would have to keep the torch alight continuously, but as over five hours still remained till daylight, there was the certainty the batteries would run low, even on both torches, if burned incessantly. So I switched off the light and relied on my hearing. When things became too silent for a long stretch, I would switch on the beam, expecting to see the creeping form of the tiger approaching me. But this did not happen and he kept his distance, demonstrating frequently till past 2.30 a.m., when I heard his growls receding in the distance. No doubt he was disgusted, but by this time I welcomed his disgust.

You may be certain I kept a sharp lookout for the rest of the night against the tiger's return, for the habits of a man-eater are often unpredictable; but the chill hours of early morning crept past without event, till at last the cheery cry of the silver-hackled jungle-cock made me grateful for the dawn and the light of another day, which on more than one occasion during the terrible hours that had just dragged by I had not thought of seeing.

Soon the halloa of my followers from the bed of the Chinar River fell like music on my tired ears, and I shouted back for them to advance, as the coast was clear. With their arrival I staggered forth from my night-long cramped position, to finish the tea that remained in my flask and to smoke a long-overdue pipe, while relating the events of the night.

All three of the men knew me most intimately, but although they did not say as much, it was clearly evident they were surprised to see me alive, for the roars and demonstrations of the frustrated man-eater had been clearly audible to them, where they had spent the night with the shivering herdsmen of Panapatti.

Byra now said that he would like to take a quick walk up the Chinar to Muthur, just four miles away, and fetch his hunting dog, which he felt would be of considerable help in following the trail of the tiger. This dog was a very non-descript white and brown village cur, answering to the most unusual name of Kush-Kush-Kariya. How it happened to possess this strange name I had never been able to fathom. In calling the animal, Byra used the first two syllables in a normal tone, but would accentuate the third into a weird rising cry resembling that of a night-heron. I had never been able to emulate him in this, and had contented

202 / Nine Man-Eaters and One Rogue

myself in the past with Kush-Kush alone, which the dog would obey without hesitation.

Insisting that he at least took Sowree as company, I returned with Ranga to Ootaimalai and had a hot breakfast, and a bath in the Cauvery, followed by a long-overdue sleep. I awoke at 2 p.m. with the return of Byra, Sowree and the much-prized Kush-Kush-Kariya, who wagged his tail at me in joyful recognition and nuzzled his cold snout against my shoulder.

Swallowing a hasty lunch and plenty of hot tea, we turned to the spot of my night's adventure, accompanied by the relatives of the dead man, who yearned to bring away his remains but were far too afraid to visit the spot unprotected.

As may be imagined, the corpse was by this time smelling to high heaven, so they decided to carry it only as far as the Chinar River and bury the remains on the bank. With their departure, poor Kush-Kush made a brave attempt to follow the cold trail of the tiger but was not very successful in going even 100 yards. Probably the stench that still pervaded the atmosphere and lingered on the quiet evening air had overpowered all faint smell that might have remained in the tiger's tracks over the hard ground. We returned to camp just before nightfall, a very disappointed group.

The following day nothing happened, but on the morning of the day after, Ranga nearly met his end.

Each day, as I have already said, Byra, Sowree and I scoured the forest in opposite directions in the hope of locating the tiger, while it was Ranga's duty to feed and water our three baits, none of which had been killed upto that time. He had made an early start that morning, with another villager for company, and had already visited the bait at the well on Mundachipallam, which was found untouched, as expected. After depositing some of the straw carried by his companion, Ranga watered the animal and then the two men moved down Mundachipallam itself, to look to the second bait tied at its confluence with the Chinar River.

The villager was leading, Ranga bringing up the rear. They had come about a mile from the road when, standing fifty yards from them in the middle of the dry stream, was the tiger.

The villager dropped his bundle of straw and shinned up the only tree at hand. For the few seconds it took him to climb a reasonable height, he blocked Ranga's progress, and within those few seconds the man-eater had reached the base of the tree, reared up on its hind legs, and with a raking sweep of its forepaw removed the loin-cloth around Ranga's waist, the end of which had hung downwards, while he climbed. The tiger halted momentarily to worry the cloth, while Ranga, minus his loin-cloth, climbed energetically, overhauling and almost knocking his companion off the tree, in his efforts to reach the higher terraces and safety. The disappointed tiger remained below, looking upwards and growling savagely, while Ranga and his companion shouted loudly for help, telling the world at large that they were being killed and eaten.

Fortunately, a party of people, travelling in large numbers for safety's sake, happened to be coming from Pennagram and were at that time in the vicinity of the well, from where they heard the shouts and recognized its message. At the double the whole group, men, women and children of all ages, covered the remaining four miles to reach me at Ootamalai with the news.

Not knowing it was Ranga who had been attacked, and Byra and Sowree not having yet returned, I jog-trotted the distance alone, arriving at the well in record time. From here I could plainly hear the shouting myself. By this time the tiger had left the foot of the tree and vanished into the forest, but the two men were afraid to descend, for fear it might be in hiding and rush forth on them. Hoping to surprise the man-eater, I refrained from answering them while hastening forward as swiftly as caution permitted. When I reached the tree, however, it was only Ranga and his companion who were surprised at seeing me, till I explained the circumstances. We then attempted to follow the tiger, but no signs of him were evident on the hard ground; so we desisted and turned back to visit the remaining baits. I accompanied the men, and we found both animals unscathed. It was past midday when we returned to Ootaimalai with the despairing knowledge that the leery tiger we were after apparently was not going to kill any of our baits. Nor, with the experience I had had with him, was he ever likely to return to a kill again. To say I was exceedingly crest-fallen and despondent would be putting it too mildly The wily man-eater of Mundachipallam looked like being one of those tigers that would stay put for a long time to come, if it did not go away of its own accord to continue its depredations elsewhere.

And then, about 7 a.m. two days later, came the event that brings this story to an end. As I have mentioned, in coincidence it remarkably resembled the events with which the tale started. Again a group of persons, except that they were ten in number for the sake of safety, had placed their baskets, laden with fish for Pennagram, on the ground, to water at the well beside Mundachipallam and to rest awhile.

Women being in the party, one of the men stepped behind the nearest tree to ease himself. There was a short roar, an elongated golden body with black stripes hurled itself as if from nowhere, and the squatter had disappeared. By good fortune, Byra, Ranga, Sowree and myself had set forth in company to visit our baits and were hardly a mile behind the *party* of ten. Soon we met the nine who were returning with the sad news of the one who was not. Running forward as fast as we could, we reached the well, where I whispered to Ranga and Sowree to climb up adjacent trees and await my further need. Byra and I crept forward and, behind the tree chosen by the unfortunate man to answer the call of nature, we picked up the trail of his blood as it had ebbed away in the jaws of the tiger.

With Byra tracking, and closely in his wake with rifle to shoulder, and scanning every bush, we had penetrated only a short hundred yards when we heard the sharp snap of a bone in the mouth of the feeding tiger. The sound had come from a half-left direction ahead of us. Laying my straining hand on Byra, I motioned him to remain where he was, while I crept cautiously forward, knowing well that under such circumstances a companion becomes an additional life to care for.

The forest was still and breathless, and the sound of gnawing and crunching could now be heard more clearly. Very carefully and silently edging closer, with downcast eyes watching each footstep, for fear I should rustle a leaf, snap a twig, or overturn a loose stone, it took me a considerable time to advance a mere fifteen yards. From there I thought I could see the slayer, crouched on the ground. A few paces nearer, and suddenly he arose and faced me, a dripping human arm, torn off at the shoulder, held across his mouth. The wicked eyes gazed at me with blank surprise, then a snarl began to contort the giant face, rendered more awful by the gruesome remains it carried.

The 300 grains of cordite, behind the soft-nosed Winchester bullet, propelled the missile with upwards of thirty-five tons to the square inch, correctly into the base of the massive neck. The human arm dropped into the grass with a plop. The animal lurched forward with a gurgling grunt. Quick working of the underlever of the old, trusted rifle, and a second missile buried itself in that wicked heart. It beat no more. The man-eating tiger of Mundachipallam lurched forward to his end in almost the same spot where he had begun his wicked career months before. A large male, he was without blemish. Undoubtedly a wicked tiger by nature, he had evidently turned man-eater through an unlucky chance. On such trivial circumstances often hang the threads of fate.

Anxious about my welfare, my wife surprised me by arriving that same afternoon in her car from Bangalore to ask me whether I ever remembered I had a home and family, and if it was not about time I thought of returning to it.

We motored Byra, via Pennagram, back to his dug-out near Muthur, where we were just in time to be present at the happy arrival of his fifth progeny. And the arrival was in this fashion. A shallow hole, hammock-shaped and about of the same dimension, had been scooped in the sands of the Chinar River, the hollow then being liberally filled with soft green leaves, freshly separated from their stalks. In this hammock the mother, about to give birth, lay when the pains of child-birth began. The husband acted as midwife. No medicines, no ergot, no hot water, no cotton wool! Only tender green leaves, and the sharp edge of a flint, to saw through the navel cord, the bleeding stump of which is staunched with ashes from an ordinary wood-fire. A couple of hours after giving birth the mother got up with her baby and went to the hole on the banks of Annaibiddahalla where they lived. The husband filled in the hammock-like hollow; leaves, placenta and all, with the loose sands of the Chinar River. In such simple and hardy fashion are the Byras of the forest born. So do they live and so do they die, true children of nature and of the jungle. Long may they continue to exist, untrammelled and untarnished by civilisation, happy and free to roam as they will over mountain, fen and forest glen, till death claims them and they return unostentatiously to mother earth, from which they have so unostentatiously sprung.

On the morning of that day I had shot a peacock, and this we had for dinner, prepared in the jungle fashion. All feathers are removed, with the entrails, head and neck. Incisions with a knife are made in the flesh of the bird, into which are inserted salt, spices, cloves and 'curry-powder' to taste. The whole is then plastered over with fresh, clean mud from the river bank to a thickness of well over an inch, so that it finally resembles a ball of wet mud. A fire of embers is built, the ball placed on it, and surrounded on all sides and above with still more embers. The fire is kept continuously alive by the addition of more wood, but the aim is to have glowing embers, rather than a blazing fire.

After some time the mud begins to crack, and finally falls away in sections. Then is the time to remove the bird before it is burnt. With a little practice in the art of mud-roasting, a truly superb roasted peacock or jungle-fowl can be prepared for dinner, the finished product putting many a housewife to shame.

11

The Tigers of Tagarthy

If you travel to the western limits of the District of Shimoga in the State of Mysore, you will at once be struck by the difference of scenery from that prevailing around Bangalore and the eastern parts of the state. For here you are within the belt of evergreen forests, fed by torrential monsoon rains, averaging above 120 inches a year west of Shimoga town itself and reaching over 250 inches at the village of Agumbe, the extreme limit of Mysore State on the Western Ghats. Giant trees, their leafy tops reaching to high heaven, and colossal tree-ferns, grow along the numerous streams that gush from forest and glen and border the roadside with a perennial supply of fresh water. Vegetation of the rankest description, among which the thorny varieties of the jungles of central and eastern South India are conspicuous by their absence, is to be seen everywhere. But little wandering in these jungles is possible, for trails do not exist, since the undergrowth densely covers every open space and struggles ever upward to reach a ray of sunshine. Beneath the towering trees everything is damp and dark; the chirp of the wood-cricket and croak of the bull-frog are the only sounds you will hear. Leeches, their bodies attached to the undersides of leaves, stretch out elastically to fasten a grip on any living creature that may brush by. They will penetrate your clothing, worm their way between the interstices of your boots, putties or stockings, and suck your blood without your being aware of their presence, for they give you no pain, until, looking downwards, you will find some part of yourself oozing blood. Attempt to pull them off, and they will leave a nasty wound that generally festers into a sore. Apply a little of the common salt you should always carry on your person in these parts, or a little tobacco juice, and they will curl up and fall off of their own accord. The wound will then heal without any attention.

This is the home of the Hamadryad or King Cobra, 'Naia Hannah', as he is known, that giant snake of the Cobra family that reaches a length of fifteen feet and more. Dark olive green in colour, with faint yellowish white circles around his body, he boasts of no visible mark on his dark, oval hood. Of amazing speed despite his great length, he feeds on other snakes, is aggressive and is said to attack on sight, a female guarding her young being reputed to be particularly bad tempered. I have twice met the King Cobra on his own grounds, once when collecting specimens for an aquarium of the beautiful red and green fish, spotted along their sides, which inhabit the forest streams outside Agumbe; and on another occasion, when out collecting orchids. But at neither time did they behave aggressively. Both specimens stopped upon seeing me, raised their heads about four feet above ground and partly extended their oval hoods while gazing at me attentively and inquisitively with their beady black eyes. Then they harmlessly glided on their way.

The higher treetops are the homes of beautiful orchids, the stick-shaped branches of the Dendrobium family being particularly represented. In summer their clusters of pink, yellow, white or mauve blooms festoon the higher terraces in colourful array.

This district embraces the Shiravati River, whose waters fall gracefully and grandiosely in four distinct streams, a sheer 950 feet at the falls of Gersoppa or Jog. Here, on a moonlit night, can be seen that rare phenomenon against the steaming spray of the waters a rainbow by moonlit.

The village of Tagarthy, eleven miles south-east of the little town of Sagar, is situated on the eastern limits of the ever-green forests, where they have been felled and cultivation has been undertaken. Because of the heavy rainfall and fertile earth, agricultural ventures in this area are extremely profitable. The grass also grows lusciously on the more open glades, and vast herds of cattle are kept in the bordering villages and hamlets, due to the abundant grazing.

Relatively few wild animals, beyond bison, inhabit the ever-green forests, owing to the denseness of the undergrowth and the presence of leeches and ticks, which annoy them. For the same reason, and due to the scarcity of game, carnivora are seldom encountered in those dark places. But as the area opens out, and the vast herds of cattle appear, carnivora collect in large numbers to feed on them and grow fat.

Tagarthy was such an area, and at no time in all my many visits were there less than four separate tigers in permanent residence. In February 1939 the peak figure of my experience was reached, with eight cattle killed in one day at various points of the compass around Tagarthy This indicated eight separate tigers operating, since the kills were reported from widely distant places.

Due to the number of tigers in the locality, panthers are rarely met with, the one or two ekeing out their existence doing so in the immediate vicinity of the villages, and living on dogs, goats and sometimes domestic fowls. For the tiger does not tolerate his smaller cousin and will without compunction kill and occasionally eat him, if the panther gets within striking distance.

Except for spotted deer, game is comparatively scarce around Tagarthy, and the tigers in that area are mainly cattle-lifters. Most of them are heavily-built animals and fat, lacking the sleek, trim appearance of the true gamekiller.

Let me tell you the story of Sham Rao Bapat of Tagarthy, and of the tiger that he shot in his garden, quite close to his house. Sham Rao was but a lad at the time, about twenty-two years; but as the sole male heir, he managed the estate that surrounded his home with efficiency and with the true love of an agriculturist. Rice grew in the lower, muddy areas, while the dry crop of ragi was cultivated on higher levels. He also had a grove of areca and cocoanut palms, up the stems of which clambered the betel-leaf vine. Moreover, Sham Rao had cattle and other livestock, and indeed was a prosperous landlord.

One day a fat tiger decided to share in this prosperity and commenced killing Sham Rao's herd, one by one. Sham Rao possessed a smooth-bore gun and nothing else, and loaded with ball, sat over the kills for the tiger's return. But for one reason or other this never happened, till it came to be surmised this particular tiger was an old hand, who had probably been shot at before and therefore would not return to his kill a second time.

And then the tiger grew bolder. One dark night it leapt the fence surrounding Sham Rao's garden and attempted to dislodge the stout bamboo screen that had been closely drawn across the entrance to the cattle shed. Sham Rao had wakened at hearing the restless snorting and stamping of his cattle. He had then detected a scratching sound and going outside met the tiger as it leapt away after having tried to force an entrance.

The next night Sham Rao placed small cut branches on the roof of his cattle shed, where he lay prone on his stomach, six feet above the ground at the entrance to his shed. This entrance had been closed. At ten o'clock the tiger presented itself and began scratching the door. Sham Rao fired both barrels of his smooth bore at point-blank range, and the marauder sank almost noiselessly to earth. He was a fine example of the heavy type of cattle-killing tiger.

The scene changes. It was 11.30 a.m. and the sun shone brilliantly down on the little forest bungalow, situated some two and a half miles from Tagarthy itself. Early lunch was nearly ready, and my wife was busy with the few finishing touches. Just then a kakar voiced his grating call from the forest that bordered the bungalow-fencing. Again and again the call was repeated, the excited note of the small deer betraying his intense alarm. Slipping on a pair of rubber boots and carrying the rifle, I crossed the forest fireline and penetrated the leafy depths of the jungle. The kakar was still calling and I went forward as fast as was possible, making the minimum of noise. I came upon a clearing, in the midst of which stood the little kakar facing away from me and voicing his intermittent bark. Slipping back into the jungle, I tiptoed around the clearing, careful not to place myself within the direct vision. of the alarmed deer. Some teak trees had been planted here and their huge leaves, dry and brittle at this season, lay where they had fallen, carpeting the forest floor. I knew that to attempt to cross them would be to give myself away. So I hid behind the trunk of a stout fig-tree, growing on the edge of the teak and strove to penetrate the shadows under them. Stare as I could, for a while I saw nothing. Then a little distance away something stirred, and in doing so gave itself away. I focussed my eyes on the spot and there I saw a tiger, lying unconcernedly on his back, all four feet in the air and apparently fast asleep. Periodically the tip of his tail would twitch, and it was this movement that had caught my eye and betrayed his presence.

It would have been unsportsmanlike to shoot the animal in his sleep. Besides he was doing no harm beyond killing his lawful food, and so I was not disposed to cause him any hurt. I leant my rifle against the tree and myself also, and for quite twenty minutes I watched that tiger sound asleep on his back. And then from the forest-lodge floated my wife's voice, calling me for lunch. The tiger heard it and sat up, turning his head towards the sound, his eyes still half-closed with sleep.

Silently I stepped from concealment, the rifle ready for all eventualities. The tiger heard me, leapt to his feet and whisked around to gaze in blank surprise at this human, who had come so close to him undiscovered. Then with a lazy snarl he began to walk casually away. I let him go peacefully and soon he was lost to sight.

On another occasion my wife and I had hired a bullock-cart, and had gone out at night shining torches, to see what we could see. We had travelled a mile and were half-way down a deep declivity, where the cart-track crossed a stream, when she picked up a pair of eyes reflecting her torch-beam, deep in the jungle to our right. Halting our cart, we dismounted, she leading the way with the torch, with me behind with the rifle. The eyes had disappeared, so we followed a narrow footpath that led at an angle in the general direction of the spot where the eyes had been. Shortly we picked them up again, large reddish-white orbs, glowing distinctly against the background of night. Fortunately the undergrowth was thin just there and we were able to advance directly towards the eyes. A few steps further and out stepped a tiger, who looked at us and then back at the place from which it had just emerged. The mystery of this strange behaviour was soon unravelled, for two cubs, the size of retrievers, broke cover and gamboled up to their mother.

She now gazed at us fixedly a few moments and then crossed into the jungle, uttering a low mewing sound, a call to the cubs to follow. They did so, and the trio were lost in the forest except for the rustle of the undergrowth that occasionally marked their progress through the bushes.

My wife kept her torch beam in the general direction where we could hear them moving, for fear that the tigress, resenting our intrusion, should change her mind and launch a flank attack. Then we both heard a distinct growl before us. Turning the beam towards this new sound, we were shaken at seeing another tiger, this time a large male, at almost the spot where the tigress had stood a few seconds before. Quite evidently we had come upon a family party returning from quenching their thirst at the stream. I might observe that it is quite unusual, however, for a male tiger to accompany a tigress with cubs of the size we had just seen. Generally she will not trust her offspring near her lord till they are fairly well grown.

The situation was now decidedly tense, as there was every possibility of one or other adult animal attacking us. My wife kept her head with commendable calmness, however, and the tiger, growling in a low tone, followed his family into the undergrowth.

At that time occurred an amusing sequel to the story, which might have had an unpleasant ending but happily did not. The unfortunate cart-driver, left alone in the dark, had heard the mewing of the tigress followed by the growl of her mate. Perhaps his bullocks then scented them, or even saw them, for suddenly they bolted with the cart, to rush pell-mell down into the bed of the stream, where the wheels stuck fast in the soft sand and water. Hearing the shouts of the cartman, and thinking he or his bulls had been attacked, we ran to the spot, to discover all was well except for the severe fright he had received. We were both glad that circumstances had not forced us to harm any of the members of that happy family party

For some time my friend, Dr Stanley of the Mysore Medical Service, was stationed by his department at Tagarthy, principally to attempt to stem the tide of malaria, which was rife and affecting practically everyone of the inhabitants. The doctor was an enterprising man, keen on shooting, and has shot quite a few tigers during his service.

Late one night he received a maternity call from a hamlet called Bellundur, about six miles away. True to his profession, he set forth by bullock-cart, armed with his bag of medicines, injections and bandages; his 'Geco' smooth bore and a five-cell torch added a touch of shikar to his duty.

They were traversing an intervening valley when a tiger leapt across the track, and sitting on its haunches by the wayside, turned to watch the passing cart. Stanley fired ball at the animal, which received the lead with a loud roar and disappeared.

Calmly he went on to his destination, relieved the mother of her baby and spent the rest of the night with the patient, returning next morning with a small boy of his acquaintance to help him and the cartman to follow up the tiger he had wounded the night before.

Coming to the spot, they soon picked up a blood-trail, which they began to follow, the cartman turning back to his cart on the plea he could not leave his bullocks alone. Stanley and the boy had gone some distance and entered a hollow, when they unexpectedly came upon the tiger lying on its side before them. Thinking it was dead, but to make certain, Stanley fired an L.G. into its rear, when the tiger came to life, turned round and charged them. As it leapt, Stanley fired his remaining barrel, this time ball, into the mouth of the tiger. Then it was on him, knocking him down and laying bare a portion of the back of his skull. At this moment the boy fled screaming, thus undoubtedly saving Stanley's life, for the tiger left him and chased the boy, whom in turn it sprang upon, biting into his side. Dazed from the wound in his head, Stanley scrambled to his feet and fumbled to reload his gun, when, unexpectedly, the tiger left the boy and jumped into the jungle.

The youngster had been badly wounded in the back and side, and blood was bubbling out of the gaping holes made by two of the great fangs. In addition, three ribs were broken. Using his torn shirt for bandages, Stanley patched him up as well as possible and carried him to the bullock-cart and the long journey of seventeen miles was begun to the town of Sagar, the doctor himself being in a bad way all the while. From there they entrained for Shimoga, about thirty-five miles away, where was a district hospital.

It is sufficient to record that both of them recovered from their adventure, Stanley to receive a severe wigging from his medical superior, who reminded him he had been stationed at Tagarthy as a doctor and not to shoot tigers.

Their fortunate escapes were undoubtedly due to the fact that the tiger had been severely wounded. Stanley's last shot into its mouth had very probably smashed the lower jaw, for it was noticeable that in both attacks thereafter it had used only its upper canines. Had the lower jaw been serviceable, there is no doubt whatever that both Stanley and the boy would not have lived to see another sunrise.

As it was, many villagers heard the wounded animal for a week thereafter, roaring night and day in agony. Then there was silence, and there is every likelihood that it crawled away into the depths of the forest to the, for the carcase was never found.

Stanley also told me of two other experiences at Tagarthy. Once while sitting on a machan over a kill, nearing sunset, a hamadrayad climbed the tree in which he was stationed. He frightened it away; but as darkness descended, thinking the great snake might come back and feeling very uneasy, he returned to the village. On another occasion, while sitting imperfectly concealed over a kill, the tiger had seen him and had demonstrated all night until the early hours of morning, circling the tree and roaring continuously. This had become a nuisance, as a drizzle set in, but the good doctor, very wisely, had not risked returning alone in the dark when he had such an aggressive tiger to deal with.

When wandering in the few areas around Tagarthy where the forest is at all penetrable, I have myself come upon a three-quarter grown tigress lying dead in a clearing, with twenty-three porcupine quills embedded in her face and chest. One of them had completely penetrated and extinguished the right eye. The tigress was in an extremely emaciated condition. A few feet away was the half-devoured carcase of a panther. The tragedy was not difficult to piece together. Evidently the tigress had attempted to make a meal of a porcupine, which had charged backwards into her face, as these animals do, embedding its quills in her head and chest and putting out one eye. Blinded, starving and still carrying the quills from the last encounter, the tigress had wandered desperately in search of food. Then she had come upon the panther, whom she had attacked, fought, killed and begun to eat, when death had overtaken her, for some unaccountable reason, perhaps through stomach or other injuries caused by the panther itself, not clearly evident to me from her decomposed carcase.

In the hamlet of Bellundur lived a mysterious individual named Buddhia, accredited by local inhabitants with great powers of witchcraft and black magic. He was reputed to have bewitched people and brought about their deaths. He was a great friend of mine and, after one of our many intimate talks late one night he presented me with a circle of plaited creeper stems, four inches in diameter, made from mysterious plants that grow, he said, deep inside the forest. He asked me to keep this with me always, on my hunting trips, and said that if any time I was in an area where game did not show up, I was to wait till the sun had set, and then pass the circle three times up and down the barrel of my gun. Within twenty-four hours, he guaranteed, I would kill something with that weapon. I still have that circle, and am ashamed to confess have used it, more than once, where game has been scarce, in accordance with the directions of its giver. Call it coincidence or luck, as you wish, but it has never failed to produce results.

Alas, old Buddhia is now no more, having succumbed to the dread scourge of malaria, from which even his powers of magic could not protect him.

Now, let me tell you about the Tiger of Gowja. Gowja is another tiny hamlet, over six miles from Tagarthy, and half-way to the forest Chowki of Amligola, situated on the borders of the great tiger preserve of Karadibetta, carefully protected by His

Highness the Maharaja of Mysore for his own shooting. Tigers are not so clever as to know that they should remain within the limits of certain boundaries. Most important of all, no cattle are permitted into the Karadibetta Preserve and tigers like eating cattle immensely. Just outside the hallowed precincts are cattle by the hundred, so what more natural than that there should be more tigers outside of the preserve than within it.

About 1938 a particularly enterprising tiger walked out of the preserve and started killing cattle around Amligola, returning afterwards to the preserve where he was safe and sound from molestation. In this manner he waxed fat, while his fame as a devourer of sleek cows spread throughout the area.

Then, as happens with humans, continued success induced greater daring, disregard for consequences, and finally that rank carelessness and overconfidence that brings undoing to both tigers and men.

Our tiger had not yet reached this last stage, though he was well on the way, for he wandered farther and farther from the protecting fastnesses of Karadibetta and disdained to return there during the daytime, as had been his custom hitherto. In this way he came to Gowja, where he took up his temporary abode on the banks of a deep nullah that scored the countryside about a mile and a half from the hamlet. From this shelter he raided the cattle herds, harrying them morning and evening, never failing to kill at least two fat cattle each week.

Letters had been written to me about this slayer, but I had never bothered unduly about his activities, for after all tigers must eat to live and this old fellow was doing no harm to humans. A few less cattle mattered little to those vast herds.

With the passage of time, however, his daring increased still more, and the last reports showed that he was loth to leave his kills, demonstrating loudly by roaring and making short rushes at the herdsmen when they attempted to drive him off. True it was that hitherto he had not hurt anyone, but I knew from the preliminary indications that this would happen almost any day now. Sooner or later another maneater would appear.

At 9.30 a.m. one morning, therefore, I alighted from the mail train from Bangalore at the wayside railway shed of Aderi. From here a walk of three and a half miles brought me to Tagarthy I was greeted by old friends and hospitably treated to coffee while a hot meal was being prepared. I occupied the time by gleaning all the news I could, but this did not amount to much beyond the usual account of the presence of tiger in all directions; the daring old tiger of Gowja having earned particular notoriety. After the meal I set forth by car to cover the six odd miles to Gowja, which, because the track was in a very bad way, we did not reach till 6 p.m. While talking with the inhabitants, my tent was erected about three furlongs away, on the banks of a smaller nullah that fed the main stream. The tiger lived a mile or so beyond.

I was told that the tiger had killed two days before. Nothing had happened since, but the next kill was undoubtedly due within the coming forty-eight hours.

Sure enough, word was brought at 1 p.m. next day that the tiger had just claimed another victim. Hurrying to the spot, I found the tiger had attacked a cow in the middle of an open field, quite 300 yards from the nearest cover, killed it and carried it away to its hiding place, which proved to be the very same nullah as that in which my tent was pitched. The soft sand of the nullah revealed tracks where the tiger had crept along the bed and then dashed over the bank towards the cow. The cow had run a short distance in an effort to escape, but had been overtaken and slain. The tiger had then lifted the cow across its back and returned to the ravine, as was evident by the absence of any drag mark, though the tiger's pugs were firmer and had sunk deeper into the rough clods of the ploughed field, due to the weight he was carrying.

I cautiously followed the tracks in the hope of encountering the animal or his kill. This I eventually did, but he did not demonstrate and show himself, as I expected he would. That indefinable sixth sense, which warns the jungle folk in the nick of time, evidently impressed this tiger that here was a human being to whom he should not show himself. While still some yards away in the undergrowth and invisible to me, he became aware of my presence, growled in a low tone and slunk away.

There was a suitable tree nearby and I arranged the erection of my charpoy machan. I was in position by 4 p.m. The tiger came at eight, but stood directly under my machan and beside the tree on which I sat. I knew of his approach by the subtle sound of his tread. No dry leaves crackled to betray his coming, but in the stillness of the silent night there was no mistaking that soft heavy footfall. He began to lick himself, his rough tongue running over his glossy coat, making the faintest of rasping sounds. Then he arose on his hind legs and began to clean and sharpen the claws of his forefeet against the bole of the tree. In so doing, he saw the machan above. A low growl and he was gone, nor did he return that night.

The following day nothing happened, so in the afternoon I tethered a heifer in the bed of the main nullah where he was reputed to have his abode and sat up on a machan in a tree overhanging the nullah at an angle of 60 degrees.

I was in position at 3 p.m. At 5.30 p.m. I heard a dragging sound and there was the tiger hauling down the bank another cow he had taken from one of the herds. He was quite eighty yards away. Aiming at his neck, I fired, but as I did so the tiger moved forward, receiving the bullet much further back than was necessary for a fatal shot. He responded to the impact with a coughing grunt and catapulted to the bottom of the nullah and was gone. I descended the tree, released my bait and returned to Gowja in the opposite direction, feeling confident I would locate and bag him next morning without undue trouble. But I was very much mistaken, as events were to show.

At dawn I was back at the scene of action, accompanied by two reliable locals from the hamlet. We picked up the tiger's blood-trail at the foot of the nullah, which traversed its bed for some considerable distance before climbing the opposite bank. We followed with every caution, but soon found that the animal had kept going, for there was no evidence that he had sat down to rest from his wound. It was almost two miles before he had eventually halted for the first time, feeling the effects of the bullet. He had then got up and continued, and I guessed that he was making for Amligola and the Tiger Preserve beyond. Once he reached this, I knew he was lost, since to carry firearms into the preserve, even in pursuit of a wounded tiger, was strictly prohibited. He had had a full night's start of us, and despite his wound it looked as if he might gain the sanctuary of the preserve after all.

Pressing forward, we came upon two more places where he had rested. At the first of these there was considerable blood, and the grass was flattened where he had been lying. At the second there was much less blood, and thereafter the trail became more difficult to follow. Evidently the flow of blood was stopping; perhaps the layer of fat beneath the outer skin had worked itself into the bullet-hole and had stopped the profuse bleeding.

We soon found ourselves in the precincts of Amligola and I knew the tiger had now but a mile to go before reaching the forest fire-line that marked the western boundary of the preserve. Here fortune favoured us, for we encountered a stream, at that time holding pools of water. The pugs of the tiger on the soft sand showed that he had now changed his mind about heading for the preserve and had gone upstream instead in search of water. We followed and came upon the first pool, at which he had drunk and had lain up for quite a considerable time thereafter, for the tracks leaving this place were comparatively fresh and had been made within the hour. This fact renewed our flagging hopes and we continued for a furlong before coming upon a second pool, where the tiger had also halted. Water still seeped through the indentations of the pugs, and it was now clear he was but a little distance ahead. He might even have heard us coming and had just moved forward.

I determined to try strategy rather than follow in his wake, for I greatly feared that he might turn tail and bolt for the sanctuary which lay so close to this spot. Motioning to my two companions to climb into a tree, I ascended the bank of the nullah soundlessly, and doubled forward in a detour as hard as I could go, parallel to the line of the nullah. I rejoined the nullah half a mile down its course and tiptoed backwards in the hope of surprising the tiger. But I was doomed to disappointment, for he heard or saw me and scampered up the bank and towards the preserve, as I had feared.

I followed his blood-trail to where he had entered a patch of dense scrub, which I circled, halting behind the trunk of a tree at the far end. Here I waited, but nothing emerged. If I attempted to summon my men I would alarm the tiger, and I was in a quandary as to what to do next. Very obligingly he provided the solution by moving, as I noticed the grass before me wave to his forward motion, although not a glimpse of his body was visible. The grass continued to wave as he crept away at an angle, so I left my protecting tree and stole forward myself. The grass began to thin then, and at last I saw him, just as he saw me. I fired at his flank and with a roar he charged. But within five paces his courage failed and he turned to receive a third shot, which took him pell-mell into the thicket from which he had just emerged.

I whistled to the men, who had heard the shots and were themselves bravely coming forward. When they had joined me I explained the situation and told them to climb to the tops of the neighbouring trees in an effort to locate the tiger. This they did, but signalled that they could see nothing. I then posted them up two separate trees about fifty yards apart, after telling them to whistle if they saw our quarry, and returned to the nullah myself, in case the tiger should have gone back.

It was a nasty business negotiating that narrow ravine, not knowing at what moment the tiger might spring upon me from the bank above or from behind one of the boulders which strewed its course. One of the fundamental principles in following a wounded tiger is never to negotiate the bed of a stream alone, when the wounded animal might be lurking above. But I was desperate, having spent the whole day in following this wounded beast, and feared that yet, at the last moment, it might escape me by dragging itself away to die in Karadibetta.

So with bated breath and rifle cocked, and with my linger closed around trigger, I negotiated that stream, to find the tiger had not recrossed it and was still inside the thicket into which it had jumped. How to dislodge him was now the problem.

Returning and summoning the men, we held a council of war. To follow the tiger into the midst of the thicket without knowing at least its approximate location would be suicidal. And then came inspiration. Returning to the stream, I removed my shirt, knotted the sleeves together and tied up the neck. Using it as a bag, we filled it with pebbles to breaking point. Then one of the men carried it back to where I had last fired at the tiger. With this store of ammunition, we began stoning the thicket in all directions, till at last we were answered by a warning growl from the bushes to the right of the point where we stood and about thirty yards away.

Evidently the tiger was severely wounded and could not move, for he did not rush out at us, but continued to answer each stone that fell near him with a series of growls.

Whispering to the men to stone intermittently to hold his attention, I made a detour of the thicket and began to enter it from the direction of the nullah. I could hear the tiger growling before me, and the occasional fall of the river stones that were hurled by my henchmen. As long as I could hear the tiger I made progress, although the thicket was dense, for I knew his attention was otherwise held. But then, as I drew nearer, he heard me, for his growling stopped. My followers also noticed this and guessed that he had heard or sensed my approach from the rear. In an effort to distract him they threw the stones higher, further and faster, but without result, for the tiger would not give himself away.

I knew I would have to be extremely careful, as he might now attack me at any moment. I halted, every sense alert, straining my ears to hear the faintest rusde preliminary to the last great bound that would bring him upon me. Nothing happened, and as the seconds rolled by in silence, broken only by the sound of the dropping stones, my nervous tension mounted and I became oppressed by an overpowering sense of impending danger. I glanced in all directions, but could detect no movement. I strained my ears, but could hear nothing. Still that sense of approaching peril grew stronger and stronger, till I could have shouted aloud to break the unnatural silence, or have turned tail and run.

And then I glanced behind me. There between two bushes was the wounded tiger, reddened with its own blood as it crawled on its belly to surprise me with its last great spring. Our eyes met, it roared and launched itself into the air, while the Winchester cracked twice, hurling its powerful bullets right into the face of the oncoming fury. I sidestepped as the heavy body crashed before me, kicked wildly in the air and then lay still, as I sped yet another bullet into its heart at point-blank range.

The troublesome old tiger of Gowja had failed to reach the sanctuary of Karadibetta and was now no more.

16355833R00134

Printed in Poland
by Amazon Fulfillment
Poland Sp. z o.o., Wrocław